"Easy, ha~~~~~~~~~~~~~~~~~~~~id. How'd y~~~~~~~~~~~~~~~~?"

Tightening her fist in the stallion's mane, Margaret gathered her muscles into vault position, then gasped.

Cold metal—round, hollow and unmistakably lethal—pressed into her neck. "Don't listen to her, Twister," a deep voice drawled from behind. "Takin' a ride with Maggie here can kill a guy."

Blood rushed to her face in a sickening wave of guilt. "You," she whispered.

"Yeah, me. The owner of the land you're tresspassin' on." The pressure on her neck eased, replaced by the sliding caress of a gun barrel. "All grown up now, are you? Let's take a look. Turn around, Maggie."

Schooling her features into a cool mask, she turned. "Don't call me Maggie."

"Seems to me I can call you any name I want. And right this minute, 'Maggie' is the nicest one that comes to mind."

Nothing had changed, she realized. He would never forget…or forgive.

ABOUT THE AUTHOR

After years of writing advertising copy, Jan Freed decided that if she could make washing machines sound glamorous, creating likable characters should be a breeze. Jan's second book combines her pride in the indomitable spirit of Texans with her lifelong love of horses. "Cowboys and the Arabian breed share a mythical appeal that makes for great romance—pairing the two was a natural choice."

Jan lives in Texas (of course!) with her husband and two children. She'd love to hear from readers and invites you to write to her at: P.O. Box 5009-272, Sugarland, Texas, 77487.

Books by Jan Freed

HARLEQUIN SUPERROMANCE

645—TOO MANY BOSSES

Jan Freed

THE TEXAS WAY

Harlequin Books

TORONTO • NEW YORK • LONDON
AMSTERDAM • PARIS • SYDNEY • HAMBURG
STOCKHOLM • ATHENS • TOKYO • MILAN
MADRID • WARSAW • BUDAPEST • AUCKLAND

ISBN 0-373-70676-6

THE TEXAS WAY

This edition published by arrangement with Harlequin Books S.A.

® and TM are trademarks of the publisher. Trademarks indicated with
® are registered in the United States Patent and Trademark Office, the
Canadian Trade Marks Office and in other countries.

Printed in U.S.A.

To Mica Kelch and Marian May, sisters in madness and valued friends. And to Jenny Hiller, blood sister and my truest fan. Thanks for the advice and support, buds!

Special thanks to Sharon and Xavier Moreau, owners of Bloodstock International, Inc., for sharing their knowledge of the Arabian horse industry. Any errors are accidental and entirely my fault.

CHAPTER ONE

MARGARET CHELSEA WINSTON crouched behind a clump of cacti, peeked over one spiny rim and forgot to breathe.

Moonlight leeched all color from the red clay and yellowed grass. Only light and dark contrasts remained. At the center of this ghostly vista stood a commanding figure, the embodiment of proud male arrogance—a shimmering gray stallion.

Twist of Fate, she'd named him six years ago, hoping she wasn't overestimating his potential, praying he'd really beaten the genetic odds. He had. His magnificence surpassed her girlish dreams. He was one of the finest Arabians in the world.

Gripped with excitement, she rose and stood tall, giving him time to study her as thoroughly as she had him. Earthy smells nettled her nose. Coyotes yipped in the distance, two, maybe three miles away. Sound carried far in this part of Texas.

He stared back across the stark landscape, his dark gaze asking, *Who watches me in the night?*

A friend, she answered, not questioning their silent communication. She'd long ago accepted her uncanny rapport with animals as compensation for the skills she lacked.

After learning the stallion still lived in this area, she'd planned on sneaking a glimpse, then slipping away unseen. But nothing had prepared her for the ambition and resentment he awakened—the burning need to reclaim him.

She walked to the fence and slipped between the strands of barbed wire. "Hey, handsome. What's a fella like you doing in a place like this?"

She kept her voice soothing, knowing he understood her tone if not the words. Ears pricked forward, he blew short and hard through flared nostrils. A fluttering snort would have indicated fear. She smiled.

"Curious, huh? I came to get reacquainted, that's all."

Her initial impression had been correct. Strong topline, wide airway, compact proportions. Perfect. Her mind whirled with possibilities. She forced her thoughts to focus, her movements to remain fluid.

Holding his alert gaze, she walked the last few feet and stood nose to muzzle. "Don't run out on me, okay, handsome? I could use a little company right now. Things've been . . ." Lousy. Miserable.

Normal.

The insidious emotions struck out of nowhere, stinging her eyes and swelling her throat. Damn, damn, *damn!* So what if she'd never felt more alone in all her twenty-six years? She'd made the right decision, and by God she would prove it. Her new life wouldn't tolerate weakness. She wouldn't tolerate weakness in herself, not ever again.

Warm breath blasted her face, jolting her back to the present.

Here is my special smell, his action said. *If you trust it, we might be friends.*

She stared at the chiseled muzzle only inches away. How many years had passed since she'd been offered simple, innocent friendship? Too many, judging by her fierce desire to hug the stallion's neck. Suppressing the urge, she responded to his overture in horse language and blew gently into his nostrils.

When he lowered his head, she laughed in delight. "I like you, too."

She squeezed a portion of silver mane between her thumb and forefinger, then rubbed the strands together. The simulated grooming action of equine teeth demonstrated her friendliness. More so than if she'd stroked him in the usual way.

Working her fingers up and down the mane, she frowned. His thick gray coat, shaggy fetlocks and furry ears hadn't felt the buzz of clipping shears in months. Trust a cowboy to let an animal of this caliber winter in the open like a second-string range pony. No warm stable for this beauty, oh, no. After all, that wouldn't be the Texas way of doing things. Lord knew this stallion's owner hated "pampered creatures." She ought to know. Memory of the tall rancher's contempt narrowed her eyes. "He ought to be horse-whipped, pardon the expression."

Finger-nibbling her way across the stallion's shoulder and ribs, she noted plenty of lean muscle but no bony protrusions. In all fairness, he appeared to be well fed and in excellent health.

Some experts considered rough terrain ideal training conditions. If true, she'd be that much ahead of the game. What she wouldn't give to put him through his paces!

Gauging the height of his withers, she glanced up at the full moon, then down at the illuminated ground. Temptation won over caution. She reached up and grasped a handful of mane.

The stallion suddenly tensed, lifted his head and shifted to the right. Margaret sidestepped his clattering hooves.

"Easy, handsome. Don't be afraid. How'd you like to go for a little ride?" Tightening her fist, she gathered her muscles into vault position and gasped.

Cold metal—round, hollow and unmistakably lethal—pressed into her neck.

"Don't listen to her, Twister," a deep voice drawled from behind. "Takin' a ride with Maggie here can kill a guy."

Blood rushed to her face in a sickening wave of guilt. She dropped her forehead against the stallion's hide, inhaling the pungent scent of warm animal and dried sweat. The gun followed her movement.

"You," she whispered.

"Yeah, me. The owner of the land you're trespassin' on. Next time you try stealin' a horse, Maggie, don't park so close to the main gate. That Porsche is a little conspicuous."

"I wasn't stealing...Twister, is that what you called him? I only wanted to see what he could do."

His mocking laugh set her teeth on edge.

"Maggie, darlin', the minute your fanny hit his back you'd be on your way to Mars. Beats the hell outta me how you ever got this close." Honest puzzlement tinged his voice.

Her head jerked up. "Don't call me Maggie."

The pressure against her neck increased. "Well now, seems to me I can call you any name I want. And right this minute, Maggie is the nicest one that comes to mind."

Nothing had changed. He would never forget—or forgive. She released the stallion's mane and straightened her shoulders.

"Put the gun down, please. I'm not going to do anything foolish."

The pressure eased, replaced by the sliding caress of a gun barrel. "All grown up now, are you? Let's take a look. Turn around."

Margaret's heart slammed against her ribs. Her entire future depended on the mercy of this man, as it had once before. She was damned if she'd wimp out this time.

Schooling her features into a cool mask, she slowly turned.

Scott Hayes lifted pistol point to Stetson brim and nudged upward. His eyes gleamed colorless and flat in the moon's glow, but she knew they were lion gold and insolent as a cat's. His gaze roved over her body now with the calculated intention of rattling her composure.

But contrary to his sarcasm, she *had* grown up. So she ignored her erratic pulse and conducted her own slow inspection. He was taller than she remembered,

around six foot two perhaps. Or maybe it was just that
damned hat he wore. At midnight, for Pete's sake. In
the few times she'd seen him, she'd never laid eyes on
his hair—other than the brownish waves breaking over
his shirt collar. Maybe he was hiding a bald spot.

She smiled at the malicious thought.

He crossed his arms and cocked one knee, the action drawing attention to his rangy legs, lean hips and
impossibly wide shoulders.

"Mind tellin' me what's so funny?"

Her smile faded. She looked him in the eye. "Yes.
I do mind."

Surprise flickered across his bold features. She
sensed a new awareness in him, a reassessing of her
will, and drew strength from having knocked the
cocksure look off his face.

He'd filled out in six years, but then, Texas ranching bred muscular men. To add to Scott's physical
workload, H & H Cattle Company was down to one
hired hand. Or so she'd heard. Word was the business
teetered on the edge of bankruptcy. She hoped to God
that was true.

Scott jammed the gunpoint down behind his belt,
against the tight denim molding everything it touched.
His gun wasn't loaded, she realized. He wouldn't risk
damaging his precious . . . jeans.

Cheeks burning, she jerked her gaze up.

His cocky smirk was back, along with a disturbing
new gleam in his eyes. "You keep lookin' at me like
that, and I'm gonna think that husband of yours
doesn't know how to keep you hap—'' His eyes widened.

She started to turn. Twister's bared teeth caught her ponytail just as Scott's strong hands gripped her shoulders and pulled. Margaret rebounded in the circle of his arms like a bungee cord.

"Dammit, Maggie! What the hell are you doin' messin' with this stud? He's mean as a javelina hog around everyone but me."

When his arms pulled her close, a strange sense of safety clouded her brain. Nose, chest, stomach and thigh pressed against Scott Hayes, she groped for concentration.

"Twister eats little girls like you for breakfast. If I hadn't grabbed you when I did, he woulda torn this pretty blond scalp of yours clean off."

His touch was so light, at first she didn't notice. Once she did, every hair follicle stood at attention.

"What were you thinkin' of, tryin' to ride that son of a bitch? At night. Bareback, no less."

Some of Scott's contempt filtered through Margaret's fog.

"Damned stupid, Maggie. Don't you have the sense God gave a goose?"

His barbed insult hit bull's-eye this time. For a moment she quivered under the impact. A lifetime of similar taunts echoed in her mind.

Melissa can read, Margaret, and she's two years younger than you.... I'm afraid Margaret just doesn't apply herself, Mrs. Winston.... That was a very important call, Margaret. Can't you even write down a simple phone number?... For heaven's sake Margaret, how could you be so stupid-stupid-stupid-stupid....

"Margaret? Margaret?" Scott gave her a shake.

She blinked twice, looked up and bumped her head against his jaw.

"Ow!" they both yelled. Breaking apart like boxers from a clench, they faced off and took each other's measure.

Feeling puny by comparison, Margaret glared. Behind her, Twister cropped grass. She jerked a thumb at the horse.

"Does that look like a violent animal to you? For your information, Twister was trying to groom me, not bite me. He was showing his trust. If you hadn't interfered, everything would have been fine." She arched an eyebrow. "Of course, breaking up relationships is what you do best, isn't it?"

Lit by moonlight, his dusky complexion darkened in embarrassment. Or anger. She didn't care which. That she'd struck a nerve at all filled her with triumph.

He tugged down his hat brim and shrugged. "I protect what needs protecting. Call it what you want."

"I call it betrayal," she said, abandoning all pretense of talking about the present. "I've spent every day since the car accident paying for my mistake, Scott. But you betrayed me. Worse, you betrayed your best friend. And my father rewarded you for it. He had no right—" She stopped, hating the quaver in her voice.

Donald Winston's action didn't bear thinking about. She'd concentrate on one betrayal at a time. "It's taken six years, Scott, but you're finally going to pay *me* what's due."

His mouth thinned. "And what's that?"

She took a deep breath. "Twister."

He ripped off his hat and slapped it against his thigh. "Like hell!"

Twister's head swept up. His tail lifted high. He exploded from a complete standstill to a full-stretch gallop in the time it took her to blink. Mesmerized, she watched him float over the uneven ground toward the far end of the field. She could no more control her elated smile than stop her heart from soaring. Man, could that horse run!

"I want him back, Scott." Turning, she caught him staring not at Twister, but at her.

"Forget it. Twister belongs to me. I've got the papers to prove it." End of discussion, his expression said.

She lifted her nose. "Papers Daddy transferred to your name without my knowledge. I never would've let Riverbend Arabian Farm give up that foal. You knew that when you accepted him. That's *why* you accepted him." Suppressed hurt welled to the surface. Why did she still care?

"Don't flatter yourself. Only a fool would've turned him down. He's a valuable animal. Special."

"Oh, right. He's so valuable you don't care if he breaks his leg in a gopher hole or cuts himself on barbed wire or throws a shoe and pulls up lame. It could happen out here and you wouldn't even know it." Her disdainful gaze swept the rock-strewn pasture. "If this is how you treat 'special' animals, I shudder to think about your poor cattle."

Scott laughed unexpectedly, the moonlight glinting off his straight, white teeth. "Lower your nose, princess. I'll have you know every one of my Santa Gertrudis has a pedigree longer than yours. I treat 'em same's I do Twister. Feed 'em. Doctor 'em when they're sick. And pretty much let 'em do what God intended."

Settling the Stetson low on his forehead, he sobered abruptly. "Pamperin' my stock would be downright cruel. They'd die come the first summer drought or winter storm." He squinted at a nearby cactus, at the moon and, finally, at her. "It takes a special breed to survive this land. But it's got nothin' to do with bloodlines. You have any idea what I'm sayin', Maggie?"

His eyes glittered with sudden intensity, as if her answer were somehow important.

She knew what he meant all right. He thought her weak and spoiled and worthless. Trouble was, so had she for too many long, miserable years.

Averting her eyes, she hugged her stomach and focused on Twister, now grazing in the distance. "I understand your hay may not last much longer. And your credit's maxed out at Luling Feed and Hardware. And you could really use some cash right now."

She risked a glance at Scott and wished she hadn't.

"Spit it out," he said as if he'd like to spit on her.

"I want to make a deal with you for Twister."

In answer, he turned and headed for the fence line, his boots crunching hard and determined on the ground. "Go home, Maggie," he called over his shoulder.

Home? She watched his bobbing hat grow smaller and felt alone. So alone. "Hey, wait!"

Even running, it took her several moments to reach his side. "Why won't you listen?" she managed breathlessly, hop-skipping every other step to keep up. "I'll treat him like he deserves. He's being totally wasted out here. H & H Cattle Company doesn't need him, but I do."

They'd reached the barbed-wire fence. Resting a forearm on the top strand, Scott tilted up his hat brim. Silvery light flooded his face.

Margaret took a half step back, as if she'd caught a snarling predator in her flashlight beam.

"You need him?" His sardonic stare traveled over her Italian half boots, designer jeans and lambskin jacket. Their gazes clashed and held. "Run out of toys to play with? That lawyer husband of yours spending too much time in court maybe?" His upper lip curled. "Too bad, Maggie. There are lots of other horses. You've got lots of money. Find another stallion to need."

Having tried, judged and convicted her, he resettled his hat, pressed down on the wire and prepared to cross.

Margaret had spent a lifetime following everyone's wishes but her own. Just this once, for something this important, someone would listen to her. Fury fueled her reflexes. She rushed forward and slapped down his arcing leg.

"Just a minute, buster! Think you've got me pegged? Think you know everything? You know nothing. *Nothing,* do you hear? I spent two years researching bloodlines before selecting Twister's Polish sire. I agonized waiting for Aladdin's Girl to be shipped home. I dreamed of her producing the perfect equine athlete, a foundation stud for the most elite line of Arabians in the world. And she did it! *I* did it. But you—'' she grabbed two fistfuls of shirt ''—have the supreme gall to deprive breeders of that line. And why?''

She leaned forward until her forehead grazed his hat brim. ''Because you think I'm rich. Because you think I'm a bored housewife looking for thrills. Because you hate my guts.''

''Mag—''

''Well, I've got news for you, Scott Hayes. I have no money. I have no husband. And I hate your guts right back. You're a selfish, judgmental jerk, and you've ruined my life for the last time!'' Her chest rose and fell in labored breaths.

''You have no husband?''

She stood close enough to count his eyelashes. Obscenely thick, they couldn't hide the stunned expression in his eyes. Her anger drained, leaving her feeling oddly at peace. She'd finally stood up for herself.

Realizing her hands still gripped his shirtfront, she relaxed her hold and smoothed the wrinkled cotton with self-conscious, outward swipes. Her fingers landed on rounded biceps, fluttered, then settled in the crook of his arm. The man was made of rock.

In the bright moonlight his throat looked strong, his chin square and stubborn. Fascinated, she stared at the dark stubble shadowing his jaw. Her ex-husband, Jim, had shaved faithfully every morning, but more from routine than necessity. Did a heavy beard feel different?

As if sensing her sudden impulse, Scott stepped back out of reach. "Okay, Maggie. We'll hash this thing out. But we'll damn well do it on my terms, not when I'm tired and mad and . . . hungry." There was a distinctly sensual growl in his voice.

Her gaze flew to his. What had gotten into her responding to his nearness like that? He was Gonzales County's reigning Lothario, and her enemy to boot.

His expression hardened. "Be at my back door by eight tomorrow. You're one minute late, we don't talk. Understand?"

"I understand."

He nodded, pressed down on the top fence strand and crossed over with practiced ease. She waited for him to turn and offer assistance. He walked on without a backward glance, his broad shoulders disappearing behind a stand of mesquite trees.

She understood all right. Perfectly.

BY SEVEN the next morning, Scott had finished his barn chores and moved on to kitchen duty. Closing the refrigerator door with one hip, he ignored the rattle of jars and bottles inside. He knew exactly how much pressure the old appliance could take before its guts spilled. The Cokes were safe.

He poured Eggbeaters into a bowl, whipped them to a froth and set them aside. Turkey bacon popped and sizzled in the skillet almost like the real thing. Inhaling its dubious scent, he hoped the stuff would tempt his father's appetite. Grant Hayes's recent heart surgery had taken off another five pounds. Pounds he couldn't afford to lose, together with the weight he'd already burned off from pure worry.

Dragging a hand down his jaw, Scott glanced at the clock above the stove. No time to shave. Margaret—*Maggie,* he corrected with a fleeting grin—would be here soon. He wanted Dad fed and out of the house by then.

His performing the cooking tasks by rote allowed his mind to dwell on the astounding events of last night. He still couldn't believe it. Margaret Chelsea Winston—model of propriety and good breeding—sneaking into his field like a common horse thief! Last he'd heard, she was married to some hotshot Dallas lawyer and was living the Junior League life. No surprise there. Her sass, though, had clipped him on the chin when he wasn't looking.

The Margaret he'd known would never have ranted till he actually doubted his own judgment. She would've lifted her oh-so-proper nose and given him her patented look. The one that said, "I don't talk to pond scum." The one that made him feel uncouth and awkward. The one that made him call her Maggie, knowing she hated the unsophisticated nickname.

Yet last night, for the first time, she'd seemed like a Maggie. Human. Approachable. Her passion for Twister was the genuine article, Scott admitted. Nothing else could explain her foolish attempt to ride the devil. He'd damn near had a heart attack when the stallion had gone for her head!

Forget all that crap about grooming. This was the same horse who'd taken a big enough chunk out of

Pete's butt to make the wrangler sit crooked the rest of his days. And she was such a little thing. Fragile as those porcelain doodads his mother had loved. Nestled against his body, Margaret had barely reached his chin.

Memory seared a path straight to his groin. She might be small, but there was nothing childish about her body. Lord, but she'd felt good in his arms. Really good.

She got under Matt's skin too, buzzard brain, and look what happened.

Scott shook off his thoughts and stared. Two plates loaded with scrambled eggs, bacon and dry toast steamed on the counter. The chipped Formica table was set for two, the juice glasses already filled. This evidence of his total absorption with Maggie scared him more than any mental talking-to could.

She'd dredged up a muck of feelings better left buried. He would listen to what she had to say, then boot her out of his kitchen—and his life.

"Breakfast!" he called, setting the plates on the table and scraping back his chair.

A door squeaked open. Boots clumped down the planked hall. Grant filled the doorway, his graying auburn hair mere inches from the frame. Faded jeans sagged at his waist; a once-tight shirt puckered at his shoulders and stomach. He seemed thinner and older than the last time Scott had paused long enough to look.

Testing the air like a coon hound, Grant cast a cautious look at the table. "Thanks, son. Looks good."

Liar. Scott forced a quick smile. "Eat up then. I'm tired of looking fat compared to you. Bad for my ego."

Grinning, Grant strode to the table and sat down. "The day your ego suffers, I'll eat a carton of ice cream to celebrate. Seems to me your sister made a similar promise not long ago, something about... flowers, was it?"

Regretting he'd ever told his dad that story, Scott grunted and dug into his eggs. Laura's exact phrase had vibrated with frustration. *Someday a woman is going to bring you to your knees, Scott Hayes. And when she does, I'll send her a dozen roses.*

His mouth twitched at the thought of poor Alec. Laura had cut him off at the kneecaps, but Scott knew his brother-in-law had dropped willingly.

Too soon, Grant put his fork down and made a show of patting his stomach. "What are your plans today?"

Scott eyed his father's half-filled plate and scowled. "The windmill up on the red hill is jammed. Pete said it looks like a tree branch. Shouldn't take more than an hour to fix, so I thought I'd ride the north fence line while I'm at it."

"Good idea. I could start at the county road and meet—"

"Dad."

Grant tightened his mouth and glared out the small window above the sink. His strong, callused fingers clenched once, then relaxed. When he turned to Scott, his leaf green eyes were calm and resigned.

"If you're not using the truck, maybe I'll take a look at the carburetor. The ol' girl could probably use an oil change, too."

Scott swallowed hard. Physical weakness demoralized a man of Grant's former vigor. "Yeah, Dad, that'd be great. If I'm not back by lunch, there's still some of Ellen's casserole in the fridge."

His father's pained groan made him grin. The vacuous widow's visits strained even Grant Hayes's good manners.

The sound of an engine's purr turned both their heads. Scott's stomach flip-flopped, a sensation he hadn't felt since his teens. He pushed back his chair, carried plates to the sink and began rinsing. Through the window, he watched a sleek red Porsche crawl up the graveled drive.

His father's mildly questioning glance suddenly deepened. "Expecting someone?"

"Margaret Winston. Remember her?" Scott forced a nonchalance he didn't feel.

"B'lieve the name rings a bell." Grant's wry tone said he remembered enough.

A thousand questions hung in the air. That they remained unasked was a measure of their mutual respect.

"She wants to buy Twister," Scott confessed. Not for a minute had he believed that crock about her having no money. Drying his hands on a dish towel, he turned and met his father's eyes. "I'm just listening out of courtesy."

Grant's expression eased. "Don't do anything rash." He rose and clasped Scott's shoulder. "I'd sell Bandolero before I'd let you give up Twister."

The prize bull was one of the few ranch assets left with a hefty market value. Scott reached up and squeezed his father's forearm. "It won't come to that."

A car door slammed. Gravel crunched.

"I'll get out of your way," Grant said, giving Scott an odd look.

The screen door twanged open. Knuckles rapped on the door.

"Why don't I get that?" Grant suggested, his green eyes twinkling now.

Scott heard his father introduce himself and exchange pleasantries, then excuse himself to work on the truck. He heard the screen door whack. But he saw only Margaret.

If he'd entertained any doubts about where she belonged, he now knew with certainty it wasn't in his kitchen.

She stood like a calla lily on the dingy white linoleum. Graceful. Delicate. Lovely in the way of women blessed with classic bone structure, rather than voluptuous curves. Her soft gray sweater and matching slacks complemented eyes the color of smoke, skin fine as bone china, hair glinting gold in the sunbeam streaming through the door.

Last night, he'd thought she must look her best in moonlight. He wished to hell he'd been right.

She squinted at the clock a long moment, then smiled hesitantly. "Right on time... aren't I?"

He checked the clock. Eight o'clock on the money. Apparently her vanity wouldn't permit wearing glasses.

He nodded toward the table. "Sit down."

She glanced at the rickety dinette, and Scott imagined her inner shudder. He hadn't even swiped it down after the meal. But she pulled out a cracked vinyl chair and sat with nary a blink.

"Thank you." She waved a graceful hand at the opposite chair. "Please, you sit down, too."

As usual, the more graciously she behaved, the ruder he felt. He might as well act the part.

Plucking his Stetson off the refrigerator, Scott jammed it low. He flipped around the chair nearest her and dropped into a straddle. "So talk."

"I'm prepared to offer you five thousand dollars for Twist of Fate... for Twister. Cash on delivery."

So much for preliminaries. He stacked his fists on the chair back and planted his chin. "That's a lot of money for someone who has no money," he drawled, waiting for her blush to peak before continuing. "But it's not a fraction of what he's worth."

"Not if he was a show-ring champion. But Twister's never been campaigned. Never sired any proven get."

"Campaigned? Proven? We're talking about a stallion, here, not a damn politician. Twister's got nothin' to prove as far as I'm concerned."

"Wasting his potential is criminal! And stupendously selfish. And... and just plain ignorant! You don't deserve to own him."

There was that passion again. So unlike the girl he'd known. So intense he couldn't take his eyes off her. He dropped his voice a husky note. "So make me an offer I can't refuse, Maggie."

Color splashed her cheeks. "I don't have any more money, damn you. I don't have a home. I don't even own that Porsche out there. The lease expires next week."

He frowned, feeling a niggle of unease. "Your husband?"

"We've been divorced a month."

He raised his eyebrows. "No settlement money?"

"The prenuptial agreement was airtight. He was a lawyer, after all."

She said it matter-of-factly, as if signing such agreements before pledging to honor and love your life mate was normal. He supposed in her privileged world, that was true.

"There's always Daddy," he said, his voice cynical. Donald Winston spared no expense when it came to his precious daughter. And his pockets were very deep.

Her mouth clamped shut. Her color heightened. She drew a cloak of dignity around her narrow shoulders.

"I'll be damned. The old man cut you off."

With sudden clarity, Scott remembered just how far her father would go to teach Margaret a lesson. Questions whirled like dust devils in his mind. He snatched at the nearest one.

"What'll you do now?"

She gave a humorless laugh and stared at her clasped fingers. Scott doubted if those creamy, manicured hands had done more than dial a phone in the past six years. With grudging admiration, he watched her trembling lips firm, her spine stiffen and her chin lift. She met his eyes squarely.

"Give me a job."

CHAPTER TWO

MARGARET FELT her courage falter, smothered beneath Scott's heavy silence. The electric hum of the ancient refrigerator mingled with the dull roar of blood in her ears. She took a deep breath. Big mistake. Musty house and strange breakfast odors wreaked havoc on her nervous stomach.

"Come again?" Scott finally asked, his amusement insulting.

"If you won't sell Twister, hire me to train him. I guarantee within six months he'll pump cash back into H & H Cattle Company. He'll bring in a bundle standing at stud."

"It takes years of training to bring a horse up to national competition level. Even I know that. H & H Cattle Company doesn't have years," he admitted grimly.

"You're thinking in terms of show-ring competition. That's not what I have in mind." The excitement she'd nurtured for weeks bubbled in her voice.

"Wanna let me in on your secret?"

"Twister has the makings of a champion racehorse."

"*Racehorse?*" Scott's incredulous stare grew pitying. "He's six years old—over the hill by at least two years. Besides, Thoroughbreds race, not Arabians."

"Oh, but you're wrong. Arabian racing is well established in Europe and the Middle East. It's a hot trend in the States now. Not only that, an Arabian's prime racing years begin at age five." She paused, savoring his dazed expression. "But that's not the best part."

"No?"

She shook her head. "The best part is, breeders are clamoring for a particular type of Arabian. One with a conformation suited to running, rather than class performance. One that is relatively rare right now and therefore brings top stud fees. There's a huge demand now for an Arabian like Twister."

Unable to contain herself any longer, she broke into a huge smile. "And we have a lock on the supply!"

"*We* have a lock on the supply?" Scott lifted one tawny brow to meet his hat band. Rising, he hooked a chair leg with his boot and slung the seat around. "I don't recall selling you any portion of my racehorse, Maggie."

She looked up into eyes the color of scotch whiskey—and lost both her smile and her capacity to speak. His lazy, masculine confidence had always twisted her up inside. But she couldn't let him intimidate her now. She had too much to lose.

As if he read her mind, his mouth quirked upward. He shoved his chair under the table and sauntered toward an aluminum percolator plugged into an outlet near the sink. Helpless to stop herself, she watched the rolling action of his lean hips and tight butt.

Jim hadn't walked like that. Neither had Matt. The truth was, no other man in her civilized experience had ever moved with quite the same feline grace and male swagger as this tall cowboy.

Opening a painted cabinet door of indeterminate color, he pulled down two mismatched ceramic mugs and looked back over one shoulder.

Caught admiring the broad stretch of his faded blue shirt, Margaret froze. He held her gaze, his own smoldering beneath sooty lashes.

"How do you like your coffee?"

He might have been asking how she liked her sex, so intimate was his tone. Margaret had never hated her fair complexion more.

"I don't drink coffee, thank you." Even to her own ears, she sounded priggish.

Shrugging, he filled his mug, turned and propped a negligent hip against the counter. "I think this farce has gone on long enough, don't you?"

"Farce?"

"This fairy tale about Twister racing. I'll give you credit for trying. But you of all people should know I can't give you a job." He took a leisurely sip of coffee, his eyes watchful behind tendrils of steam.

She stiffened. "Can't? Or won't?"

He lowered the mug. Those eyes were glittering dangerously now. His dark stubbled jaw clenched and unclenched. "Need a refresher course, Maggie? Okay. My hay won't last, my credit's maxed out, and I could really use some cash right now—you seemed to grasp the situation clearly enough last night. So what makes you think I can afford to pay you a salary today?"

Her stomach roiling, Margaret picked a nonexistent piece of lint from her cashmere sleeve.

"Run on home to Daddy while you still can, Maggie. You'd be plain stupid not to."

Margaret's chin came up. She skipped angry and went straight to livid. "Don't call me Maggie. *And don't call me stupid.*"

She jumped up and stalked to within an arm's length of his slouching form. "Who said anything about a salary, Einstein? I'm interested in a joint venture. My expertise and seed money in exchange for fifty percent ownership of Twister, plus room and board."

Scott set his mug down with a snort. "Dream on, princess. Twister is mine and that's that. Besides, he's half-wild. What makes you think he'll even respond to you?"

It was Margaret's turn to snort. "He'll respond."

On sure ground at last, she dismissed his skepticism and prowled the room. "I'll take care of insurance, feed, farrier, veterinary and transportation costs for the first five months. With creative management, five thousand dollars ought to just about cover it. After Twister wins the Armand Hammer Classic in August, we'll split the bills fifty-fifty." She slanted him a challenging look. "And, of course, the profits, too."

Scott straightened, forcing her to tilt her head back. His thick brows drew together into a daunting V. "What profits are we talking about here? A couple of grand a month in stud fees? That'd be nice, but hardly enough to pay the note due on H & H Cattle Company." His features hardened. "Frankly, putting up with you isn't worth it."

My life in a nutshell, cowboy. Her throat constricting, she examined one smooth coral fingernail with forced indifference. When she could safely speak again, Margaret met his gaze.

"The Armand Hammer Classic offers a fifty-thousand-dollar purse. Top racing sires command stud fees of up to five thousand dollars a mare. By conservative estimates, Twister could earn over a half-million dollars a year for the next ten years. Would that be worth putting up with me?"

His slack-jawed surprise did wonders for her bruised ego. Thankful she'd done her research, she played her ace. "If you won't do it for yourself, think of your father. With that kind of working capital, you could hire all the hands you need, make a big dent in his medical bills."

Muttering a foul word, he spun around to brace both palms on the lip of the rusted sink and stare out the window. She followed his gaze. For once, fate was on her side.

Blurred by the dirty glass panes, Grant Hayes stood outside the barn wiping his fingers on a faded red cloth. Pausing, he lifted the rag with trembling fingers to his forehead and blotted twice before continuing his listless cleaning. If she hadn't heard about his triple-bypass surgery, she would have suspected worse. He looked pale and exhausted.

Watching Scott's chin drop and his knuckles whiten, Margaret felt her satisfaction slink away in shame. If anyone understood the sickening helplessness of emotional blackmail, she did. She'd had no right to bring his ailing father into their battle.

Scott slowly raised his head and spoke without turning. "All right, Maggie, you win. But I swear to God, before we're through you'll wish you hadn't."

TWENTY-FOUR HOURS LATER, Margaret parked just outside H & H Cattle Company's gate and listened to the powerful engine idle. This was it. Her chance for independence and the fulfillment of a dream she'd cherished since first becoming enchanted with Arabians as a teenager. Scott's agreement to a joint-venture partnership yesterday could establish her as a top breeder and trainer, a woman to be respected, instead of ridiculed. A woman who didn't need a man to survive.

True, she was dependent on Scott now. But then, he was equally dependent on her. With luck, they'd separate in less than six months in a position to pursue their individual goals and change their lives. Money had that power, she'd learned early in life. Her father made sure she never forgot it.

Morning sunlight winked off the eighteen-karat-gold initial key ring her parents had presented—along with a flashy silver Corvette—for her sixteenth birthday. A reward, she recalled wryly, for winning four blue ribbons in a class "A" horse show.

After years of disappointing them with poor grades, botched recitals and social faux pas, she'd been pathetically happy at the proud smiles on their faces. Her riding instructor had mentioned that with a finer horse, Margaret had the potential to become a national champion. Donald Winston's eyes had gleamed at the prospect.

Margaret dropped her forehead against the steering wheel and succumbed to bittersweet memories of the Arabian horse farm her father had established adjacent to Scott's ranch. Riverbend. In many ways, her life had begun—and ended—at the prosperous breeding and training facility.

She'd spent five summers and many holidays there under the tutelage of Liz Howarth, Riverbend's manager and a former member of the U.S. Olympic equestrian team. Yet Liz's lessons had been a joy. Her instructions had been easily understood. Wonder of wonders, her teaching hadn't been hindered by her student's dyslexia.

Margaret squeezed her eyes shut, remembering the incalculable frustration and humiliation her impairment had caused throughout her childhood. The exclusive girls' boarding schools she'd attended had been staffed to train future matrons of society, not detect learning disabilities. She'd often wondered why she advanced to the next grade each year. Later, she'd learned her father was a most generous benefactor of each school she attended.

Heaven bless Miss Jenkins. The seventh-grade English teacher had possessed the perception and integrity to insist Margaret be tested by a specialist. Donald and Gloria had first denied, then been embarrassed by, their daughter's problem. But Margaret had received the news with profound gratitude.

She wasn't stupid. She wasn't! There was a medical reason for the jumbled mess her mind made of letters and numbers. With specialized tutoring, she could learn to decipher the world in ways she could understand. Her relief had been shattering. Liberating.

Lifting her forehead from the leather-wrapped wheel, Margaret blinked at the rutted road winding beyond the open gate. She'd almost conquered her debilitating insecurity six years ago, only to be knocked down again with brutal force.

Matt. Oh, Matt, I'd turn back the clock and start over, if I could.

But she couldn't. She could only go forward and live with her guilt as best she could. Funny how life had brought her full circle to the man least likely to help her forget Matt's death.

Straightening her shoulders, she shifted gears and drove over the rattling cattle guard, past the sagging aluminum gate propped against a fence post. Scott Hayes was every bit as domineering as her father and ex-husband. Maybe more so. Living with his contempt on a daily basis, striving to earn his respect, would be the toughest challenge she'd ever faced.

As the Porsche climbed an ungraded road and topped the steep rise, Margaret set her jaw. Scott might call her Maggie, but it wasn't the first nickname she'd been given. Teachers and schoolmates alike had awarded her another epithet after experiencing her tenacious, dogged . . . persistence, she preferred to call it.

Scott would have his own challenge to deal with, Margaret vowed, looking down the hill at a dilapidated barn and house. Her new partner was about to face The Mule.

IN THE FARMHOUSE BELOW, Grant stared at his bedroom ceiling and watched the fan blades whirl. Pitiful, he thought. There was a time he would've already put in four hours of hard labor by ten o'clock, and here he lay weak as a kitten from washing the breakfast dishes. Damn his traitorous heart! Fifty-three wasn't *that* old. Yet his ticker had given out when Scott needed him most. And now the medical bills, on top of the bank note . . .

He closed his eyes and willed himself to rest. To heal. The fan motor whirred. The pull chain ticked against the swaying brass casing like a metronome. He fingered the nubby chenille bedspread Patricia had bought their first year of marriage and sighed wistfully.

After eighteen years, he still missed her. She'd been too fine and cultured for a simple rancher like him, but he'd accepted the gift of her love and tried to be worthy. They'd had ambitious plans for H & H Cattle Company once. Then cancer had struck, and his dreams had died with her. His body had gone through the motions of ranch chores. He'd loved his children and kept a roof over their heads. Occasionally he'd slaked his physical needs with an equally lonely widow in Gonzales.

But his heart had remained insulated. He simply hadn't cared about improving the place or making it profitable. And now Scott was paying the price.

Pain that had nothing to do with his operation made Grant wince. For eighteen years, he'd been sleepwalking through life, his memories of Patricia more real to him than the deteriorating ranch. Damned if he'd asked to wake up, but he didn't seem to have much choice in the matter these days.

A loud ruckus broke out in the barn. Masculine shouts. Twister's whinny. Grant listened for a tense moment, then relaxed back against his pillow. No point in getting up really. If there was a problem, Scott would handle it.

He always did.

THE DOUBLE CRACK of iron-shod hooves against wood reverberated throughout the barn.

"Dammit, Pete, I told you to stay back! You know he hates the sight of you." Scott threw an irritated glance over his shoulder.

"Well, he don't exactly make the sun shine for me, neither," the peppery old cowhand grumbled, shuffling to a safer distance.

Scott ignored Pete's injured feelings and concentrated on the greater problem at hand. What the hell was wrong with Twister?

The stallion danced restlessly on the far side of the twelve-by-twenty-foot stall, his bunched muscles rippling beneath a pearl gray coat. Charcoal velvet nostrils fluttered in distress. His silver tail swished up and down, side to side.

"Come on, boy. Don't you want to get out and stretch your legs?" Scott moved slowly into the stall and clasped a lead rope to the nylon halter. Thank goodness he'd forgotten to remove the halter last night before returning to the house.

Noting the full feed bin, he frowned. "What's the matter, Twister? You're usually a pig. Are you getting sick maybe?"

A coil of dread tightened Scott's belly. Ranch life had hastened his mother's death, crushed his younger sister Laura's spirit, weakened the heart of his once-invincible father. He sent up a silent prayer. *Please God, not Twister, too.*

Backing out the open door, Scott pulled the rope taut.

Twister planted his forelegs and refused to budge. Eyes rolling, sides heaving, sweat lathering his neck and flanks, he nickered low and deep.

Scott turned toward Pete. "Go up to the house and ask Dad to call Doc Chalmers. Something's wrong with Twister, but hell if I can figure out what."

"Car's comin' down the road," Pete observed from the barn doorway. "Fancy thing, just like the girlie drivin' it."

Scott drew in a hissing breath. *Maggie.* Damn. He'd thought it would take her at least a day to pack whatever a princess needed to live among the common folk. He didn't have time for her royal crap now.

"Just do what I ask and get the Doc out here. Tell him it's an emergency."

"I'm goin', I'm goin'." Pete pushed off the doorframe and ambled toward the house, his voice drifting back in mumbled snatches. "Too dang mean to be sick...into some loco weed...do this, Pete, do that, Pete..."

Doc Chalmers wouldn't go into a stall with the fractious stallion for a truckload of money. The veterinarian had made that clear the last time Twister had landed a well-aimed hoof.

Scott dug in his heels and pulled harder on the rope. "Come on out, dammit. You don't even *like* being in there." Sweat trickled into his eyes, stinging like hell. He lifted one arm and rubbed his forehead, knocking his hat off in the process. His T-shirt clung damply, his jeans felt hot and scratchy—and he was playing tug-of-war with a friggin' elephant!

Twister nickered again, but something about the sound was different this time. And suddenly Scott knew. Knew even before the light, fresh scent filled his lungs with spring flowers and his mind with images of sunlit hair.

"What is he afraid of?" the cultured, feminine voice asked from several feet behind.

Scott slackened the rope and watched his proud, beautiful stallion shiver. "He's not afraid. He's sick. Doc Chalmers is on the way."

"He's terrified," Margaret insisted, walking up to stand beside Scott in the stall doorway.

In the dim light, her shoulder-length hair glimmered palely—her translucent gray eyes more palely still. She wore a sleeveless yellow dress sprigged with blue cornflowers. A thin blue satin ribbon threaded the puckered scoop neck, drawing his gaze to delicate collarbones and the hint of creamy breasts. The cotton material hung waistless, beltless, yet skimmed her curves more alluringly than spandex.

He felt like a smelly, hairy Neanderthal next to a magical fairy princess.

"Let me see what I can do." With ethereal grace, she slipped into the stall and moved toward the wild-eyed stallion.

Scott's heartbeat stalled, sputtered and roared to piston-pumping life. He was afraid to yell, afraid to do anything that might startle eleven hundred pounds of horseflesh into explosive action.

"Hiya, handsome. Remember me? Of course you do." She reached up, grabbed the halter cheek straps and pulled Twister's head down. "You wouldn't forget your new friend."

Damned if she wasn't blowing in his nose!

"Now what is it that's got you so scared? Why don't we check it out together, okay?" She took the rope from Scott and shooed him back from the doorway.

Dazed, he stumbled backward as she moved forward, her pink toenails flashing bright next to Twister's tough, yellowed hooves.

God almighty! Sandals in a horse stall. *Twister's* horse stall.

"Ready, handsome?" She did something to his mane with her fingers. Amazingly he seemed to calm down a little. "All right then, let's go."

Paralyzed, Scott watched the powerful haunches gather, the pricked ears flatten. In two tremendous leaps Twister catapulted through the door, Margaret trotting close behind. Fifteen feet away he wheeled to face the stall and backed up, snorting all the while.

Pete's skinny form darkened the barn entrance, but Twister ignored his long-standing enemy. Nothing else could have demonstrated his fear so well.

"You okay, Maggie?" Scott choked out.

Her steady gray eyes were inspecting the stall. "Whatever has him spooked is over there. See anything new or unfamiliar?"

Scott scanned the area and rumpled his hair. Nothing looked different to him. Same frayed leather bridle drooping from a rusty nail. Same packed dirt floor covered with matted straw. Same shovel leaning against—

"The hay," Pete said, moving toward Margaret with surprising hustle.

With the right incentive, those bowed legs of his could sure get up and go, Scott noted wryly.

At the wrangler's approach, Twister jerked his head back. Margaret laid her small white hand against his arched neck and murmured soothingly. Once again the stallion marginally settled.

Pete's light blue eyes widened.

"What about the hay, Mr. . . . ?" Margaret paused politely.

"Pete. Just call me Pete, miss."

She flashed a dazzling smile. "Pete, then. And please, call me Margaret."

Scott rolled his eyes. He was at a goddamn tea party.

"Were you talking about that hay over there, Pete?" She indicated two bales stacked next to the stall doorway.

"That's right, mi . . . M-Margaret." Pete doffed a battered straw hat and ducked his head, revealing a shiny brown bald spot surrounded by crinkled gray hair. "I put it there myself yesterday evenin'."

"Would you mind very much moving it away from the wall for me?"

"Don't mind a'tall, not a bit, no." He hurried to the hay and heaved the top bale down with the strength of a much younger man.

It landed with a heavy thud, missing Scott's toes by a dust mote. He narrowed his eyes and glared.

Supremely indifferent, Pete stooped over and lifted the second bale. A long black snake slithered between his boots.

Twister squealed and rode his haunches. Pete dropped the bale and cursed. Scott grabbed a shovel and swung it edge-side down at the snake.

The reptile's body and head separated; the one writhing and flipping, the other yawning pink and grotesque in search of a target.

Pete shuddered. "Ain't nothin' on this earth I hate worse'n a damn snake, even a piddly ol' bull snake. No wonder Twister went nuts. Want me to get rid of it, boss?" He looked none too thrilled at the prospect.

Scott had the shovel, after all. Grimacing, he walked toward the motionless form. "Call Doc Chalmers and see if he's left yet. I'll—"

"Wait," Margaret interrupted. "Don't move the snake yet."

Shovel extended, Scott frowned.

"Twister's been scared for hours. His territory's been threatened. He needs to protect it, to vent his fear. Let him kill the snake."

Pete glanced down at the severed, triangular head and scratched his neck. "Uh, Margaret? It's—"

"Go on and make that phone call, Pete. She knows what she's doing." Scott waited for her smug comment. When she flashed him a look of gratitude, he hid his surprise behind a scowl.

Twister's whole manner changed as she led him forward. Head high, eyes flashing, ears pricked toward his enemy in the dirt, he screamed a high challenge and rose on hind legs. Down came his front hooves, again and again, his rage elemental and awesome to watch. When finally he stood still, blowing hard and trembling with exhaustion, the snake lay scattered in pulpy bits. Lowering his head, Twister gave the pieces one last contemptuous sniff before turning toward his stall.

Margaret scratched beneath Twister's chin. Grunting in ecstasy, he raised his head and stretched his neck like a contented tabby.

"Good work, handsome. I'll bet you're hungry now. How about some nice breakfast and a nap?"

Somehow the sight of Twister calmly following her into the stall didn't surprise Scott. Her confident assurance yesterday that Twister would respond to her training didn't appear boastful now. The woman seemed able to read the stallion's mind. She'd bewitched him. And much as Scott hated to admit it, he couldn't blame the poor animal. Her fairy-princess act was pretty potent.

He reached down, hoisted the nearest bale to his shoulder and staggered blindly toward the stall.

"No! Don't ever stack hay outside his stall again or he'll think there's a snake there," Margaret explained.

Scott felt his face heat. She was right of course. If she hadn't tied him in knots he wouldn't be acting like a total greenhorn. Wishing she'd never slipped into his moonlit field, he turned and headed for an empty stall at the far end of the barn. The makeshift storage room housed bags of feed, salt blocks and his tooled Western stock saddle. He slid the hay from his shoulder and stepped back. Dust and fragments of summer meadow mushroomed up, tickling a violent sneeze out of him.

"Bless you." Margaret's gentle laughter wafted from Twister's stall.

Every masculine instinct he possessed whispered danger.

Margaret Chelsea Winston was nothing but trouble and always had been. Look how she was already ordering him around. It'd taken her all of five minutes to hook her little finger in Pete's nose ring. And when Scott'd told his father about her scheme to turn Twister into a money machine, Grant had been sickeningly enthusiastic.

Scott tightened his mouth and brushed off his arms and shoulders. He'd exhausted all options for making the bank-note payment or he never would've grabbed at the solution she offered. Honor dictated he try his best to make the plan work. He would tolerate her because he had to.

But damned if he'd play lapdog to the woman who'd killed his best friend.

CHAPTER THREE

MARGARET REACHED for a stick of margarine, paused, and cautiously sniffed the air. Oh, no! Slamming the refrigerator door, she cringed at the ominous clatter of glass and raced to the stove. Acrid smoke billowed from a frying pan.

Coughing, she turned off the burner and stared down at the gooey mess in the pan that had once been a rubber spatula. A second skillet lined with uncooked strips of bacon sat on the adjacent burner. Not good, not good. Cooking meals was part of the agreement she'd made the day before, and now she'd botched Scott's breakfast. Her ex-husband would have had a field day with this if he knew. Jim's patronizing still stung.

You can't even tell left from right, Margaret, and you want a career? Now don't pout, honey. You already have a job. Just keep being the prettiest hostess any Jacobs and McMillan associate ever had, and I'll make partner yet.

Grimacing, Margaret carried the ruined pan to the sink and twisted the cold water tap. Hot rubber hissed and foul-smelling steam rose to cloud the window. She slumped against the counter and marveled at human nature.

After three years of enduring similar put-downs from Jim, there was no reason that particular insult should have aroused The Mule in her. But it had. Oh, she'd done her job, such as it was—and filed for divorce the day Jim announced he'd made partner.

Marrying the ambitious lawyer had been a mistake of course. At the time, she'd still felt numb with guilt over Matt's death and undeserving of happiness. Even knowing that Jim had prized her only for her ornamental value and social connections, she'd grabbed the chance to escape her father's control. Margaret huffed and straightened from the counter.

Some escape. Her husband's handling had been no less confining for being velvet-gloved. He'd been truly shocked when she'd called him chauvinistic. And now she was working with a man who made Jim seem practically a feminist.

She had no doubt Scott would be horrified or, worse, pitying, if he knew about her disability. It would be just the excuse he needed to renege on their agreement. Well, she wouldn't give him the chance! She would succeed on her own, depend on herself and maybe, just maybe, win back her self-respect in the process.

Boot steps and a twanging screen door jerked her thoughts to the present. Her good intentions cowered. *Please let it be Grant.*

The back door opened. She spun around. Scott stepped inside, whipped off his hat and fanned the air. His brows formed a fierce line.

"What is that godawful smell?"

He glanced at the stove top, then peered over her shoulder at the hardened glob of rubber and defaced metal. His frown deepened.

She hung her head, realized what she was doing and summoned the courage to meet his eyes. "I'm sorry. It was...an accident."

"I can't afford careless accidents, Maggie."

"I'll buy you a new pan."

"Save your money and time for Twister. We're twenty miles from town and there's a full day of work ahead—" he gave her white shorts and sneakers a scornful once-over "—even if you *are* dressed for tennis at the club. Guess we'll have to make do with one fryin' pan from now on."

Sliding his hat on with a grieved expression, he nodded toward the bacon. "That was for Pete, you know."

"P-Pete?"

"He lives in a trailer behind the barn. We take turns running into town for supplies, but he hasn't come up to the house to pick up his stuff yet. Dad and I eat the turkey bacon." He heaved a long-suffering sigh. "But since you've opened the package, go ahead and cook it. We don't waste things on this ranch."

She sidled by his looming form and moved to the stove, wishing he were somewhere else, wishing she were some*one* else. She couldn't think with him watching her, couldn't sort out the confusing letters beneath each knob on the electric stove. Let's see, she'd turned this one before. Three choices left. Reaching blindly, she turned a control. Coils glowed, but not under the frying pan.

"Gawd," Scott muttered from behind.

Her face grew scorching. Sensing he'd turned, she frantically twisted knobs until the correct burner lit. The refrigerator door clunked open.

"What the...? Dammit, Maggie, I told you about this door. Half the stuff in here is broken or spilled." Each word wallowed in disgust. Each clink of glass hitting the trash can punctuated his censure.

Biting her lip and blinking furiously, Margaret tried to concentrate while he cleaned up her mess. Eggs. She'd planned on scrambling some. But those were probably Pete's, too. How thoughtless to fry bacon for someone who'd just had heart surgery. How negligent to ruin a pan. How *stupid* to botch a simple task like cooking breakfast.

The shame she'd been holding at bay all morning attacked full force. Her nose lifted, her muscles froze, her sight glazed—the defense mechanisms developed as a child were automatic now. She was only vaguely aware of the bacon sizzling. A popping noise produced a corresponding sting on her arm, but she didn't flinch.

"Turn down the heat, Maggie! What are you trying to do, burn breakfast *and* the house? Can't you even fry a batch of—"

"That's enough, Scott."

Gentle hands gripped her shoulders and pulled her back from the stove. Grant adjusted the control, reached for her wrist, and slowly uncurled her fist. His work-worn fingers moved up to probe an angry red circle on her pale skin.

"Let's get some ice on that burn before it blisters."

She searched his eyes and found only compassion, as if he knew her pain went much deeper than a grease burn. Her senses slowly thawed.

"I'm sorry about the pan, Mr. Hayes, and the bacon. I shouldn't have been so... careless." Scott's accusation was convenient, and much kinder than the truth she had no intention of revealing.

Grant released her arm with a pat. "Call me Grant, remember? That ol' skillet should've been tossed out along with the Nixon administration. And don't apologize about the bacon. I like my meat on the burned side—just ask Scott. Been eatin' his cookin' for years and never complained."

The older man's lopsided, teasing grin added lines around his eyes and subtracted years from his face. It was easy to see where Scott's masculine good looks came from. Heaven help her if the son ever emulated the father's conscious effort to charm.

"Scott, you get an ice cube on this girl's arm while I make us all some pancakes." He led Margaret to the scratched kitchen table, pulled out a chair with courtly grace and waited.

"Really, Mr. Hayes... Grant. I can make pancakes if that's what you want."

"Let the princess fix her own breakfast," Scott said.

"I'll make you some Eggbeaters, Dad." Hunkered in front of the refrigerator, Scott threw down his sponge and rose to a standing position.

"Mind your manners, son. And take off that hat. Sit down, Margaret. Please."

To refuse would be an insult. Carefully avoiding Scott's eyes, she sat.

Grant rubbed his neck, drawing Margaret's attention to his frayed sleeve cuff. She frowned. The cost of a single custom-made shirt from her father's closet could buy a dozen replacements for the one Grant wore.

He dropped his arm and sighed. "If I eat one more bite of Eggbeaters, Scott, you'll see last night's dinner again. Only it won't look near as appetizing this morning."

"The doctor said—"

"Stirring batter is *not* going to raise my blood pressure. And one normal breakfast every now and then is not going to clog my arteries. Dr. Hearn was clear about that. You gotta quit treating me like an invalid, son, and trust me to take care of myself."

The moment stretched, Grant's obvious frustration gaining Margaret's sincere sympathy. How many times had she encountered the same lack of trust in her own abilities?

Scott relented first. Setting his hat on the refrigerator, he opened the tiny freezer compartment and cracked loose an ice cube from a dented metal tray. Cube in hand, he stepped aside.

"Make my order a double stack," he said wryly.

Breaking into a relieved smile, Grant moved forward and began rummaging for ingredients. Scott gave him a look of affectionate exasperation, then slowly turned his head.

Margaret tensed.

Their eyes met.

She felt his contempt like a physical blow. It simmered in his tawny eyes, along with something else, a sexual charisma that was as genetically inherent as his square jaw, as unconscious for him as breathing.

Her gaze faltered and dropped. He wore a white, Western-style shirt like his father's. But where the material swallowed Grant's gaunt torso, it strained against Scott's muscular frame. She focused on a pearl snap button near his tooled leather belt, refusing to look lower, unable to look higher as he walked to stand in front of her.

"Hold out your arm, Maggie."

He was too close, and he hated her. She tilted her head back. "I can take care of myself. I'm not an invalid any more than your father is."

One minute he was towering over her, the next he was sitting in a chair with her hand on his thigh, his fingers clamping her wrist.

"Hold still now, this might get a little uncomfortable," he said soothingly, his glittering eyes and vise-like grip hidden from Grant.

Scott raised the dripping ice cube and pressed it against her burn. She yanked her arm and gasped, more stunned at his immovable strength than the shock of cold. Jerk. He knew she couldn't do anything with his father mixing batter not fifteen feet away. She pressed her bare knees primly together and pretended they weren't sandwiched between denim-covered muscles.

He looked different without a hat, she realized, staring. Up close, his hair was a thick, swirling mixture of chocolate browns and caramel highlights. It begged a woman's fingers to plunge right in. As if sensing her thoughts, he looked up through sun-tipped lashes and smiled, a lazy curl of lips that did funny things to her stomach. Returning his focus to her burn, he rubbed the ice in small circles.

Her hands flexed, the one on his thigh noting muscles gone suddenly concrete. The ice cube released a fat drip. It rolled down the curve of her skin and joined the spreading wet spot on his jeans.

He gentled his hold on her wrist. "Feel better?"

The skin on her forearm felt frozen, the skin underneath on fire where he massaged her wild pulse with his thumb. She felt flustered, aroused and very, very confused. But *better?*

"I'll be fine now, thanks." She pulled back her arm, freeing her wrist and dislodging the ice. It slithered over her thigh and fell to the floor.

"How many pancakes can you eat, Margaret?" Grant called from the stove.

She tried to answer. She tried to do anything but shiver from the combined impact of frigid ice and a predatory gold stare.

"One," she managed breathlessly.

"What was that?"

She dragged her gaze to Grant. *"One."*

"Lost your appetite, princess?" Scott asked softly, his eyes slitted with knowing amusement.

He was insufferable. He'd been insufferable from the time they'd first met. But she wasn't a painfully shy teenager anymore. She was her own person, a woman strong enough to stand alone.

She scraped back her chair and stood.

"I changed my mind, Grant, I'll have a short stack . . . with bacon." She sent Scott a scathing look. "Suddenly I could eat a pig."

LATE THAT AFTERNOON, Ada Butler cut the engine of her pickup and resisted the urge to check her face in the rearview mirror. Silly fool. Powder and a dab of lipstick wouldn't disguise forty-nine years of hard living. Besides, Grant wouldn't notice if she dyed her salt-and-pepper hair green and danced naked on his bed.

She smoothed her jeans, anyway, and wished briefly she hadn't changed from her Sunday dress. The minister'd said the blue silk matched her eyes. Then again, it was his Christian duty to say something charitable about everyone—especially aging spinsters.

With a huff of self-disgust, she slid out of the truck and scanned the dirt yard. Her squinted eyes widened on a flashy red Porsche by the barn. Who on earth was here? She spun toward the house and shaded her eyes with one hand.

The yellow clapboards shimmered in the midday sun, every curl of paint glaringly exposed. Missing shingles pockmarked the roof. The long front porch sagged in the middle, surely more so than the last time she'd stopped by? Dropping her hand, she frowned and moved toward the house.

Scott had assured her that after the surgery his father was fine, that there was no reason for her to visit the hospital or drop off a casserole when Grant came home. Yet Ellen Gates had done both. Every congregation member sitting within five pews of the new

widow heard how she'd read scripture by Grant's
bed—no doubt wishing she was in it, the hypocrite—
and taken him her famous Chicken Delight the next
week. Baiting the trap for a husband, that's what she
was doing.

A series of grunts from the back of Ada's pickup
gave her pause. It was true Ellen had boobs the size of
Canada. But Ada had fifty times more brains. Surely
that gave the widow only a moderate edge.

She was halfway up the porch steps when Grant
opened the door.

"Ada, what a nice surprise."

Hand pressed to pounding heart, she allowed herself one devouring look. He was so thin! Yet the rak-
ish smile and lively green eyes were as irresistible as
ever.

"Hello, Grant. How're you feeling?"

His eyes lost some of their sparkle. "Oh, good as an
old man with one foot in the grave can feel."

She arched a brow. "Glad I came by in time. Dead
men are so boring."

When he chuckled, her pleasure pulsed bone deep.

"Come on in out of the sun, Ada. I think I can
manage a little conversation before the funeral."

"You're sure I'm not intruding? Looks like you've
already got company." She glanced pointedly at the
Porsche.

"That'll take some explaining. Come in."

She climbed the remaining steps while he held open
the door. His fingertips branded the small of her back
as she swept into the oak-planked parlor. He made her

feel protected and utterly feminine when she didn't need the first and certainly wasn't the second.

And that, she supposed, was why she'd loved Grant Hayes most of her adult life.

He settled her on the camelback sofa and squeezed into the room's only chair, a wooden rocker far too delicate for his large frame.

"The car belongs to Margaret Winston. You remember, Donald Winston's daughter?"

"I'm not likely to forget."

No single family in the county had provided as much juicy gossip as the Winstons. People still wondered what really happened the day young Matt Collins died. One thing was clear—a body never mentioned Margaret's name around Scott unless she wanted her head snapped off. And Ada was rather fond of hers.

"I thought Margaret lived in Dallas now. What brings her here?" she asked, listening enthralled to Grant's account of the past three days. When he finished, she slowly shook her head.

"If that doesn't beat all. To hear Doc Chalmers tell it, Twister was spawned from the bowels of hell. Do you really think a little thing like Margaret can handle that devil?"

"She saddled him up not twenty minutes ago and took off on their first ride. Damnedest thing I ever saw. You'd have thought he was a Shetland pony at the kiddie park. Margaret'll handle Twister just fine. But handling Scott...now, that's a whole different ball of wax."

Did he know his eyes were as green as fresh mint? Did he know how masculine he looked in that dainty chair or what happened to her stomach when he smiled?

"But enough about us, Ada. What brings you away from your sows during spring farrowing? Can't be my charming company."

Of course he didn't know. She was plain, practical Ada Butler, raiser of hogs and peaches, not men's pulses. She glanced from his jutting arms and knees to the empty cushion beside her and blinked back the horrifying sting of tears.

"Ada? What is it?" He unfolded from the chair and left it rocking wildly to sit on the sofa. Reaching for her hands, he gave them a squeeze and searched her eyes. "Has something happened at the farm? Do you need help?"

Concern had accomplished what her pitiful charms could not. It would be easy enough to let the tears flow, to find a plausible problem and see where it led. Already prickles of excitement from their joined palms spread up her arms. Heavenly.

She drew a deep breath and pulled her hands away. "Nothing's wrong, Grant. It's my silly allergies. They always act up this time of year."

Avoiding his gaze, she rose and walked to the door, clearing her throat and sniffing for effect. "You're right, I really can't stay away from the farm long. But I ran into Scott last week in town, and he mentioned wanting to raise a hog for fall slaughter." *Some day* was what he'd said. She opened the door and stood half in, half out.

"Morning Glory's last litter was a beaut," she babbled on. "Twelve in all, but the runt barely made it. He'll bring next to nothing at market and less than that as breeding stock. You're welcome to take him if you want. He's in the truck now."

"Really? One of your prize Hampshires? I don't know what to say, Ada."

Neither did she, since he'd moved to peer out the door and driven every coherent thought out of her head. Her spine hugged the doorjamb. Her chest rose and fell an inch from his arm. Oh, to be Ellen Gates now.

He turned and looked down, his evident pleasure shifting to surprise, then keen awareness. She could count on one hand the number of times she'd seen that expression in a man's eyes. Never had it thrilled her body and soul like now.

She saw his gaze fasten on her mouth, felt her lips soften in response, watched him frown in confusion and step out onto the front porch. As he stared into space, realization hit. Lord in heaven, he'd almost kissed her!

Her heart soaring, she breezed across the porch, floated down the steps and turned to call up teasingly, "C'mon, old man. Let's get your pig unloaded."

Spinning on one serviceable work boot, she was amazed at how naturally her walk had an extra sway when she knew Grant was watching. One thing about working a farm sunup to sundown—it kept her figure trim and supple. From this view, she might even have the edge on Ellen.

At her truck, Ada dropped the tailgate, grabbed a flimsy chicken-wire cage and pulled. Excited grunts erupted from the black-and-white shoat inside. She'd always had a soft spot for runts. She'd only postponed this one's inevitable fate, but still, she felt noble.

"Hush, little guy. We'll get you out of there in a minute," Ada crooned, dragging the cage to the edge of the tailgate. The eight-week-old pig trembled miserably, his tail tucked as low as the curl would allow. Intent on getting the poor creature settled, Ada tightened her grip on the cage and heaved.

"Let me help," Grant rumbled unexpectedly in her ear.

Her fingers slackened. The cage hit the ground. Wire crunched, popping the door open. And thirty pounds of squealing, outraged pig dug in his toes and raced wildly for the barn.

After exchanging a stunned look with Grant, Ada took off in hot pursuit.

She focused with dizzying results on the corkscrew tail twirling counterclockwise to anatomy. Ah, good. The rascal was headed straight for the first stall. Easy pickings. She plunged through the stall just behind the pig, waited tensely while he bobbled against three walls and grasped empty air as he squirted between her legs and out the door.

"Get him!" Ada shrieked at Grant, who stood watching with an infuriatingly superior male smirk.

Stumpy legs pumping, the runt streaked into the next stall. Grant leapt into manly action. Ada stumbled into the corridor just in time to see the frenzied

pig rounding the stall like a fresh-shelled pea in a bowl.
When Grant zigged with hands open, the black-and-
white terror zagged straight out through the door.

It was a beautiful moment.

"Get him!" Grant roared, lurching out of the stall
with murder in his eyes.

There were advantages to being a runt, Ada discovered during the next ten minutes. Never again would
she feel sorry for nature's pip-squeaks. Runts were
faster than their heftier siblings, for one thing. And
small enough to wiggle under sawhorses, between
stacked well pipe and behind metal storage cabinets.

In a distant part of Ada's awareness, she registered
the sound of an approaching vehicle, then closed out
all distractions save the pig eyeing her with myopic
defiance four feet away. For some reason, he'd skidded to a stop in another stall. Afraid to move, she
spoke in a soft, singsong voice.

"That's a good piggy, just stay where you are and
we'll stick an apple in your mouth yet, yes we will. If
you're there, Grant, close the stall door *now,* because
our little friend here looks very nervous."

She watched the pig's beady eyes follow Grant's
movement toward the door.

"Yoohoo. Oh, Gra-ant?" came a woman's glass-
shattering voice.

Hide bristling, the runt bolted for the stall door.
Ada lunged, groaning as a piece of his tail slipped
through her fingers. Dusty, sweaty and completely
alone, she hung her head.

Outrage brought her chin up. She charged out of the
stall and spotted Grant pounding down the corridor,

hard on the tiny rump of Turbo Pig. A voluptuous woman in a flowing, ankle-length dress stood silhouetted in the barn entrance, holding a cake aloft.

"My, it's dark in here. Is that you, Grant? I brought you my famous Molasses Spice Cake everybody raves abou— Eeeeek! Get away! Get away, you nasty thing!" Spinning in a circle, Ellen Gates trapped the thrashing, frantic pig in her swirling skirt.

You should have changed out of your Sunday dress, Ada thought smugly.

"Stand still, Ellen," Grant ordered. "He won't hurt you."

"What won't hurt me? What won't hurt me, goddamn it!"

Tsk-tsk, what would the preacher say?

"It's a pig. A small pig," Grant explained with a superior male smirk Ada didn't mind at all.

Just then, the animal in question caught scent of his favorite flavor in the world, the one Ada used to sweeten his sorghum and tempt his runty appetite, and snuffled as high as he could reach beneath Ellen's skirts.

"Eeeeeyuu!"

The cake hit the ground with a succulent splat. The pig fought his way out of Ellen's skirts with a squeal of ecstasy and began gobbling scattered molasses shrapnel from the dirt floor. The last of Ada's hostility toward the little runt faded.

"Do something!" Ellen wailed.

Ada pushed past Grant, grabbed the warm, quivering pig, and repositioned his leathery snout dead center in the cake. "Enjoy yourself, runt. It's famous."

SCOTT CAUGHT a loose strand of barbed wire with his hammer claw and pressed the tool back against a worm-eaten mesquite post. He waited for the telltale twang of maximum tension before plucking a staple out of his mouth, lifting a second hammer from his belt and securing the strand with two solid whacks. Only then did he straighten and wipe the sweat from his brow.

Repairing fence alone was tricky work and required all his concentration—which was exactly why he'd declined Pete's offer to help. If Scott had time to think, he might remember Maggie's stricken expression earlier today when he'd lectured her about ruining a frying pan. Or her startled awareness when he'd forcibly held her wrist. Neither reaction spoke well of his behavior. But then, she'd always brought out the worst in him.

Frowning, he dropped both hammers and noted the belch of dust on impact. Damn, it was dry for April. Unless a gully-washer hit soon, the approaching summer would dry up his stock tanks. They were dangerously low as it was.

He peeled off his work gloves and walked to the pickup parked in the dubious shade of a young mesquite. This part of the ranch hadn't been cleared in two years. The profusion of cactus, scrub brush and spindly trees depressed him. Pulling his shirttail free, he wrenched open the snaps in one movement and threw the wadded material into the open window.

He'd had big plans for this place once. Now he just got up, worked until he couldn't see straight, then fell into bed—day after day after day.

Lifting out the thermos of water he always carried, Scott gulped and then backhanded his mouth. If only watering his cattle was so easy. Inevitably, irresistibly, his gaze drifted to the thick stand of oaks and cottonwoods edging the horizon.

The trees sheltered the Guadalupe River, whose far bank sloped up to the foot of a manicured green lawn. His mind provided details of the plantation-style house, massive horse barn and various outbuildings he'd seen only twice in his life.

Riverbend. The embodiment of everything he wanted, yet couldn't have.

As a kid, he'd listened to his dad talk about buying the riverfront acreage from old man Perkin and improving H & H Cattle Company's holdings. Then his mom had grown ill. The medical bills stacked up, and the talk stopped.

After she died, they'd all handled it differently. Laura found comfort in excelling at school, Grant relinquished his dream, and Scott grabbed hold of it with both hands. At the ripe old age of twelve, he'd extracted a promise from Andrew Perkin to give Scott first crack at purchasing the prime riverfront land one day.

For seven years he'd worked any job his spare time would allow and saved his earnings. After high school graduation, Mr. Perkin had made noises about being too old to keep farming, and Scott had picked up a loan application from the bank. While his friends dreamed about college, he'd fantasized about his Santa Gertrudis herd drinking from the Guadalupe.

Until someone with more money, more clout and more *cojones* beat him to it.

Scott pushed off from the truck with a snort and headed for the fence post. He'd do well to forget the past if he hoped to show any degree of civility in the next few months. Stooping over, he jerked his gloves on and attacked his work with a vengeance.

Ten minutes and two fence posts later, he heard the jingle of a bit, the clack of a hoof connecting with rock. He straightened at the sight of Maggie riding Twister slowly up the fence line. The stallion looked foreign but magnificent, with an English saddle and slender woman in jodhpurs on his back.

She stopped about twenty feet away, one hand holding the reins loosely while the other scribbled on paper against the saddle pommel.

Scott walked forward, straining to see. Some sort of drawing, it looked like. Bracing against Twister's nudge of greeting, Scott watched her quickly fold the paper and slip it into the pocket of her pale blue shirt.

"I thought you weren't going to ride today," he said, reaching up to hold the bridle.

Her gaze fluttered over his bare chest and darted away. "The farrier rescheduled for tomorrow. I decided to scope out possible training sites. Twister hasn't given me a bit of trouble—" she leaned over and rubbed the glossy neck "—have ya, handsome?"

Her sleeveless shirt gaped at the neck. Scott's breath snagged on a glimpse of milky flesh and scalloped cream lace.

She straightened and stared out over the fence. "I never realized Riverbend was this close to your ranch."

"No, I don't suppose you did. It's beneath a princess to notice the peons."

Her head snapped around. Twister snorted and sidestepped. She collected the reins and eyed Scott with regal scorn.

"Quit calling me a princess."

He almost smiled, but shrugged, instead. "It's what you are."

"Because my father bought Riverbend out from under your nose?"

His grip tightened on the bridle. How did she know about that?

"I spent some time at the feed store last week. I found out you worked there off and on all through high school. Apparently the whole town knew about your bargain with Mr. Perkin. My father didn't win any friends around here by offering a deal the old man couldn't refuse. Still, that has nothing to do with me."

Like hell. "Donald Winston bought that land for you, for his little princess, so she could win horse shows."

"So I'm the daughter of a man obsessed with winning."

"A *rich* man."

"Okay, a rich man. I can't help it if I have wealthy parents. They don't define me. When have I ever treated you like I was a princess, Scott Hayes?"

She sat there with her nose in the air and her posture church perfect and her eyes frosting the air between them, and Scott felt his control snap. He moved closer and gripped the supple riding boot that epitomized her privileged world.

"Since the first day I met you," he said, all the confusion and humiliation of that day resurfacing. He wanted to shake her ivory tower till her teeth rattled. "Do you even remember that day, Maggie?"

Her cheeks flushed to match her sunburned nose. She remembered.

"Must've been quite a social comedown for you to hang out with the locals, huh?"

"No, I was grateful to be invited. Being new to the area wasn't easy."

"Our nasty red dust get your Corvette dirty?"

"You're not being fair!"

"That's life in the big country, princess. It ain't fair and it ain't easy. You don't belong here any more than you did ten years ago."

He'd spotted her right off when he'd walked into Lucy's Café. Her sophisticated haircut, her expensive clothes, her French-restaurant table manners—hell, everything about her had screamed *class*. He'd been fascinated—and intimidated.

"My buddies bet me ten bucks I couldn't get your phone number. I gotta admit, Maggie, you were good."

She shifted in the saddle and frowned. "Good?"

"I thought I'd been around, knew all the tricks. But you played me like a puppet for thirty minutes before cutting the strings. I didn't even see it coming." He'd bought into that shy smile, the pleasure in her dove gray eyes, one hundred percent.

"I don't know what you're talking about."

"Oh, I think you do. I think you waited for the exact right minute to put me in my place. Everyone there saw me asking for your phone number. Everyone there knew I didn't get it."

He'd held out that pen and napkin for a hundred excruciating years while she'd given him the Snow Princess treatment. Her friends had giggled when he'd snatched his hand back. His own friends had snickered as he joined them in a corner booth. Losing the bet wasn't the half of his shock.

Mr. Stud had finally been rejected, his friends had told him, by a Dallas blueblood—daughter of the millionaire who'd just bought old man Perkin's place.

Twister tossed his head and stamped, jolting Scott back to the present. He focused on Maggie's overly bright eyes, the pressed lips, which trembled nonetheless. She didn't look cold now. She looked close to tears.

"It wasn't you. It was me. I'm..." Her swallow was audible. She shook her head and fumbled with the reins.

Scott resented his pang of sympathy. "You're what, Maggie?"

Her eyes hardened. Her chin came up and out. "I'm a damn good horse trainer, that's what. That's all you need to know about me."

Twister launched forward into a fast trot, wrenching Scott's hand from her boot. Stunned, he watched horse and rider kick up dust until they melted into the brush.

Absently rubbing his right glove, he stared unmoving at the horizon. The sun beat down hotter than ever, but he scarcely noticed. Something important had happened just now, no doubt about it.

He wished like hell he knew what it was.

CHAPTER FOUR

MARGARET FOUGHT the powerful undertow. Clawed her way toward wakefulness and blessed peace. But the current was invincible. It swept her past the sweetness and plunged her into panic. Into despair. . .

Into the car.

Cracked rubber tape on the steering wheel pricked her palms. Sweltering heat compressed her lungs. Matt's voice implored her to slow down, to pull over. A red-white-and-blue beacon flashed in her rearview mirror. Too close. Too fast.

She couldn't go back. Wouldn't go back, or she might never have the courage to leave again.

Get away—get away—get away. The refrain pounded in her mind with each heartbeat. She pressed down on the accelerator and clutched the steering wheel tighter, willing her grip to hold the vibrating car together. Her muscles ached. Dizziness blurred her vision. She tried to slow her shallow breaths and only panted faster.

Get away, get away, get away— Boom!

The steering wheel was wrenched from her hands. Matt yelled. The horizon spun around and around and

*around. Metal screeched. Pain exploded in her legs
and chest. Glass stalactites trembled.*

Silence throbbed.

*She slowly turned her head. Matt's flesh and bone
fused with jagged metal in a gruesome sculpture of
death.*

*Anguish filled her soul. She threw back her head
and screamed at fate, "It should have been me.
It should have been me. It should have been
me-e-e-e—"*

"Maggie!"

She jerked into consciousness with a gasp, her eyes
popping open unfocused in the dark. Where...? Her
vision cleared. The farmhouse, her second night here.
Scott sat on the four-poster bed gripping her shoulders hard. She wondered how many times he'd shaken
her.

"You were dreaming, Maggie. It was just a bad
dream."

Just a bad dream. She would've laughed if her teeth
weren't chattering like a set of windup toy dentures.
Violent trembling seized her body in rhythmic waves.
A terrible cold penetrated marrow deep. It would pass.
Eventually. Closing her eyes, she waited...and endured.

"Damn," Scott muttered, pulling her upright and
into his arms.

She nearly whimpered with relief. His bare chest was
hard beneath her cheek, his heartbeat loud and steady.
She wrapped her arms around his waist and shamelessly clung. Maybe he hated her for what she'd done
to Matt, maybe her present weakness disgusted him,

but it didn't matter. He felt strong and warm and *alive,* and she needed the human contact.

He rubbed her spine hesitantly, then more firmly, his callused fingers snagging on her cotton nightgown. "You're shiverin' like a spooked colt. Must've been a helluva nightmare."

Swallowing hard, she nodded.

"Wanna talk about it?"

To this man? "No," she whispered. "I'll be fine in a minute." Humiliating, but she couldn't seem to unlock her fingers from the waistband of his jeans.

"You were dreaming about the accident, weren't you?"

She tensed. His room was right next door. "Was I talking out loud?"

"Sounded more like screaming to me."

She unpeeled her fingers and started to push away, thwarted by the iron band of his arms.

"Relax, princess. No need to get your nose out of joint."

Somehow that nose was buried against his chest now. He smelled of soap and sleep-roused male, and radiated heat like a healthy animal.

"At least you don't feel like a damn ice cube anymore," Scott said, satisfaction deepening his voice.

Not hardly. Grateful he couldn't see her face, she turned and pressed her cheek to his chest. "I'm sorry I woke you up."

His body shifted toward the window. "Looks like it's close to dawn. I'd have gotten up soon, anyway."

"What did I..." *Go on, coward, spit it out.* "What did I scream?"

He hesitated a fraction too long. "Damned if I know. One thing's for sure. My money's on you, instead of Ada, at the next county fair."

She struggled to make the connection.

"The pig-calling contest," he explained. "You pack a mean set of lungs for such a little thing."

His chuckle rumbled pleasantly against her ear. She managed a shaky smile, surprised to realize her trembling had stopped. Dangerous. She was too warm, too content, too willing to stay in his arms indefinitely. This time when she pushed away, he let her go.

She lay back and pulled the quilt to her chin, uncertain how their relationship had changed, sure only that it had.

"I guess I should thank you," she finally said.

"No need. I didn't want you to wake Dad." He sprang up as if released from an unpleasant duty and headed for the door. Halfway there, he paused and looked over his shoulder. "You gonna be okay?"

"I'll be fine."

He didn't linger to make sure.

Margaret stared at the closed door in bemusement. Normally it took her several hours to recover from the dream. Never in her lifetime would she have expected Scott Hayes to speed the process. She almost wished he hadn't. His compassion increased his virility by a thousandfold. As her horror had receded, every nerve ending in her body had tingled with awareness.

Funny. She'd never been as physically conscious of Matt, although she'd planned to marry him. He'd been a handsome young veterinary student working the summer at Riverbend when they'd met. She'd craved his unconditional love, so different from her parents' embarrassed tolerance, but never his touch.

Nor had Jim ever caused this distressing reaction. She'd found him attractive, but that was secondary to the opportunity he'd offered—the chance to start a new life unfettered by guilt or her father's censure. If truth were told, the physical side of her marriage had been disappointing. All those disconcerting noises, all that sweaty skin...

... that tanned, sweaty skin. An image of Scott as he'd looked the day before mocked her thoughts.

Far from distasteful, Scott's glistening torso had fascinated her. When he'd reached up and held Twister's bridle, his biceps had bunched and the corded sinew of his forearms flexed. Leather work gloves only emphasized his hard muscles, the kind earned through strenuous physical labor, not honed and perfected in a gym.

Blinking, Margaret shook off both the vision and her sappy smile. She yawned and stretched. The first blush of dawn tinged the lace curtains. Shadows solidified into an armoire, a scarred dresser and silver-spotted mirror. Margaret fingered the Wedding Ring quilt beneath her chin and admired the workmanship.

Scott was right. Everything on this ranch had been made or purchased to last through generations of hard wear. The sense of permanency charmed her, challenged her to be just as strong, just as capable of earning her keep.

Muffled kitchen sounds told her Scott was starting the first pot of coffee. Grant would be up soon. What could she make for breakfast that would be appetizing, as well as low in fat?

Cereal. That she could handle.

Throwing back the covers, she indulged in one last joint-popping stretch. Anticipation spread like caffeine through her blood, vanquishing fatigue. There was a long, exhausting day ahead of her. She couldn't wait to get started.

THREE HOURS LATER Margaret's enthusiasm had faded considerably. "Hold still, darn it!"

Twister swished his tail, jerking the currycomb from her hand—but not from a nasty snarl. He swished again, avoiding her frantic grab. His third, violent swish sent the heavy metal comb rocketing into the back plank wall like a deadly missile.

Freed of the annoyance, he turned and gazed at Margaret with liquid brown innocence.

"Nice try, handsome, but no bananas. You're going to look respectable for Dr. Morley if it kills me." Which it almost had.

Pete's worried face appeared over the stall door. He swept off his disreputable hat and wiped his brow. "Praise the Lord, you ain't dead."

"Save your prayers for Scott. I'm going to shoot him for letting Twister's tail get in this condition." She glared at the long, tangled mess, filled with burrs and range debris. "Hasn't Scott ever combed it?"

Pete plunked on his hat and draped his wrists over the half door. "Can't say he has. Should he do it before he tends the herd or after he tends his pa?"

Margaret smoothed her palm down Twister's freshly brushed coat, as soft and sleek as sealskin now. "I'm sorry. Scott didn't deserve that." She sent Pete a challenging glance. "He doesn't like me much, and I get defensive, say things I shouldn't. He's a hard man to get along with."

"No harder'n he's had to be, I reckon."

She knew H & H Cattle Company had once been a thriving operation. For the first time, she allowed herself to consider its imminent failure as something other than her good fortune.

"He really loves this ranch, doesn't he?"

Pete's light blue eyes studied her kindly, and Margaret had the strange feeling he saw right through her skin to the knot of guilt and confusion inside.

He appeared to make some decision. "His ma got the cancer when he was little, y'know. Part of Grant up and died with her, seemed like. Scott sorta took over after that. Been doin' the work of three men since he was fifteen." He paused, his gaze sharpening. "If he expects a lot from other folks, it's 'cause he expects even more from hisself. No need—"

Twister's head snaked forward, his ears flat and teeth bared.

Margaret simultaneously smacked his shoulder and shouted, "No!" The stallion's strong teeth clacked a hairbreadth from Pete's fingers.

The wrangler stepped back with a yelped curse.

"You all right?" a voice boomed from the make-shift tack room.

"Oh, just dandy, boss."

Margaret shot Twister a dark look and elbowed him aside to lean over the door. Scott was heading this way fast. Stopping outside the stall, he folded his arms and waited.

"Nothin' like almost losin' a hand t'get your blood singin' Dixie." Pete smiled weakly, going from pale to ruddy under the younger man's disgusted stare. "He's acted so different lately, guess I thought he might've mellowed some."

"Guess you thought wrong." Scott snorted a laugh. "How many chunks does he have to take outta your hide before you learn some sense?"

"It was my fault." Margaret spoke up, wanting to ease Pete's embarrassment. "Stallions are unpredictable at best—" she cocked her head at a moist blast of air on her neck "—and should be handled with extreme caution at all times—" she swatted at the muzzle nibbling her hair "—but I wasn't paying close enough attention. I'll be more careful from now on." Twister planted his chin on her shoulder and heaved a noisy sigh. She studiously ignored the heavy weight.

"Yeah, I can see how vicious he is around you." Scott moved forward and rubbed Twister's forehead in a slow circle. "Some friend you are. Meet a pretty girl and you've got no time for me anymore." He looked up. "Stealing my buddies must be a hobby of yours, Maggie."

Being a jerk must be yours. She arched a brow. "I was Matt's girlfriend. Preferring a girlfriend's company over a buddy's is normal for most men. What does that make you, Scott?"

Her implication seemed to amuse him. He gave her a lecherous smile and lowered his voice. "I'll be happy to show you, darlin'. Any time. Any place."

A trill of sensation rose from the vicinity of her stomach. Irritated with herself, she shoved Twister's muzzle off her shoulder. He promptly returned it.

"Smart guy." Scott's raspy growl stroked her nerves.

Damn his insolent, sexy hide. How could she respond like this to a man who didn't even like her? To cover her confusion, she reached up and massaged Twister's throat, blurting the first thought that came to mind. "Here's the reason Twister will win the Armand Hammer Classic."

Scott's lazy arrogance fled. "What are you talking about?"

Pressing the back of her hand against Twister's throat, she ran her flexed fingers forward between the wings of his jaw bones. Her thumb slipped in beside the four finger joints with room to spare.

"Watch this," she ordered, unable to quell a triumphant grin as she placed the thumb of her opposite hand next to the fingers already in place. "Count 'em and weep, ladies and gentlemen. A *six*-finger jaw!"

Scott looked at her blankly.

"Twister's the only six-finger foal Riverbend ever produced. You might act a little happier."

"Why?"

Lowering her hands, she suppressed her disappointment. Scott couldn't realize how hard she'd labored to match the perfect sire and dam for just such an occurrence. He couldn't know what a miracle beating the genetic odds really was.

"The airflow factor," she said. "Some experts think the airway—the throat and voice box—is more important than the lungs when it comes to winning races. I happen to agree."

"And a six-finger jaw is good?"

"Jump-up-and-shout-Hallelujah good."

He nudged his hat brim back, a devilish glint in his eye. "Why?"

He was teasing her, she realized in amazement, and the novelty made her smile. "Twister doesn't have to work as hard as other horses. More oxygen reaches his lungs, and he converts his body's fuel more efficiently."

"Lord help us," Pete said on a moan. "The last thing that stud needs is more energy."

Scott slowly turned. "What do you care? You've got a woman doing all your work."

"I insisted," Margaret said.

Pete sent her a grateful look. "I ain't never seen the likes of her with critters, boss. She even had that killer pig actin' like a pussycat."

"Speaking of which, weren't you supposed to get that front stall ready for him?"

Pete's face screwed up in a mutinous mass of wrinkles.

Scott folded his arms.

"I'm goin', I'm goin'." He turned and shuffled off, grumbling under his breath. "A cowboy workin' with pigs. It ain't natural, I tell ya. S'pose they'll be callin' me a *pig*boy, next. Just ain't natural . . ."

Margaret met Scott's eyes, then broke into peals of laughter. It took her a moment to realize he hadn't joined in, but was watching her curiously. She lowered her gaze and cursed the heat searing her cheeks.

"That's the first time I've heard you let go and really laugh," he said.

She looked up, captivated by a glimpse of the man who'd banished her nightmare in the circle of his arms. "I don't suppose I've had much reason to laugh around you in the past."

They exchanged a cautious look, filled with *what-ifs*. What if she hadn't frozen up all those years ago when he'd asked for her phone number? What if she'd actually gone out with him then, as she'd longed to do? Would they be friends now? Margaret studied the rugged structure of his face, the width of his shoulders, the sudden alertness in his eyes that made her both wary and excited—and admitted the truth. They would be much more than friends.

She would've made sure of it.

Twister pricked his ears forward and lifted his head, interrupting the tense moment. The distant whine of a truck engine announced Dr. Morley's arrival. Margaret threw the stallion a dismayed glance.

"Rats. I never finished your tail." She smoothed her own hair, then hurriedly retucked her shirt into the waistband of her jeans.

"Must be some vet," Scott said, his familiar sarcasm back.

"One of the best," she agreed, grabbing Twister's lead rope and unlatching the door. "He's Riverbend's veterinarian. Frankly I'm surprised he agreed to accept us as clients.''

Pushing the door open with her boot, she led the stallion into the corridor. The truck had crested the hill by the sound of it. She wanted Twister ready and waiting for Dr. Morley, not vice versa.

Scott closed the half door and slouched back against it, his elbows propped on the ledge. ''How old is he?''

''Wha...who?'' She quickly cross-tied Twister and tightened his halter.

''Dr. Morley.''

''Oh, I don't know. Late thirties, maybe?'' Hmm. If Dr. Morley used a stomach tube for worming, she'd probably need the twitch to control Twister.

''There's your answer.''

''Huh?'' She headed past Scott for the tack room.

''That's why he agreed to go slumming here.''

Margaret stopped in midstride. Slumming? She turned and inspected Scott coolly. ''That's an ugly chip on your shoulder, mister. I suggest you get rid of it before Dr. Morley walks in. He's doing us both a favor by examining Twister.''

Scott shoved away from the door and advanced with catlike grace. ''You just don't get it, do you, Maggie?'' Wrapping callused fingers around her chin, he drew her face closer to his. ''A man would have to be dead to say no to you. If Morley's in his thirties, you couldn't keep him away with Mace. So don't talk like he's doing *me* a favor, lady. I've got nothing to do with it *or* your crazy scheme.''

Releasing her chin, he stalked off down the corridor, leaving the tingle of his fingers behind.

SCOTT SHOVED one shoulder against the door of Luling Feed and Hardware and stumbled into a wealth of scents. Grain and leather, fresh-cut lumber and insecticide—the mingling smells had been irresistible to him as a boy. They still had the power to stir up vague yearnings, remind him of unfulfilled dreams.

He closed the off-kilter door with a thrust of his rump and grunted. After Maggie's startling nightmare, followed by his own jealousy of Dr. Morley two days ago, her departure for Dallas yesterday had suited him fine. His priorities were clear now.

The sooner he found a practical solution to his problems, the better. He'd reached for the sky once before and hit the ground hard. He wouldn't survive another fall.

Behind a counter near the door, Pudge Webster lowered the *Luling Gazette*. His round face, rounder body and black button eyes hadn't changed much since high school. Scott supposed that was what inheriting a debt-free business and sitting on your ass all day did for you.

"Well, look what the cat dragged in, boys," Pudge said, folding his paper and laying it beside the vintage cash register.

Scott tipped his hat brim. "H'lo Pudge. Ben, Lester. How y'all been?"

The two ancient "boys" playing dominoes on an upended spool of chain never glanced up. Lit by a tall window frosted with spiderwebs, they looked eerily frozen in time.

As usual, Pudge answered for them all. "Fair to middlin'. Can't complain. How's your dad feeling these days? I heard tell he was up and around. Spry enough to chase some pig, according to the widow Gates. Was she pulling my leg or what?''

Scott wandered to a display of tick spray without answering. Pudge wouldn't notice.

"Funny you should come in today. Must be ESP or sump'n. I says to Ben just this morning, Ben, I says, we ain't seen Scott Hayes around here in a while. He knows I'll let his feed bill ride another month...." Pudge met Scott's eyes and paled. "H-hell, what are friends for, I says, didn't I, Ben? And then dang if you didn't walk in."

The door burst open. Four heads turned as Maggie stumbled in clutching a Neiman Marcus shopping bag.

She stood blinking in the dim light, wearing a belted silk jacket with pants in the same dusky rose fabric. Her ash blond hair, swept back into a low bun, shone as richly as the gold clips at her ears. Matching suede flats and shoulder bag completed the pricey getup.

Judging by Pudge's rare silence, Scott wasn't the only one feeling outclassed right now.

He watched her search the store, find him and walk quickly forward, looking better with each step. She didn't seem depressed. Trading a Porsche for a Greyhound bus would've made *him* miserable.

"You're early," he said gruffly. Her bus wasn't due for another ten minutes. "How was the ride?"

"Actually not too bad. I enjoyed looking at the scenery."

His surge of gladness shocked him.

Setting the Neiman's bag on the floor, she pawed through her purse. "I had the most interesting woman sitting next to me. She's moving to Gonzales— Ah, here it is!" Pulling out a business card, Maggie waggled it under his nose.

Distracted by the silver mischief in her eyes, the unexpected dimple in her left cheek, he finally focused on the hot pink lettering: Lorna Lane, Dance Instructor and Massage Therapist.

Maggie seemed to be waiting for his comment.

"Just what a farm and ranch community needs," he drawled.

"That's what I told her. After the Armand Hammer Classic in August, we might trade our services. You know, I teach her how to ride, she teaches me how to two-step. What do you think?"

He thought this animated woman should slip back into her haughty-princess peg hole where she belonged. Folding his arms, he looked her up and down.

"I dunno, darlin'. Learning massage would be a whole lot more...interesting." He gave her a lazy tomcat grin. "You can practice on me."

Her nose lifted on cue. She dropped the card into her purse and gave him a chilly glare. Unfortunately the idea of Maggie practicing interesting things made more than his brain perk up. He slipped behind the pyramid of insecticides.

"No problems turning the Porsche in?" he asked, touching a bottle here, a jar there.

"The mileage was a little high, but the dealership owner let it slide. He even gave me a ride to the bus depot."

I'll bet he did. "Looks like you squeezed in a trip to Neiman's first." He eyed her shopping bag with disgust. "There go Twister's shoes for the month."

Her silence ground him under her dainty foot.

He blew out a breath. "I would've picked you up at the station. You didn't have to walk here."

She hesitated just long enough to irritate him. "It wasn't far. I saw your truck pass by and figured you were killing time here. Besides, I need supplies for Twister."

Dismissing him with a regal turn, she smiled at Pudge in that soft, feminine way she reserved for other men.

"Hello, Martin. Nice to see you again." She moved to the knotty-pine counter, tossed her purse in front of the cash register and nodded politely at the domino players. "Mr. Drake. Mr. Tobin. You're both looking well."

Martin? Scott nearly tripped over the abandoned shopping bag in his effort to see Pudge's reaction. The name only his mother had used had him sucking in his paunch and puffing out his chest. "H-hello, Margaret. Good to see you, too. Sounds like you'll be staying awhile."

"That's right. I'm training a horse at the H & H ranch," she explained, waiting until Pudge's shocked expression grew self-conscious under her cool regard. "I'll need a high-performance feed mixed up please." She ticked off the items on her fingers. "Cracked corn, whole oats, soybean meal, molasses, calcium carbonate, brewer's yeast . . . oh, and dicalcium phosphate."

She fumbled in her purse and withdrew what looked like an index card, handing it to Pudge. "Here's the quantity and percentages for you to keep on file."

He studied the card and nodded. "This looks like what I used to help Mom mix up for Riverbend every month. But Liz Howarth doesn't buy from me anymore." His black eyes hardened, strangely at odds with his plump face. "Even if I stocked everything she wanted, I can't compete with San Antonio's volume-discount prices."

"Don't take it personally, Martin. Training race-horses isn't cheap. Liz has to take advantage of cost efficiencies wherever possible. But *I* certainly have no intention of taking my business elsewhere."

Laying her forearm on the counter, Maggie traced the scarred wood with one fingertip. "The thing is, though, I really need my first month's feed order by tomorrow morning." Her finger stopped. "In fifty-pound bags." She looked up through her lashes. "Cash on delivery. If that wouldn't be too much trouble?"

Pudge nearly fell off his stool shaking his head. "Shoot, no, Margaret. I'll deliver it to Scott's place myself first thing tomorrow."

"Perfect! I knew I could count on you. And by the way, I'll need about twenty bales of good clean timothy hay, also."

Scott snorted loudly from behind the display. So much for counting on Luling Feed and Hardware. When Maggie sent him an over-the-shoulder glare, he couldn't control his smirk.

She turned back to Pudge. "You don't have it?"

He looked crestfallen. "Not *timothy* hay, no. But I can order it, Margaret. Shouldn't take more'n a coupla days—"

"The Taylor farm puts in a few fields of timothy each year for their stock," a querulous voice interrupted.

Maggie swiveled to Ben and favored him with her luminous gaze. "Mr. Drake, you're a genius! Martin can buy Bill Taylor's surplus and pick it up on the way to the H & H. I'm *so* glad that's settled. Now, how's that new great-grandson of yours doing?"

Ben cracked a gummy smile, fumbled in the pocket of his bib overalls and pulled out a wallet-sized photograph.

"Asked Nancy fer a pitcher like y'said."

Maggie glided to his side and draped an arm over his shoulder. Watching blond head meet silver, Scott felt an odd little catch in his chest.

"He's going to break the ladies' hearts," Maggie predicted. "I'll bet you shattered a few in your day, too, didn't you?"

Ben ducked his chin in a surprisingly boyish gesture. Across the scattered dominoes, Lester scowled fiercely, his hands fisting on the makeshift table.

The old coot was jealous, Scott realized, turning a measuring gaze on Maggie. She'd certainly made the most of her earlier visit to the store. No wonder she knew too damn much about his business.

Just then she straightened and patted Lester's gnarled brown knuckles. "How's your arthritis, Mr. Tobin? Did you try that cream I told you about?"

He jerked back his hand and crossed his arms. "Don't need no cream."

"He fergot the name, is what," Ben said with a reproving glance at his friend. "I can't recollect it, neither. Our memories ain't so good no more."

Lester sent a pained look Scott's way.

Taking pity, Scott turned his back and pretended to study a jar of screw-worm ointment.

"My memory's terrible, too." Maggie's voice was matter-of-fact. "I forget everything unless it's written down. You know, Mr. Tobin, I'd be happy to get a tube of that cream at the pharmacy for you. It wouldn't be any trouble."

"Why don't you just write down the name for Lester?" Pudge suggested.

Something about her absolute silence prickled Scott's neck. He turned. She was staring vacantly at Pudge's puzzled frown.

"I ain't dead yet," Lester groused, breaking her trancelike state. "I'll write it here on my score pad if you'll spell it out, Margaret."

"N-no, this is silly." Grabbing her purse, she headed for the door. "I know exactly what to look for, and the pharmacy is right across the street. Be back in a minute."

Jerking the door open, she slipped out as two strangers walked in.

Scott picked up Maggie's Neiman Marcus bag from the floor and strolled to the hardware section. Damn, what had she bought that was so heavy? Certainly not the clothes he'd suspected.

Everything about the woman confused him. One minute high society, the next down-home country. One minute supremely confident, the next incapable of speech. She'd had a dream about Matt's death and screamed, "It should have been me." She'd fussed over two lonely old men without demeaning their dignity. Could it all be an act?

He reached the last aisle, set the shopping bag at his feet and found the roofing nails he wanted. Hell, he *wanted* everything in the store, what with all the repairs and improvements needed around the place. His leg jammed against a hard edge, and Scott focused all his anger, all his seething frustration on Maggie's hapless bag.

Of course her concern had all been an act. The spoiled little princess thought nothing of shopping at a ritzy store while he had to think twice about buying a friggin' bag of penny nails!

With a mindless growl, he gave the bag a kick that toppled it over and sent three items sprawling.

Scott stared down at the boxed Teflon-coated skillet and smoke alarm for a long moment before crouching to pick up a partially hidden book. A cookbook, actually, titled *Heart-Healthy Eating for Life*.

He squeezed his eyes shut and fought the nameless emotion tightening his chest. He'd damn well better find a practical solution to his problems soon.

Another fall would destroy him.

CHAPTER FIVE

YAWNING SO HARD her jaw popped, Margaret leaned back against the headboard. The long bus ride from Dallas, her close call at the feed store, Scott's silence on the trip back to the ranch—the day's tension was catching up to her now. A normal person would go to sleep. But then, that was the crux of her problems. She wasn't normal.

Stifling another yawn, she pulled out a sheet of notepaper, clutched her pencil in a death grip and hunched over. Careful. Don't forget the smile, or it will be a *c* instead of an *e*. Oh, so slowly, she formed the letter.

Of all the tasks dyslexia made difficult, writing was the hardest. Her tutors had explained that a phonetic-based approach wouldn't work for someone with her poor auditory memory for symbols. She'd learned, instead, how to recognize words on sight like the faces of friends, sometimes drawing picture notes that captured the word's meaning. By matching the picture note to the printed word, she linked meaning to symbol and was able to recall the word thereafter. Sweet liberation!

Focusing now on reproducing each letter, she glanced frequently at the cookbook lying next to her on the bed. An hour passed. When she straightened at last, it was after midnight. Her nightgown clung to damp skin, her shoulders ached, and she shook from exhaustion.

But a list of fifteen grocery items marched somewhat unevenly down the page.

Absurd to feel so proud. Yet she didn't deny herself the moment. There'd been all too few such moments in her life.

Tucking the grocery list into Grant's cookbook, she smiled fondly. She'd given the book to him that afternoon, along with the frying-pan replacement and smoke alarm. He'd wrapped her in a bear hug so warm and safe and affectionate she'd ached with the pleasure. She would've tried to move a mountain if he'd asked. Writing the grocery list had only been slightly harder.

Scott had grumbled something about her paying top dollar. But she'd rather he think her extravagant than admit entering an unfamiliar store would disorient her. It had taken her years to learn the layout of Neiman-Marcus.

She picked up her hairbrush from the nightstand and began the one-hundred strokes ritual. As a young child, she used to close her eyes and imagine that it was her mother brushing her hair. Later, the action soothed her ego, affirmed her sense of self when she felt particularly worthless. Particularly stupid.

Sighing now at the memory, Margaret slid the brush onto the nightstand, switched off the lamp and snuggled under the covers. Silence engulfed her in a soothing balm. It was always this way after completing a demanding task. Fatigue was a common symptom of dyslexia. She'd learned to pace herself and catnap when she could.

Ten minutes later she was still staring at the ceiling. Moonlight filtered through the ligustrum bush outside her window and created fluttery shadows on the plaster. The longer she looked, the wider awake she felt. Maybe some herbal tea would help. It was the only item besides her clothes she'd brought to the ranch.

Slipping out of bed, she groped in the closet for her knee-length kimono and gave it a tug. The wire hanger did a half gainer off the rod and clattered against the wood floor. Cringing, she belted her robe and tiptoed to the door. The groaning hinges made her wince again. Did all old houses make this much noise?

Once past Scott's door, she let out her breath and scuttled into the kitchen. Teabag, sugar, mug—everything was here but a kettle. She filled a pan with water and set it on the stove, turning on the proper burner with ease. Only on-the-spot pressure caused her to freeze up as she had her first morning cooking breakfast, or yesterday at the feed store in front of Pudge. Propping her backside against the counter, she folded her arms and felt her muscles relax.

Despite its shabbiness, she loved this kitchen. With a fresh coat of paint, some new curtains—okay, maybe new linoleum, too— it would look warm and homey. Far different from the stainless-steel-and-black-tile-marvel in her parents' home. The cook had never allowed her inside except on rare occasions.

Frowning, she glanced out the window. The night looked so peaceful....

Minutes later she sat on the cement stoop holding a mug of tea, gazing at nothing, just absorbing the quiet. Mingled smells teased her nose. Loamy soil. Rusty metal. Sweet clover. Tangy steam. Odd how much sharper odors were at this hour.

Not a breath of wind stirred. She took a slow sip, her swallow sounding unnaturally loud. The barn stood iced in moonlight, camouflaging weathered boards and peeling paint and...*Scott.*

Her spine stiffened. She squeezed the ceramic mug in her lap until the heat penetrated her brain. Shifting her grip to the handle, she watched him push off the shadowed wall and amble toward the stoop. Loose-limbed. Broad-shouldered. All cowboy, despite the fact he wasn't wearing a hat. Or boots. With every step his feet flashed pale, three shades lighter than his muscular arms. Had this been a commercial, his low-slung jeans would have sold millions of Levi's.

He reached the steps and stopped, pushing two fingers up at a nonexistent hat brim. His face darkened. Was he *blushing?*

Margaret smiled.

"Habit," he said, shrugging. His gaze swept her slowly, taking in silk hitched high above her knees.

She tugged her kimono hem down, her toes curling against the cement. "It's beautiful out here, isn't it?"

He shot her a surprised look. "You think so?"

"Well, it can't compare with the Austrian Alps or the canals of Venice. But I guess in a pinch it's okay." Irritation sharpened her voice. His sheepish expression didn't pacify her. "Every place has its own unique beauty. Why do you assume I can't appreciate your ranch?"

He stared off somewhere into the yard and frowned. "It's just that...well, you're not the kind of woman..." Blowing out a breath, he looked down at his feet, then back up at her. "You just don't fit here, that's all."

She hadn't expected the truth to hurt so much. Taking a quick sip of tea, she rubbed the glazed daisy on her mug. "What kind of woman *do* you think fits here?"

When she peeked through her lashes, he wore the pained "how did I get myself into this" expression of a man thigh-high into a knee-deep conversation. She decided to modify her question.

"Did your mother and sister fit?"

At first she thought he wouldn't answer. Then he mumbled, "Yes and no."

She arched a brow.

He rumpled his hair and hooked a thumb in one pocket, the action pulling his waistband farther down. "Do you have any idea how hard ranch life is on a woman?"

Her gaze snapped up. He was deadly serious. "I'm sure it's not easy. I've had a small taste of it."

He snorted a laugh. "This ranch is a skeleton operation. No hired hands to feed, the cattle herd down to twenty head, no chickens, milk cows, goats, cats. Hell, most ranches are a regular zoo compared with this one. You can't judge ranch life by the way the

H & H is now. But when Mama was alive, her work never stopped.''

The way he said Mama brought a lump to her throat. Oh, to be loved like that! She took another sip of tea and ached for the boy inside the man. "Was your mother a frail woman?"

He seemed startled. "Frail? No, but she was the only child of older parents. She never lifted a finger growing up, except for her piano lessons. When she married Dad, she married a lifetime of hard labor. Cooking, cleaning, doing laundry—we didn't have a dryer until Laura was in high school—tending the farm animals, along with the calves that always manage to get sick." He folded his arms and widened his stance. "Then of course there was the isolation."

His eyes dared her to dispute him. She set her mug down and hugged her knees. "Luling's not so far."

"Too far to have a cup of coffee with a neighbor. Not big enough to offer theater or the symphony or any of the finer things Mama grew up with in Boston. Living on this ranch killed her—" He stopped and shook his head, as if regretting his outburst.

"Pete told me she had cancer," Margaret said gently.

"Doctors still don't know what causes cancer. Who knows, if she'd had an easier life..."

"She had a *happy* life. That's all a woman wants."

He cocked his head. "How do you know she was happy?"

Margaret smiled, completely confident. "She was married to your father."

He stared, the stern angles and planes of his face softening.

Her insides turned to mush. She struggled for composure. "Tell me about Laura," she blurted.

His eyes lit. A full-scale smile transformed his face into a younger, carefree version of the one she knew.

Her lips curved in response. "I take it you're rather fond of her."

"Laura's just like me. Strong-willed, opinionated, exasperating..."

Irresistible, Margaret supplied. The thought wiped the smile from her face. An irresistible man could control her, ruin her plans for an independent future. Better he stay insufferable.

"Laura hated living on the ranch, even though she was a tomboy. The routine crushed her spirit. A college scholarship was her ticket to the big city, and there's no stopping her now." He chuckled, obviously proud.

"What's she doing?"

"She and her husband, Alec, own an advertising agency in Houston. A real 'hot shop,' from what I understand. She's expecting their first child in August." He unfolded his arms, a veil of wistfulness settling over his features.

He's lonely, just like me. "Why haven't you ever married, Scott?" She'd wondered before but had never had the nerve to ask.

His expression closed up. He propped his foot on the first step and brushed something from his jeans. "I plan to someday."

"When you find a woman who 'fits,'" she guessed intuitively.

"Something like that. No sense us both being miserable."

Oddly depressed, Margaret rested her cheek against her knees. Minutes passed and her lids grew heavy.

"You should be in bed," he said.

She looked up. "We both should be."

His gaze sharpened. The innocent words took on a loaded meaning. Her sleepiness vanished, replaced with heart-stopping awareness.

For an instant his eyes held suppressed wildness and frustration—suggesting sweaty skin and tangled sheets and come-and-get-it promise.

Then he blinked and looked away, banishing the promise as if it had never been. "Go on in, Maggie."

Rising on shaky legs, she turned, opened the screen door and shoved against the inner door. A low mutter followed her into the kitchen, "One of us should get some sleep."

Slamming the door shut, she fled before the urge to stay grew stronger.

SCOTT SQUINTED at the Lexus heading down the hill and muttered a curse. It was pure bad luck he was stuck on the roof with no time to escape.

Pete had driven into town for the weekly grocery run, Dad had tagged along for the change of scenery, and Maggie was off with Twister somewhere. Scott had gotten maybe three hours of sleep after their little chat on the back stoop last night. And most of that had been filled with dreams of moon-spun hair and shapely legs and eyes so full of compassion he'd ached and felt comforted at the same time.

Pounding shingles had seemed like a good idea this morning. Right about now it ranked up there with getting an enema.

Hammering down a cedar shake, he stole glimpses of the approaching luxury car and its blond-haired driver. Scott hadn't talked to Maggie's father since the day Donald Winston had brought her dream foal to the H & H. The colt was a gift, he'd said, for preventing his daughter from eloping with a penniless veterinary student. The fact that Matt had died during the course of events hadn't seemed to bother Donald much.

But it had ripped Scott apart.

With shattering grief over the needless death of his best friend. With agonizing guilt over his own role in the tragedy. And with bitter contempt for the woman primarily responsible—a woman he'd blamed so blindly, he'd accepted the foal she loved out of sheer meanness and a desire to punish.

He'd felt justified and vindicated—at the time. But time had a way of moving on, of putting details into perspective. In retrospect, he saw that accepting Twister smacked of a payoff. Scott had managed to avoid thinking about it for years. And then Maggie had shown up in his field eight days ago.

Shifting his knees on the pitched roof, he heard a car door slam and the sound of crunching gravel. The footsteps stopped directly below.

"Can you tell me where Margaret is?" Donald asked without preamble.

Scott pulled the last nail from his mouth and positioned the head carefully. Driving it home in one whack, he sat back on his heels, tugged off his gloves and squinted down.

The older man gazed up, his gray eyes the exact color of Maggie's and filled with impatience. The hand riding his hip flashed Morse-code signals off a diamond on his pinky. His sports jacket alone probably cost more than Scott's entire past-due feed bill.

"I expect she'll show up soon," Scott finally answered, tucking the gloves into his back pocket. "The farrier just left. Maggie took Twister out for a quick test drive."

"So it's *Maggie* now, is it?"

"What of it?"

"Sounds like you two are pretty cozy all of a sudden."

"Get to the point."

Donald smoothed his graying blond hair and blew out a breath. "The point is, people are talking. And not about your stallion, either. They're wondering why a woman with Margaret's prospects moved in with a confirmed bachelor."

"Dad lives here, too."

"Oh, excuse me. *Two* confirmed bachelors."

The thought that others might have the wrong impression of Maggie's living arrangement knotted Scott's stomach. "Maggie gets room and board, period. If folks want to make more of it than that, there's nothing I can do to stop them." He tossed his hammer in the toolbox with a jarring clatter.

"I disagree. Anyone who can keep my daughter from marrying Matt Collins is smart enough to nip a little gossip in the bud."

Slamming the toolbox lid shut, Scott glared down. He'd been wrong earlier. This man's eyes were nothing like Maggie's. Nothing at all.

"Why do I get the feeling you don't like me, Scott? I thought we had an understanding."

"What I understand is that you haven't visited this ranch in five years, and both of us wanted it that way. What are you doing here, Donald?"

All pretense at civility fled. "I've come for Margaret," Donald admitted, flinging a hand at the stack of shingles by Scott's knees. "The least my daughter deserves is a decent roof over her head."

"If you'd helped your daughter when she needed you, maybe she'd have one."

"Why you . . . I'll have you know I asked Margaret to move back home and she refused! What did she tell you?"

"Nothing, Daddy."

Scott jerked his gaze toward the sharp voice. Maggie stood several feet from the ladder, facing Donald with quiet dignity.

"I was too embarrassed to admit my wealthy father wouldn't grant me a loan."

Giving in to a compelling need he couldn't explain, Scott maneuvered to the edge of the roof and climbed down.

Donald stepped aside to make room. "And why would I throw away good money to help you start your own breeding farm? You don't have the skills to survive as a receptionist, much less run a prosperous stable."

"How do you know?" Maggie demanded.

He walked up and squeezed her shoulders. "Margaret, honey, don't make me list the reasons. Look at this ridiculous scheme of yours to race a cow pony. If that doesn't prove you've got no head for business, I don't know what does."

"Come on, Daddy. You of all people know this 'cow pony's' potential. We used to discuss his pedigree for hours, remember?"

"You're the one who forgot it and ran away with the first boy who gave you a second glance."

Margaret shook her head. "I always intended to come back for Twist of Fate. I *would* have, if you hadn't given him away."

Their gazes locked, shimmering with pain and resentment.

Donald looked away first. His arms fell to his sides. "Pack your bags, Margaret. I'm taking you home."

Her eyes widened. "I have responsibilities here. A job." Her voice rose as he started to turn. "What would I do at home?"

He spun around, his hands fisted. "Dammit, girl, how do I know? Have lunch with your friends. Join your mother's bridge club. Do whatever you did when you were married to Jim, but do it where I can keep an eye on you."

"Where I can't embarrass you, don't you mean?"

Ignoring her, he cocked a belligerent eyebrow at Scott. "Try to stop us, and I'll press charges so fast you'll be sleeping in a cell tonight."

Scott took a combative step forward.

"I'm not going, Daddy."

Scott stopped, some instinct telling him not to interfere.

"Don't be stupid, Margaret. Now get your things together and bring them to the car."

Her chin came up. "*Don't call me stupid.* And believe me, I am *not* going with you."

Scott hooked his thumbs in his belt loops and grinned.

Donald's shocked expression revealed volumes about their relationship. "Be rational, Margaret. I'm...sorry I spoke to you that way. But why struggle so hard if it's not necessary? Your mother and I agree you'll be much happier living with us at home."

"You have no idea what makes me happy. No idea what I'm capable of accomplishing outside of a show ring. I want the chance to succeed—or fail—on my own."

"But there's no need." He seemed truly puzzled. "With your looks, you won't have any problem finding another—"

"No! I won't be pawned off on some man again."

"Now see here, young lady, I won't tolerate your attitude! When this ridiculous plan to race Twist of Fate blows up in your face, don't expect your mother and me to welcome you back with open arms."

She laughed, a bitter sound totally devoid of joy. "Don't worry, Daddy, that's the last thing I'd expect. Now if you'll excuse me, I have a job to do."

Donald threw up his hands and heaved a sigh. "All right, let's talk about what it'll take to make you come home. There's an SC 400 Coupe on the lot with your name on it.''

Scott noted Maggie's stricken expression and moved to stand beside her. ''Since you don't hear so good, Winston, I'll put it to you another way. Get the hell off my property. And don't come back without an engraved invitation.''

GRANT STOOD before the rows of canned vegetables and tried not to look as foolish as he felt. All around him, shoppers—every damned one of them women—tossed items into their carts with decisive plunks while he stared at the overwhelming selection. Luling's new mega grocery store was too modern, too bright, too *mega* for Grant's tastes.

He squinted at the childish scrawl on the crumpled notepaper in his hand. He never should have offered to tackle Margaret's list by himself. But Pete had few enough opportunities to do personal errands, and Grant had wanted to give him a break.

Pulling down a can of peas at random, he read the label. Loaded with sodium. A definite no-no, according to his new cookbook. He'd been touched by Margaret's gift, even more so by her gentle insistence that he follow the book's guidelines, but dammit...

He shoved the can back into place, found a brand labeled Sodium Free and threw it into his basket. Bland food. Mild exercise. Restrained activities. Why hadn't they just put a gun to his head and been done with it?

Rolling the cart forward, he blew out a guilty breath. He was lucky. He knew that. The doctors as-

sured him he would eventually feel stronger than he
had in years. But ever since his first heart attack, he'd
been confused and grouchy and, yes, deeply ashamed.

His brush with death had jolted him awake, opened
his eyes to the way he'd retreated from life and allowed his son to carry the burden of H & H Cattle
Company's problems alone. It wasn't fair or honorable. He couldn't undo years of indifference, and it
sickened him.

"Uh, sir? Are you looking for a particular brand or
something?"

Grant frowned at the stock boy shelving cans of
tuna ten feet down the aisle, then flashed a sheepish
grin. "No, son, you caught me daydreaming is all. I'm
not exactly a pro at this."

The teenager nodded self-importantly. "My name's
Bruce. You need any help, just ask for me. I've been
here three months."

"Will do, Bruce."

Three whole months, eh? Grant headed for the next
aisle, his smile mutating to a scowl at the sight of Ellen Gates fondling tomatoes in the produce section. He
whipped around and rolled back toward Bruce at a
fast clip.

"You never saw me," Grant told the startled young
man, who broke into a knowing grin.

At the far end of the store, he finally slowed. Damn,
that'd been close! Ellen was turning into a major nui-
sance. At first her bedside attention had been flattering. He'd been weak, not dead, and he couldn't help
reacting to the sheer bounty she offered.

Now his eyes glazed over at the mere sight of her. The woman was dumb as a stump, and he avoided her as much as possible without hurting her feelings. Patricia had ruined him for other women.

So why are you having those dreams, hmm?

Turning into the last aisle, he stopped at the sight of his nighttime fantasy in the flesh. As if conjured by his taunting mind, Ada Butler stood studying the shelves. His pulse picked up speed.

What the hell was wrong with him? This was Ada. His neighbor. His friend.

And one fine-looking woman, you idiot.

She wore ordinary jeans and boots with a plain white shirt. But her figure was trim and youthful, with enough curves to fill his palms nicely. Short, dark hair threaded with silver curled around a heart-shaped face. In profile, her nose tilted up in a kissable curve. She reached high, the action lifting her breasts, and grasped something on the top shelf. He knew the exact moment she sensed him.

Her head snapped around and their gazes met. His eyes narrowed with intensity. Hers widened in shock.

They were turquoise, those eyes, and fringed with short, thick lashes untouched by mascara.

He dragged in a lungful of air. "Hello, Ada."

Her hand jerked back. A beat later, she crouched beneath a waterfall of tumbling pink boxes. When the last one trickled off the shelf, Grant was there to catch it. She uncovered her head and straightened.

He cleared his throat and held out a pink box of tampons.

Blushing furiously, she snatched it from his hand and turned to put it into her cart. The bottom was filled with pink. She stared for a long moment, shrugged and dropped the box on top of the others.

"That oughtta hold me till menopause."

She looked up with a grin that raised his spirits and had him chuckling along with her. The sizzling tension of moments before had vanished.

As they restacked boxes in companionable silence, he chided himself for acting like a randy kid. He had more important things to focus on. Like pulling his own weight at the ranch.

Sliding the last box into place, Ada gestured to their handiwork. "Thanks for the help, Grant." She glanced at the single can of peas in his cart. "Is there anything I can do for you?"

"No... no, I'll manage. But thanks for asking."

Nodding, she stared straight ahead, then hesitantly back at him. "Well, then, I guess I'll finish my shopping now." She gripped her cart handle, but didn't move.

"Sure, go ahead. I've got quite a bit left myself." He gripped his cart handle, but didn't move.

She was his neighbor and his friend and a lot smarter than a stump. There was no crime in enjoying her company, for God's sake. He watched her start to roll forward and experienced a stab of alarm. Snatching up the crumpled shopping list from his cart, he smoothed the paper against his stomach and held it out.

"Maybe you could help me a little."

Brightening, she took the list from his hand and gave it a cursory glance. "I can take you right to these items."

"But can you do it without running into Ellen Gates?"

"Ellen's here?"

Grant nodded, unconsciously comparing Ellen's vacant blue eyes with Ada's penetrating gaze, alive now with mischief. "Think you can do it?" he repeated.

She snorted and arched a brow. "Does a hog like molasses spice cake?"

CHAPTER SIX

MARGARET ENTERED the cool barn and allowed her rigid spine to sag. Facing down her father had sucked the heart right out of her. She'd held on to her control while watching his car drive off. She'd calmly brushed Twister and turned him out to pasture. She'd even managed to thank Scott for his support and send him back up the ladder with a casual wave.

But now that her guard was down... Oh, God, would she ever grow indifferent to disappointing her parents? Their scorn still had the power to wound her, to make her feel like a frightened twelve-year-old lying awake, pillow hugged tightly to her chest, listening to their shouting drift down the hallway.

"I've donated a fortune to that school, goddammit. You'd better talk this new teacher out of testing Margaret, or they'll have no choice but to kick her out."

"Me talk to her? This is all your fault! None of my family ever had these problems. Your own brother never made it past the sixth grade...."

Margaret shoved back the hurtful memory, only to have others take its place.

They'd blamed her for the failure of her marriage naturally. Berated her even more for signing a prenuptial agreement that left her virtually out on the streets. "You should've taken Jim to the cleaners," her mother, charity fund-raiser extraordinaire, had said with a sneer. But Margaret couldn't in good conscience take assets she'd had no part in accumulating.

Hugging her stomach, she remembered the smug satisfaction in her father's eyes when he'd refused her request for a loan. She hadn't asked for much. He would hardly notice the loss. But it wasn't money he was afraid of losing. Donald Winston was afraid of losing face.

Armed with a high school diploma and a keen instinct for trends, he'd made millions securing some of the first import-car dealerships in the country. The elite strata of society he'd worked so hard to enter contained the very people who owned racehorses. He expected her to fail big time. And he wanted her to crawl back home before she had the chance to embarrass him.

Well, think again, Daddy.

An unfamiliar curl of pride straightened her shoulders. Perversely, tears battled for release. As she had since childhood, Margaret sought the nearest animal for comfort.

Slipping into the front stall of the barn, she closed the door and turned. Four cloven-hoofed feet stepped back. A flat, glistening snout sniffed the air. Licorice-drop eyes never wavered from hers.

"A real tough guy, huh? That's okay. Trust shouldn't be given lightly. Believe me, I know." She sank down and sat cross-legged in the straw, gazing at the weanling pig in sympathy.

"It's strange here without your mom and brothers and sisters, isn't it? You don't have to pretend with me. I know you're lonely and scared."

And she did know. She'd always known how creatures felt, a gift she attributed as much to reading animal body language as to instinct. She watched the shoat lower his snout, sensed when his impulse to flee became curiosity and groped deep in her pocket.

Withdrawing her hand, she held it out and crooned, "C'mere sweetie. I wouldn't hurt you for the world."

Squat legs braced, he stretched out his nose.

"Mmm, just smell that yummy grain." She swayed her cupped palm, the better for him to whiff its contents.

Led by his quivering snout, he took a stiff step. Then another and another. He covered the final distance in a greedy lunge.

Margaret smiled at the feel of his shoveling mouth, the sound of his snuffling grunts. His little tail whirled in a blurring circle. As he scarfed up the last particles of grain from her palm, she scratched behind his ear with her opposite hand, replacing one pleasure with another. Soon he was pressing against her fingers in ecstasy.

She arched a brow. "Killer pig, humph! You're nothing but a pussycat, you big fake."

A baritone chuckle unrolled above her head. When she slapped both hands over her thumping heart, the leaning animal fell into the nest formed by her crossed legs and snuggled there contentedly.

How long had Scott been watching her, his tanned forearms braced on the half door, his amber eyes slitted with lazy amusement?

"You scared me to death!" she snapped.

"How do you do that, Maggie?"

"Do what? Have a heart attack?"

He flashed an unrepentant grin, then flung a hand at the pig reclining in her lap. "No, how do you tame wild studs and killer pigs? That animal won't go near me or Pete, and we're the ones who feed him. What's your secret?"

Wiping a sticky palm on her jodhpurs, Margaret smiled down at the runt. He gazed back with porcine adoration.

"He knows I love him," she said simply, stroking the purebred Hampshire from his white-haired collar to his sturdy black rump.

"Did you love Matt?"

Her head whipped up. Scott's eyes were inquisitive, not accusing. For some reason, that made her furious. "It's a little late to be asking that, don't you think?"

"Maybe. But I'm asking, anyway."

"Why?"

"Because I didn't before."

No, he hadn't asked. He'd vehemently warned his friend against eloping with her, filling Matt's ears with prejudiced assumptions. Had last night's talk in the moonlight softened Scott's attitude toward her? Rattling snores rose from her lap and filled the stall. Intent on each other, neither she nor Scott paid attention.

She searched his eyes, wishing they weren't eternally shadowed by a hat. "Will you believe what I tell you now?"

His jaw clenched, then relaxed. "Yeah. I'll believe you."

But he didn't want to, that much was obvious. She picked at a snarl of straw on her boot and thought about lying just to spite him. In the end, she knew that was a coward's answer. Analyzing and accepting her feelings for Matt had been painfully hard. He'd been her admirer and defender, her last act of defiance against her father—but he'd never been her lover. Scott deserved the truth.

Sweeping the hollow stalks aside, she lifted her gaze. "Yes, I loved Matt... as a friend. A best friend."

Scott snorted. "That job was already filled. He didn't need a best friend."

She smiled sadly. "But I did."

"Dammit, Maggie, that was no reason to marry him." He lifted his hat, finger-raked his hair, jammed the hat down low. "Rural veterinarians work long, grueling hours for chicken feed. Matt deserved a wife who wouldn't hightail it back to her cush life when the going got rough."

Enough was enough! "If you'll recall, I was running *away* from the cush life to be with Matt. I am sick to death of people thinking they know what I want. Daddy. Jim. *You*. Matt was the only person who understood me. A word of praise from him was worth ten Corvettes, a dozen Riverbends. He didn't care a fig about my money or my looks or my roomful of trophies. He loved me. *Me*—can you believe it?"

She noted his expression and laughed, the sound a half sob. "No, I can see you can't. I couldn't, either, but I wanted to. I wanted to so much I panicked at the thought of losing him, and I forced him into that car, and—" she drew a shuddering breath "—I destroyed the most precious person on earth to me. So go on and hate me all you want, Scott, it really doesn't matter. Because you'll never hate me as much as I hate myself."

Margaret bowed her head, unable to face his inevitable scorn. Or worse, his pity. The pig slept on, content and oblivious in her lap.

"Maggie."

Blinking rapidly, she curled her fingers around a warm, floppy ear.

"Maggie, look at me." Scott's voice sounded as ragged as her emotions. "Please."

She slowly raised her chin and thrust it out.

His mouth quirked once before compressing into a grim line. "I miss him, too, darlin'."

It wasn't an apology. He hadn't said he didn't hate her. But for just an instant he shared his loneliness and grief, and some of her own pain eased.

"I would've been a good wife to Matt," she said, wondering why it was vital he believe her. "Friendship isn't a bad foundation for marriage. Eventually I would have loved him the way a wife loves a husband."

"The way you loved your lawyer." He tipped up his hat brim as if to see her better.

"My law...you mean Jim?" She huffed and idly rubbed the ear in her hand. "Not hardly."

"You didn't love your husband?"

"No." Let him draw his own conclusions. "At least not that way."

He cocked his head and studied her with keen interest. Gradually his eyes darkened, held hers captive while the mood shifted, became something thick and languid and undeniably sexual. "I'm curious, Maggie. If you didn't love Matt or your ex that way, how do you know how a wife should love a husband?"

She'd read books, and seen movies. She'd imagined feelings she'd never experienced with Matt or Jim.

"I..." Margaret moistened her lips, distracted when his gaze dropped to her mouth. Her heartbeat accelerated to jackhammer speed.

"Yes?"

"I just know, okay?"

"Okay. So tell me. How should a wife love a husband?"

The Mule had nothing on Scott Hayes. He wasn't going to drop it. "She should w-want to be with him all the time and feel miserable when she's not."

His gaze climbed up, smoky topaz and filled with speculation. "That's it?"

"Sh-she should want to take care of him. And ease his mind when he's worried." Her voice sounded far away even to her own ears.

"Very...sweet. But surely there's more?"

The fantasy gripped her. She couldn't breathe or look away from Scott's glittering eyes. Heat swirled and pooled low in her belly.

"She should want to plan a future with him, full of hope and . . . and babies."

A tic pulsed in his cheek. "And?"

And? She squirmed, her cheeks burning.

"Tell me, Maggie. Tell me what you're thinking."

When she found her voice, it came out as a husky whisper. "A wife should want to touch her husband, should want to be touched by him."

Scott straightened slowly, his eyes never wavering from hers. The click of the door latch rang in her ears as he slipped inside the stall. From her vantage point he literally towered, six feet plus of lean cowboy so overwhelming she lowered her gaze.

His dun-colored boots were darker at the toes, his jean cuffs frayed at the heels. He walked forward with athletic grace and eased down into a crouch. The stall shrank. His wide shoulders blocked her vision, his musky male scent flared her nostrils. She felt small and quivery and thoroughly female as she gazed up at his taut, rugged face.

"How does she want to be touched, darlin'?"

She couldn't answer, could only stare with unconscious yearning into his eyes. His pupils dilated, his brown irises swirling with gold flecks. He lightly stroked a thumb down her cheek.

"Like that, maybe?"

Her lips parted on a sigh.

His blunt fingertips tunneled beneath her hair and curled around her sensitive nape. "Like this, do you think?'' Her lashes fell steadily as he massaged her neck.

"Or how about something a little more intimate...something a husband would claim by rights?"

Warm fingers cupped her breast and lifted. Her lids popped open.

His cheeks and mouth were drawn tight, his eyes fierce with predatory concentration. She should slap his face. At the very least, push him away.

Her fist came up, catching the brim of his hat and flipping it off his head like a bottle cap. Spreading her fingers, she plunged her hand into his shaggy hair. Ahh, just as she'd thought. The twining chocolate-and caramel-colored strands felt sinfully delicious.

"A wife has her rights, too," she said, enjoying his stunned expression.

The moment froze as they both considered the possibilities. The masculine fingers around her neck exerted a steady pressure, pulling her mouth closer. Closer. His breath was warm and tinged with mint. Unable to look directly into the golden blaze of his eyes, she lowered her lashes. Their lips touched. Everything in her melted. She parted her lips to the masterly coaxing of his tongue.

He wasn't worshipful like Matt or smoothly polished like Jim. His tongue swirled and teased and... mated, she realized with a thrill.

He clutched her hair and tilted her head back. She welcomed his tender roughness, welcomed the heat that incinerated the past and left only the here and now. Her tongue learned his salty, unique taste and dipped for more. His hand left her breast to press between her shoulder blades and crush her against his chest.

The rumble in his throat was cut short by a piercing squeal slicing up from her lap.

"Son of a bitch!" Scott sprang up and clutched his thigh, aiming a murderous glare at the pig now sheltered in Margaret's arms. "He bit me! That ungrateful little runt bit me, and you're comforting *him?*"

Lost in a sensual fog, it took a moment for his words to register. She struggled to look contrite, instead of disappointed at the interruption. "Is the skin broken?"

Gingerly probing the site of attack, Scott raised his head. A fallen lock of hair covered one eye. "I guess not. No thanks to that little...psychopath you're protecting."

The man who'd expanded her sensual horizons moments ago now wore a boyish pout. Cute. Very cute.

Scooping his hat from the floor, he brushed it off and crammed it home. "Sure, go ahead and smile. But Pete's right. That pig is dangerous, and I'm not going to put up with much more from him."

The inspiration struck from nowhere.

"I've got it!" Margaret said, gazing down at the runt's distinctive black-and-white markings.

"Huh?"

"His name. I've been trying to think of one for days, but nothing was right."

"How about calling him Supper?" Man and pig exchanged a look of mutual hostility.

"No, that's cruel. Leave the poor thing some dignity. But Orca—now that's a name to respect."

"Orca?" Scott stared reflectively at the black-and-white animal. "Orca...killer pig." He met Margaret's eyes and grinned crookedly. "I like it!"

Cute. *Very* cute.

Boy, was she in trouble.

MARGARET ADJUSTED her reins and tried to concentrate on Twister's rocking canter. Instead, images flashed in time with his hoofbeats. The confrontation with her father. Her confession of self-hatred. Scott's kiss.

After the ups and downs of the past few hours, her emotions were mincemeat.

One fact remained perfectly clear. She would need all her energy and concentration to establish her reputation as a winning trainer. She had nothing to spare for a charismatic and surprisingly complex cowboy—even if his kiss had blown her boots off!

It wouldn't happen again, she vowed. She wouldn't jeopardize her dream for the transient thrill he offered.

That decided, she settled down to business. Spine straight, knees and ankles flexed, heels down, stirrups on the balls of her feet. The correct riding form had been instilled in her muscles by years of practice, leaving her mind free to focus on Twister.

Oh, he was glorious! Fit beyond her wildest hopes. Smoother-gaited and more responsive than his dam, Aladdin's Girl, despite having no formal training. If things had been different, Margaret had no doubt he would already be an international champion. Regret twinged and passed, swept away by the wind in her face, the urgent expectancy of spring in the parched land.

She rode past mesquite branches furred with green buds. Brown scrub fallen in preparation for new growth. Darting birds with twigs in their beaks. And everywhere the tender, green tips of sprouting grass.

Life. Renewal. Second chances. The signs were all around her, bolstering her confidence in a plan her father obviously believed would fail. But Twister would succeed. She knew he would.

They'd covered about three miles of hilly terrain, alternating walk, trot and canter. She'd planned on turning around and heading back to the barn until she spotted a graded dirt road ahead—a long, flat stretch connecting the main compound with an obscure county highway.

How do you feel? Her question flowed through the reins to Twister.

She read his response in the tug of his bit, the raised flag of his tail, the unlabored sound of his breathing. *Impatient. Eager. Strong.*

Licking suddenly dry lips, she turned him toward the road. When his hooves struck the packed red dirt, she slowed to a stop and faced the substitute race-track ribboning into the horizon. Wispy clouds drifted across a marine blue sky. A gentle breeze stirred the hair against her shoulders. Her stomach churned, but she had to know.

Dismounting, she shortened the stirrups and swung back up into the saddle. "All right, handsome," she murmured, gathering the reins and crouching forward into jockey position. "Let's see what you can do."

With hands and knees and heart she commanded *Go!*

Only her training saved her from falling. Nothing could have prepared her heart for the sensation of being shot out of a cannon while perched atop the hurtling cannonball.

Pounding hooves thundered in her ears. Strands of mane lashed her cheeks. Equine muscles extended and bunched in rapid succession. She narrowed her eyes against a wall of stinging wind and smiled with pure joy. Never had she felt such unleashed power, such...freedom. She settled her weight over Twister's withers and soared.

After three, maybe four furlongs, common sense nagged her to stop. Reluctantly she pulled on the reins.

Twister shook his head and struggled to resume a full gallop. It took every ounce of her strength and a good measure of The Mule to bring him to a bowed-neck, trembling halt. Even then he danced in place.

"You need to learn some manners, boy," she scolded, grinning hugely. He was barely winded!

She'd exercised enough Riverbend hopefuls to know Twister was special—a virtual running machine. Apparently roughing it on the open range had been a blessing, after all. The sloping, rocky surfaces of the H & H had stimulated both his muscles and hooves to grow hard and strong in defense. Dr. Morley had said as much after examining the stallion three days ago. This little experiment verified his theory.

Suddenly she couldn't wait to tell Scott. He might smile that boyish, lighthearted way she'd glimpsed in the barn. Not that she cared if he worried himself sick of course.

Pulling out the rough map she'd drawn last week of the ranch layout, she pinpointed her present location. Directions were tricky for her. Without the diagram, she would've been hopelessly lost.

As it was, she added thirty minutes to her ride by cutting over to the north fence line and following it back. In her experience, the axiom Better Safe than Sorry was exceedingly good advice.

Cresting the final hill, which sloped down to the house, she reined in. A beige pickup, sporting the forest green silhouette of a running horse on the door panel, sat next to the barn.

Three people stood near the tall ladder propped against the house. One of them turned and waved. Love, respect and a touch of apprehension propelled the hand Margaret lifted in return.

THE LORD DIDN'T WANT him to fix the roof today, Scott decided. No, this was one of those days He felt like testing Scott's mettle. Why else would He send forth the plagues of Donald, Lust, and now these two characters—all before noon?

"Look, there she is!" Liz Howarth said, waving with one hand and tugging on Thomas Morley's sleeve with the other. "Oh, my God, what a beauty."

Maggie and Twister were headed down the hill at a trot. "Posting," as she called her fluid up-and-down movement, seemed a waste of energy to Scott. But he had to admit she looked damn good wasting it.

Dr. Morley smiled. "What did I tell you? Wait'll you see that chest. It's magnificent!"

Scott glanced sharply at the tall, black-haired veterinarian. *Get a grip, Hayes. He's talking about the horse.*

Wearing creased black slacks, loafers and a black linen shirt, Dr. Morley was as different from Doc Chalmers as a Doberman pinscher was from a basset hound. The younger vet had handled Twister's examination three days ago capably and without fear, Scott admitted. So why did he feel like shoving those perfect white teeth down the man's throat?

Because he's not looking at Twister now, buddy boy.

Horse and rider had stopped in the yard. Maggie's normally smooth blond hair appeared tousled and snarled. Her cheeks glowed pink, her eyes sparkled with excitement. Her white shirt was rumpled and unevenly tucked into tight black jodhpurs. She looked fresh from a session of heavy petting, and Scott wanted to drag her from the saddle and finish the job.

Morley reached her first.

When she swung her leg over the stallion's hindquarters and kicked out of the stirrups, he grabbed her slim waist and set her on the ground.

"Thank you Dr. Morley," she said, slipping from the doctor's fingers seconds before Scott would've pried them off and broken each one individually. "Is everything okay? I mean, the lab tests didn't show...?"

"No, no, everything's fine. In fact, that's the reason I came with Liz—to go over the results."

Maggie nodded vaguely, her attention somewhere else. "Would you excuse me a moment, Dr. Morley?"

Beside Scott, Liz opened her arms.

Tossing the reins to Morley, Maggie ran forward and fell into the taller woman's embrace. "Liz, oh, Liz. It's so good to see you again. I've really missed you."

"I've missed you, too, honey. How've you been?"

Scott's mouth twisted cynically. Liz Howarth was going on forty, but came in a timeless package. Three years ago those pouty red lips and sultry blue eyes had sauntered into the Silver Spur saloon after Scott's fourth shot of tequila. He'd been drunk enough to unwrap the package and sober enough to feel cheated.

Studying Maggie's softened features now, Scott was genuinely surprised. Liz was one of the most selfish, egotistical women he'd ever encountered. He found it hard to believe she'd inspired and kept Maggie's loyalty all these years.

Pulling back, Liz held Maggie at arm's length. "Shame on you, training a Riverbend-bred horse and not letting me know. I had to hear about it from Thomas." She gestured at the veterinarian.

"I wanted to, but ..."

Liz chafed Maggie's wrists. "But what?"

"I was embarrassed. You defended my decision to quit showing horses when nobody else did, and here I am trying something even riskier."

"*Now* she admits it," Scott muttered under his breath.

"Racing is a crapshoot," Liz agreed, draping an arm around Maggie's shoulders. "That's why I wanted to see you. Not everyone's cut out for the stress, hon. It's not too late to admit you made a mistake."

Maggie slipped from beneath Liz's arm and lifted her narrow nose. "I've managed stress before. Just check out the trophies in Riverbend's guest lounge."

Liz looked as startled as if her pet kitten had turned into a snarling cougar. Her expression cooled. "You mean the ones next to my Olympic gold medal?" she asked, neatly establishing seniority and rank.

Scott tightened his mouth as Maggie blushed.

"I'm sorry, Liz. Daddy was here earlier and I guess I'm still feeling defensive. I appreciate your concern, I really do. But now that I've seen Twister, I have to utilize his potential. Just *look* at him."

Scott, too, found himself turning to analyze the horse he'd raised from a foal.

Although Morley held his reins, Twister gazed into the distance as if the man didn't exist. His large, dark eyes held a thousand secrets, a knowledge of searing deserts and lush oases. Perpetually flared nostrils quivered, as did the tips of small, inward-curving ears. He stood quietly. Unmoving. Yet the powerful, flowing symmetry of muscle and bone made him a creature of motion, an animal bred to run.

For the first time, Scott understood why Maggie had called him selfish for using the stallion as a cow pony. Twister's kingly bearing spoke for itself. He was destined for great things.

"I'll take him now, Dr. Morley," Maggie said, walking toward the vet. "He needs to be cooled down gradually after the workout I gave him."

She recaptured the reins and slanted a secret wait'll-I-tell-you glance at Scott.

"If he had a hard workout, it sure doesn't show," Morley said. "His condition is remarkable actually. I still can't get over how fit he is."

Resettling his hat, Scott spoke for the first time. "What about the Coggins test? Don't we need the results to run Twister?" Maggie'd told him a horse testing positive for equine infectious anemia wouldn't be allowed on any racetrack.

She rewarded his question with a brilliant smile. His heart responded with a surge.

"As I'd started to tell Margaret earlier, the test was negative. Twister has a clean bill of health to race," Morley said, his dark eyes sullen.

"That's perfect!" Maggie sandwiched Twister's cheeks between her palms and loudly kissed his muzzle. The stallion lowered his head, nestled the bridge of his nose between her breasts and cocked his rear fetlock in a pose of pure contentment.

So much for kingly bearing. The poor schmuck was no different from the lowliest smitten male.

"You always could calm down the troublemakers in the stable." As Liz briskly approached her student, Twister flung up his head, eyes rolled back, and whinnied long and piercingly. His ears grew flatter the closer Liz came.

"Liz, stop!" Margaret turned an anxious gaze on the stallion. "What on earth is wrong with you?" When Twister continued his restless, hostile behavior, she cast Liz an apologetic glance. "I'm sorry. He gets like this sometimes. I'd better start walking him so he won't be sore tomorrow. But thanks for coming by. Your support means a lot to me. Dr. Morley, please set up Twister's next inoculation with Scott. He'll fill me in."

This last was said breathlessly as Twister lived up to his name. She finally gave up and headed in the direction of Pete's trailer. Scott could hear her scolding the stallion even as she stroked his neck.

Two pairs of eyes met Scott's with equal resentment. Morley pulled an appointment book from his pocket, flipped it open and scanned a page.

"Hmm, I have some time free on Wednesday. Would that work for Margaret?"

Elbows propped behind him on the ladder, Scott lifted one boot and hooked his heel on the first rung. "Gee, I dunno, Dr. Morley. Our schedule's kinda tight. Got anything else open?"

As the handsome vet scowled, Scott decided maybe the day wasn't a total loss, after all. He was almost starting to have fun.

CHAPTER SEVEN

"HOLD ON," Scott warned, clutching the steering wheel the way he would a bronc ready to bust out of the chute. The old pickup hit a crater in the road and bucked once, twice. The crown of Scott's hat mashed into the cab's torn headliner both times. When the jouncing squeaks subsided to a steady rattle, he glanced at his passenger.

"You okay?"

Maggie's response was somewhere between a laugh and a groan. "I think I bit my lip." She ran the moist pink tip of her tongue over her bottom lip in a testing manner.

Gnashing his teeth, Scott turned back to the two dirt ruts serving as a road. Damn his father's unfailing courtesy. She'd expressed a casual desire to see the cattle herd up close—one little comment between a bite of oatmeal and sip of juice—and the next thing Scott knew, he was being forced to include her in his morning routine. He never should have agreed.

She had her agenda. He had his. As long as the two remained separate, he just might come out of their joint venture with his sanity intact. Maybe. If he could ever forget that incredible kiss.

After two weeks, he still couldn't shake the memory.

Her soft mouth, her passionate response—the touch and taste and smell of her had filled him with a wild yearning, a driving need to possess that went beyond mere lust. He'd wanted to replace the haunted look in her eyes with new memories. Memories of *him*. And nothing short of a killer pig could have torn him away from her.

Scowling, he wrestled the truck through another deep hole. The cab rolled and pitched. Maggie bounced along the bench seat and jammed against his thigh and shoulder. His elbow pressed into the once felt, never forgotten softness of a female breast.

"Sorry," Maggie said a bit breathlessly.

Scott grunted as she scrambled back to her side of the cab. He would feed the herd as quickly as possible and get the hell back to the house. His usual thorough check of each animal could wait until tomorrow.

"Is that your herd?" She pointed to the scattered red cows grazing beyond a fence ahead.

In spite of himself, he felt a spurt of pride, a rising eagerness to show this woman who loved animals some of the finest examples of their breed.

"Yeah. Hang on while I open the gate." He braked and shifted to neutral.

"I'll get it."

She was out of the truck and jogging toward the gate before he could move—if the mesquite-post-and-barbed-wire contraption could be dignified with such a name. Managing the H & H was a matter of prioritizing. Aluminum gates were expensive. The cows wouldn't notice the inconvenient substitute, but they'd damn sure miss their daily ration of corn, cottonseed meal and hay.

The unburied gate post tilted toward Margaret, snubbed at the top by a loop of wire attached to the grounded barbed-wire fence. Without straightening the post and pulling it from the bottom, it could be the very devil to open. Maggie studied the thing carefully to see how it worked. After a moment, she pulled against the leaning mesquite to loosen the wire loop. Nothing happened.

Scott started to get out, then saw her rounded chin jut. His lips twitched and he settled back to watch.

Bracing her ridiculous red boots, she cupped both palms against the wood and pulled, her snug denim jeans straightening against surprisingly muscular thighs and a tight little bottom.

Straining, she dug her heels in. The post quivered, but didn't budge. Relaxing her stance, she blew a few wispy strands of hair from her face.

Popping the door handle, Scott slid out. The look she threw him broke his stride.

He raised his palms high. "Don't shoot. I'm here to help."

But she was already at it again, her jaw set, her eyes flint gray. He was torn between admiration and puzzlement. Damn, the woman was stubborn! In one swift move, he straightened the post, positioned himself behind Maggie and placed his palms above hers on the wood. Her delicate spine and curvy backside flowed into his hollows and planes like hot wax into a mold. Her peach-scented hair tickled his chin. He squeezed his eyes shut at the sweet torture, then pulled back with his arms. The wire snub loosened as his body did the opposite. His hard-on could have dug postholes.

Stumbling back, he hoped to God she hadn't noticed. "Hold it open while I drive through," he ordered gruffly.

Escaping to the truck, he climbed inside and cursed under his breath. Why, of all the women in the world, did this one ignite his blood without even trying?

He roared through the gap and hopped out of the truck as she was dragging the unwieldy gate back into position. Grasping her shoulders, he set her firmly aside and completed the procedure while she sputtered.

"I had it under control, Scott."

But I didn't. "I'll let you handle it on the way back. C'mon. My girls are hungry."

Sure enough, every cow had lifted her head and now ambled toward long, wooden troughs standing in a large dirt clearing. He urged Maggie into the cab and drove over tender grass toward the gathering herd. She cast him a wry glance.

"Your girls, huh? I thought you didn't believe in pampering your cattle."

He felt his neck heat as she grinned. When she turned to stare out the window, he let out a relieved breath.

"They're huge," she said, her tone awed.

"Gilda, the one in front, is close to 1400 pounds. Liberty Bell, behind her, topped 1600 pounds the last time we weighed her. I guess that'd qualify as big. 'Course, Bandolero dwarfs these ladies, but he's in another pasture.''

Scott stopped the truck, pulled a notebook binder from the glove compartment and flipped it open. Forms, sleeved in clear plastic, held the recorded dates of heat periods, breeding attempts, calving and vaccinations for each animal in the herd. He turned to the page he wanted.

''Let's see, Gilda's due to drop her calf in about two weeks.''

Maggie scooted closer and peered down a long time, as if concentrating intently. ''We have a computer program at Riverbend that compiles and stores similar information. It will even combine different dam and sire pedigrees and predict dominant foal characteristics. I'm sure Liz would let you take a look if you're interested.''

Right now, he was far too interested in the dizzying smell of peaches and warm female skin for his peace of mind. Hoping to establish mental distance, he slammed the book shut and harshened his voice.

''What's the point? If I could afford a computer, I'd more than likely be able to afford an irrigation system, a new tractor, maybe a bulldozer, grader and harvester. This truck would hit the scrap-metal heap, and I'd get a fully loaded four-by-four Chevy with a winch and, hell, maybe a cellular phone.

''I'd clear the trash trees and cactus, and fence the pastures with steel posts, instead of worm-eaten mesquite. I'd keep a small remuda of quarter horses for heavy brush roundup, and dirt bikes for general work and riding the fences." He noted her startled look. "On this terrain, bikes cost and eat less than a well-trained cutting horse, and won't pull up lame, either."

Sometime during his outburst, the vision he'd guarded closely—especially from himself—had emerged from hiding. "The H & H could support two hundred head of cattle, with proper management and adequate funding," he said stubbornly, bracing himself for her skepticism.

She laid her fingers over his hand and squeezed. "I *know* it could, with you in charge. And you'll prove it, too, just as soon as Twister establishes his reputation as a winner."

A warmth ten times more dangerous than lust heated his body. He reacted in self-defense, refusing to return her vote of confidence. "Excuse me if I don't hold my breath. Right now I've got mothers to feed, or I won't be able to count on their calves to sell."

Pulling his hand free, he steeled his heart against her wounded expression and opened his door. Better he be a first-class bastard now than involve them both in a dead-end relationship sure to hurt her later. The idea of exacting revenge for Matt's death had completely lost its appeal.

The herd was lowing impatiently, several young calves adding their raucous bawl to the chorus. He dropped the tailgate, tugged on his gloves and hoisted a bale of hay to his shoulder. Heading for one trough, he spoke soothingly.

"Hold your cud, I'm coming. You can't be that hungry with all this spring grass popping up." Thank the Lord for that. He'd be able to save money and cut down on supplemental feed soon.

He slid the hay into the trough and pulled a pair of clippers from his back pocket. Cattle could pick up parasites from hay left on the ground. He never took chances with these beauties. Snipping the baling wire, he spread the hay evenly and checked the second trough. Several blocks of salt, minerals and systemic insecticides had been licked to varying lumpish shapes, but all were intact. He headed back to the pickup.

Maggie had slipped out of the cab and was scratching the head of a particular favorite of Scott's. Lady Love would be bred for the first time next month, sure to produce her weight in gold in quality calves. He watched the beautiful heifer lip something from Maggie's palm.

"What do you think you're doing?" he bellowed.

Feeding grass by hand could be dangerous for someone Maggie's size. The cows were docile, but big enough to inflict damage with a casual toss of their heads.

Maggie spun around guiltily. Lady Love shuffled off toward the troughs.

He crossed his arms and tilted his head. "You wouldn't be *pamperin'* that little lady now, would you, Maggie?"

Her gaze filled with relief, then devilment. "Why, of course not. That would be cruel come the first summer drought," she drawled, mimicking the words he'd spoken to a lovely horse thief a lifetime ago.

He went about the task of adding corn and cotton-seed meal to the trough with a silly grin on his face.

There, that ought to hold the spoiled brats. Wiping his hands on his thighs, he joined Maggie where she leaned against the front fender.

"You've done a fine job, Scott. They're glowing with health. Their calves must bring top dollar."

He grunted, noting with deep satisfaction the sleek red hides absent of protruding ribs or clinging flies. "They'll be bought as breeding stock to upgrade the quality of commercial herds all over the country." He refrained from adding they were the only thing standing between H & H Cattle Company and bankruptcy.

"I would think Bandolero is in great demand. Do you have a good supply of frozen sperm in storage?" She might have been referring to frozen steaks, so matter-of-fact was her tone.

"Actually, no. The service is expensive, and I'd have to develop a market, and...no, dammit, I haven't had time." It was a lousy excuse, but a valid one. He *didn't* have time to be both acting foreman and business administrator for the ranch.

She gave him a considering look before turning back to the herd. "I'm not familiar with this breed. What country originally developed it?"

Scott relaxed and slanted her a grin. "Texas."

She seemed startled, then delighted. "Really?"

"Yep. The King Ranch experimented for ten years with a cross between Brahmans and shorthorns before producing the founding bull. Santa Gertrudis was the first breed of beef cattle developed in America."

"I'm impressed. So where is the famous Bandolero your dad— "

"Shh!" Scott cut her off and listened carefully, dread tightening his belly. Another wheezing cough confirmed his suspicion.

"What's wrong?"

Ignoring her question, he searched the cows crowding around the trough. Lady Love stood with feet splayed and tongue stretched out, coughing incessantly now. A steady stream of slobber dripped from her mouth.

"Oh, God," Maggie said, obviously spotting the heifer at the same time he did.

Scott ran toward the distressed animal. The signs were unmistakable. She was choking, but on what? He turned to Maggie, who'd followed him.

"Something's stuck in her throat. What did you feed her a minute ago?"

Her face drained of color, but she met his eyes squarely. "An apple. I fed her an apple."

"Son of a *bitch!*" He studied the wheezing cow anxiously, hoping she would cough up the lethal object.

"I—I'm sorry. I didn't know it could hurt her. Horses love them."

Feeling the heifer's rapidly swelling left flank, he spoke curtly. "Horses can bite off chunks. Cattle don't have incisors. They practically swallow food whole. It digests in their rumen and comes back up as cud to chew." Lady Love's bloat had grown to alarming proportions.

"What should we do?" Maggie whispered.

If he'd had a cellular phone, he would've called Doc Chalmers. If it'd been bloat without choking, he would've drenched the rumen, or first stomach, with peanut oil. As it was, the stomach gases were trapped and building into a lethal situation. *Prioritize,* he told himself sternly.

He would deal with the bloat first and then tackle the apple.

"There're two knives in my toolbox. Forget the pocket blade and bring me the long, curved one like you clean fish with."

Maggie ran off. Lady Love suddenly staggered, but stayed on her feet, praise the gods. He would never have been able to lift her with just Maggie to help him.

She rushed up and handed him the knife. The herd had stopped feeding and now encircled the unfolding drama as if watching from an operating theater. Scott drew a deep breath and struggled to recall the emergency procedure he'd read about in his *Cattleman's Veterinary Handbook*.

Picturing a circle on the heifer's left flank, he sighted a spot equidistant from her last rib, the top of her spine and the point of her hip. "Be bold," the book had said. "You won't harm the cow and you won't do any permanent damage."

Balancing the knife tip on this imaginary spot, he plunged the blade down to the hilt.

Maggie gasped.

Partially withdrawing the blade, he turned it in a full circle, then pulled it out. Gas bubbled from the incision with a slight hiss. The flank slowly sank to normal.

Now the apple. The poor animal was wild-eyed with suffering. He would have to try to remove it by hand.

"Come hold her horns as steady as you can," he directed Maggie, positioning himself at the heifer's mouth.

Holding the muzzle with his left fingers, he cupped his right hand as small as possible and pushed it palm upward into the cow's mouth. As she thrashed her head from side to side, he forced himself to concentrate on what he had to do. Molar teeth cruelly scraped his arm. The cow's throat grew smaller and smaller. His hand lodged and stuck.

"It's too big," he told Maggie. "My goddamn hand's too big to reach far enough." As he withdrew it from the heifer's throat, he noticed Lady Love's coughing had weakened considerably. The thought of losing her sickened him. He bowed his head and willed himself to think.

"Move!" Maggie ordered, shoving him aside with surprising strength. "Get back there and hold her horns."

Grabbing the heifer's nose, she cupped her hand and pushed it slowly into the slobbery mouth.

After a stunned moment, Scott grasped the heifer as instructed and spoke quietly to Maggie. "Keep your palm pressed to her top palate and slide between her molars. Push your way to the back of her throat."

Maggie's hand disappeared, then her wrist. She wore the absorbed expression of inward focus. Despite Scott's grip, the heifer swung her head from left to right. Maggie winced, following the movement as best she could, and continued her hand's slow advance. When her arm was swallowed past the elbow, her face brightened.

"I feel something. I think it's the apple." She met his eyes, her excitement turning into panic.

"Okay, that's real good, Maggie. You're doing great, darlin'. Now slowly turn your hand and try to get a hold on it."

He watched her absorbed concentration return and knew the instant she'd accomplished her objective.

"I've got it in my hand!" Her gaze returned to his for reassurance.

"Good girl. No, don't yank it out—you might hurt her. Turn your palm up and press the apple against the roof of her mouth. Now work your hand out slowly. That's it. Take it easy."

He tried his best to keep the heifer's head still, but once her air passage was cleared, she was wild to get rid of the foreign objects in her mouth. Most cattlemen Scott knew would have given in to natural instinct and hurried past those grinding molars.

This little slip of a woman gamely held back and followed Scott's instructions to the letter. At last she pulled the apple free and held it aloft. Perspiration beaded her forehead and upper lip. Saliva dripped from her elbow and smeared the front of her T-shirt. Nasty, jagged scrapes marred the creamy skin of her hand and arm.

"We did it!" she whooped, her smile more beautiful than anything Scott had seen in his life.

Unable to cope with his roiling emotions, he turned to watch Lady Love. Within a minute she was breathing normally. Another two, and she was nuzzling the trough for remnants of food.

Scott tried to focus on the immediate situation. He would clean up Maggie's arm as best he could, then drive back and call Doc Chalmers to take over where they'd left off. It looked as if the heifer would make a full recovery, unchanged by the dramatic rescue.

If only the same was true for himself. If only he could keep Maggie in the neat little slot that had kept him safe all these years. If only...

His thoughts whirled, spinning backward to a time he hadn't allowed himself to revisit in six long years....

"SO WHAT D'YA SAY? Will you help us, buddy?"

Scott met the pleading brown eyes across the booth table and clenched his fists. What *could* he say? Matt had been his best friend since the sixth grade. They'd drunk their first six-pack together and puked it up side by side minutes later. They'd made the football team together and scored a combined total of twenty-two touchdowns by their senior year. They'd shared homework, cars and even dates with the offhand casualness of blood brothers.

What the goddamn hell could he say?

"All right, you can borrow my car. Can you find a ride and be here by 9:00 a.m.?"

Matt grinned lopsidedly and kissed the cheek of the girl at his side. "By noon tomorrow, Miss Margaret Chelsea Winston, you'll be Mrs. Matthew Rayburn Collins. And there's nothing your dad can do about it!" He squeezed her narrow shoulders. "I told you Scott would come through for us."

For the first time, Scott looked directly at the girl. She was watching him with an odd expression, part wary, part hopeful, as if she wanted to trust him, yet didn't dare.

He had to get away. Scooting out of the booth, he dropped tip money onto the table and focused on the spinning quarter—anywhere but her huge, dove gray eyes.

"I expect a breakfast outta this, Collins," Scott growled, walking away to the sound of Matt's good-natured laughter.

All that night Scott lay awake. Matt was crazy in love, and had been since he'd first met Riverbend's resident princess.

Matt had sworn she wasn't a snob, just shy. There were reasons, but he wanted Margaret to tell Scott herself, when she knew him better. She'd helped Matt in the barn and was interested in his plan to open a veterinary clinic. After he'd proposed, she talked of being his assistant until he could afford to hire help. She and Matt were perfect for each other. If Scott would make the effort to become friends with her, he would *see* that, Matt insisted.

Scott did see her Corvette, and wondered if she'd be willing to sell it to pay off student loans. He saw her fancy clothes, and wondered if she had any idea how messy delivering a calf was. He saw her affection for his friend, and wondered if it ever changed to the passion he saw in Matt's eyes. Matt deserved her passion. He deserved to be happy.

The couple wanted to borrow Scott's car tomorrow and drive to San Antonio to get married. No one would recognize them there. Donald had confiscated the keys to Margaret's Corvette until she showed proper remorse for dating the "shit-kicking son of a grocer." And as usual, Matt's truck was out of commission— something about a bad fuel line this time. Scott hadn't paid much attention.

Tossing fitfully, he imagined Donald Winston's reaction to the elopement. Margaret's father had fired Matt last week. A secret marriage would send Donald over the edge. He would make Matt's life a living hell.

Someone had to show some sense, force the couple to slow down and confirm their feelings for each other before taking such a permanent step. Matt was making a terrible mistake. Someone should save him.

At five in the morning Scott gave up trying to sleep, made coffee and did his barn chores. Breakfast was on the table when his dad and Laura got up. They drove off to the school-bus stop by seven. Scott slumped in the kitchen chair, his eyes gritty, his mind fuzzy. If he didn't leave soon, he'd be late.

Rising like an old man, he shuffled to the telephone and dialed the number he'd looked up earlier.

All the way to Luling he practiced what he'd say. "It was for your own good, buddy." Or, "She wasn't the right girl for you. She would've made you miserable." The closer he got to town, the weaker the excuses sounded. In a horrifying moment of clarity, Scott realized they *were* weak. Not because they weren't true, but because he had no right to play God with his best friend's future.

Entrusted with the most important decision in Matt's life, Scott had taken steps to change fate, instead of honoring his friend's request. Bile rose in his throat, followed by a frantic desire to make amends.

He would tell them what he'd done, then send them off immediately rather than join them for breakfast as he'd planned. His palms grew slick against the steering wheel as he entered the outskirts of town. Lucy's Café was right up ahead. Please, Lord, don't let him be too late.

The parking lot wasn't crowded. His gaze swept the few cars, and his hands relaxed. Pulling into a front space, he checked the gas gauge and wished he'd filled the tank. The tires needed air, too. Some friend he was. Oh, God, please don't let him be too late.

Matt and Margaret pushed through the glass front door, their arms around each other's waists. The sheer beauty of their youth and brilliant smiles was painful to look at. Scott killed the engine and moved to get out. In his peripheral vision, a car pulled up in the space beside him. One glance at Margaret's face was enough to tell him who was driving.

"No-o-o," she moaned, echoing Scott's inner scream.

As long as Scott lived, he would never forget the look she turned on him then—accusing, wounded, thoroughly betrayed. That look castrated him as effectively as a scalpel. He didn't have the guts to meet Matt's eyes.

Opening the door, Scott climbed out talking. "I can explain everyth—"

His breath whooshed out as Margaret barreled into his shoulder, knocking him aside. He staggered against the car.

"Get in!" she shrieked at Matt.

Matt blinked in the morning sunlight.

"Move!" When she slid behind the wheel, Matt appeared to wake up from his trance. He ran to the passenger side.

The adjacent car door crashed open, slamming Matt in the stomach. *"Stop right there, you son of a bitch!"* Donald Winston planted a tassled loafer on the blacktop and prepared to climb out.

Matt never gave him the chance. Younger, stronger and fueled by panic, he shoved the door against Donald's leg, forcing him to pull it inside or be crushed. In seconds, Matt jumped in beside Margaret and slammed his door.

Scott barely leapt aside in time to avoid the swooping rear bumper. He watched in horror as Margaret sent the car squealing backward, then screeching forward in an instinctive flight from the man Scott had phoned that morning.

"They won't get away, dammit! They're headed for the interstate. One call to Ken Browning'll take care of that." Donald slid out of the car and hobbled toward the restaurant.

"They're scared now," Scott called to Donald's back, his own alarm growing by the minute. "Give them a chance to cool down. A patrol car on their tail might set Margaret off."

But he was talking to a closed glass door. Donald had entered the restaurant to phone the sheriff, whose election campaign he'd supported heavily.

Eventually Scott went inside and slid into the same booth he, Margaret and Matt had occupied the night before.

Donald sat across the room looking flushed and triumphant.

Time passed, and the lump of dread in Scott's stomach grew to nauseating proportions. Something was wrong. Terribly wrong. When the sound of sirens wailed in the distance, he wasn't even surprised. Donald rose along with the few customers in the restaurant to look through the windows. He didn't look smug now, Scott noticed. And then Scott's senses shut down.

The ambulance, the sheriff's report, the ride to the hospital—they were all a distorted blur.

Later he learned the full story from the deputy sheriff who'd given chase. Instead of slowing down and pulling over when she saw the flashing lights, Margaret had sped up. Only a princess used to driving a Corvette wouldn't have sensed the rattletrap's limitations. At eighty miles an hour, the old car had probably started to come apart at the seams. The bald right tire had exploded, spinning the chassis around and around across the highway. A concrete overpass post had stopped its progress.

Margaret suffered three broken ribs, a fractured tibia and a mild concussion. She hadn't been able to attend Matt's funeral.

Scott had wanted her there, had wanted her to see the tears and the agonizing grief she'd caused. He'd wanted her to bear the crushing guilt, to bear the blame—and he'd succeeded in convincing himself she deserved them.

Until lately.

Until she'd come back into his life and blown all his previous perceptions to hell.

CHAPTER EIGHT

SCOTT'S BEDROOM DOOR creaked open right on schedule. In the next room, Grant sighed and looked out the window. Not quite dawn yet. Something had happened four days ago to give his son itchy feet. Something besides Lady Love's close call with death.

Throwing back his covers, Grant dressed hastily and rushed to the kitchen. Even so, he almost wasn't fast enough.

"Whoa, son, hold up a minute. What's your hurry?"

Scott paused with his hand on the back doorknob. A canvas backpack was slung over one shoulder. "The chute-head gate was acting up yesterday. I want to get it workin' before Pete comes to help with the sprayin'."

"Sit down and have a cup of coffee with your ol' man. It won't even be light yet for another fifteen minutes."

"I really should—"

"Scott." Grant used a tone of voice he hadn't exercised in years. It had the same effect now as it had when Scott and Laura were children.

Withdrawing his hand from the knob, Scott moved to a chair and slouched down with a sulky scowl. He slipped the backpack to the floor.

Grant pulled coffee from a cabinet and got the percolator going. He inhaled with appreciation and
wished he had a cup ready now to fortify himself. This
wasn't going to be easy.

He nodded toward the canvas bag. "Plannin' on
another long day?"

"Not plannin' on it. Just prepared."

Scott had been leaving before dawn and returning
after ten at night ever since the morning he'd shown
Margaret the herd. Grant had a pretty good idea why,
but wanted to hear his son's explanation. He propped
his rear against the counter and crossed his ankles.

"You missed a good meal last night. Margaret's a
fair hand with roast chicken." Scratching his jaw, he
hid a smile at Scott's instant wariness.

"There was a plate wrapped up on the stove when I
came in. I figured you left it out for me."

"Wasn't me. Anybody stubborn enough to stay
gone all day and half the night deserves to starve.
Margaret must think different, though."

Scott stretched out a boot and appeared to find the
toe fascinating.

"That's a fine young woman, Scott, even if her father is lower than a dung beetle." Grant's mouth
thinned ruefully at his son's startled glance. "I always thought so, son. I just didn't have the gumption
to do anything about it. By the time Donald Winston
bought Perkin's place, I was so used to lettin' you fight
the battles, I'd forgotten how."

"There was nothin' you could've done, Dad. We
never could've matched Winston's price."

For a minute Grant couldn't speak for the emotion swelling in his throat. "Maybe not then. But if I'd taken a more active role in runnin' the ranch after your mother's death, we might've managed to buy the place before Winston came on the scene." He swallowed thickly. "I should've let you grow up a little slower, Scott. I should've stayed grown-up a little longer."

Shaking his head, Grant turned and busied himself pouring coffee. His maudlin rambling wasn't helping anyone. When he had himself under control, he carried two steaming mugs to the table.

Scott straightened in his chair. Grant sat and shoved a mug across the table.

"What's done is done, and I can't give you back those years. But maybe I can keep you from throwin' away the ones you have left."

Scott took a sip and studied the curling steam. "That's kinda cryptic."

"Let me be blunt, then. It's time you stopped treatin' Margaret so poorly."

Scott's golden brown eyes flickered once and grew blank. He'd learned to hide his feelings well. That was fine, Grant thought, as long as he didn't hide them from himself.

"I don't see her enough to treat her poorly." Scott's voice revealed the irritation his face didn't.

"That's as good a form of punishment as any. How did you feel after your mother's funeral when I withdrew from you and Laura?" Grant winced at the flash of pain his son couldn't conceal. "You were probably hurt. You might even have blamed yourself, damn my soul."

Scott's jaw clenched. His fingers gripped the mug so tightly his joints whitened. "You're a lousy shrink, Dad. Maggie's here to do a job, and the more I stay out of her way, the better she likes it."

"You're runnin' scared, son, and that's not like you. Slow down and give yourself a chance—"

Scott slammed the mug down on the table, ignoring the slosh of coffee that had to have burned his hand. "I don't know where the hell this is comin' from, unless it's your new love life."

Grant blinked and forced his mouth to close.

"C'mon, Dad, did you think I wouldn't hear? You've had lunch at the diner with her four times. You may as well have run an ad in the *Luling Gazette*." He picked up his backpack and thrust to his feet. "Don't get me wrong. I think Ada's great. But I'll thank you to quit analyzin' my life and drawin' ridiculous conclusions. It's a little late for fatherly advice." Slinging the pack over one shoulder, he flung the door open and didn't bother to muffle the closing whack of the screen.

Grant sipped his coffee and sighed. He deserved that last dig. But damn, it hurt. He'd made a fine mess of the whole thing when all he'd wanted was to save his son from making the same mistake he'd made.

All these years, he'd avoided serious relationships because no woman could measure up to Patricia. Ironically Scott had used her as a standard of what to *avoid* in a mate. He equated cultured femininity with an inability to survive ranch hardships. His son was as blind to Margaret's strength as Grant had been to Ada's womanly grace and fun-loving spirit.

Grant lowered his mug, aware he was smiling. Ada did that to him. Hell, if the town gossips were watching his courtship, anyway, maybe it was time he gave them something juicy to chew on.

"May I join you?"

Startled, Grant twisted to see Margaret hovering in the doorway. "Of course. I could use the company."

She moved to the stove and started a pot of water for the tea she drank every morning. "Looks like you've already had some. Company," she clarified, waving a hand at the second coffee mug.

"I could use some *pleasant* company."

Her smile didn't reach her eyes. "That bad, huh?"

"He makes Orca seem like Porky Pig." Ah, her eyes weren't so sad now. She had lovely eyes. "I would've taken him over my knee if he didn't top me by an inch. Where've the years gone? I'm tellin' you, Margaret, enjoy every minute of your youth before you get old like me."

"Oh, quit fishing. You're not old."

"I'll be fifty-four soon. Seems like yesterday I was twenty-four."

"Your birthday's coming up?"

He grimaced. "In six days, more's the pity."

She looked thoughtful. "Oh, I don't know. I've always thought birthdays should be celebrated. They have a way of bringing people together, if you know what I mean." She slanted him a conspiratorial glance.

His mouth curved up with his rising spirits. He really liked this girl. She was smart and sensitive and exactly what Scott needed. He lifted his cup in a mock salute.

"I do believe I know exactly what you mean. And I'm gettin' a distinct cravin' to blow out some candles."

ADA STUFFED her jeans into her knee-high rubber boots and checked her watch. Where *was* Clive, anyway? He'd promised to be back by ten, and it was damn near eleven now. She'd bet Morning Glory's next litter he was gabbing with Pudge Webster at the cash register, instead of heading back here with the nozzles she needed. And men said women gossiped. Humph!

Straightening, Ada wondered if people were talking about Grant Hayes's seeming preference for her over Ellen Gates. As her pleasure swelled, she forced herself to be sensible. So he'd bought her lunch at the diner after she'd helped him at the grocery store. He'd been courteous, that was all.

Only... he *had* shown up at the market the following three weeks on her shopping day and repeated the lunch offer. And he *had* given her that look—the one that'd dried up her mouth and sucked the air right out of her lungs—when he thought she wasn't watching. Surely that meant their platonic relationship was on the verge of changing.

Shaking off her distracting thoughts, she headed for a long, low building with a metal roof and concrete walls about waist high. A gap of open space between the roof and walls let air enter and circulate. Inside, a dozen finishing pens with concrete floors and partitions held fifteen to twenty hogs each.

Her father, a transplanted Midwesterner, had built the pig parlor with the idea of raising as many market hogs as possible with as little human intervention as necessary. The pens had everything. Self-feeder bins. Automatic drinking fountains. Fogging nozzles that sprayed a fine mist of water in hot weather.

And today promised to be a scorcher.

Ada glanced toward the farmhouse and frowned. Heat waves shimmered off the pitched roof. The potted impatiens on her porch already drooped. And three of the dag-blame misting nozzles were malfunctioning.

Where was that Clive?

He was avoiding cleaning the pens of course. It was a messy, loathsome chore even with the new high-pressure washers she'd installed. She couldn't blame him for wanting to dawdle, and she couldn't fire him, either. This was cattle country. No one else in the area would work with hogs, much less for such low wages.

Entering the building, she ignored the racket of feeder bins slamming, hogs murmuring and the occasional squeal or scuffle breaking out. She'd grown up with the symphony. She was, in fact, a damn good "pigman," the title bestowed in states that respected her occupation. When her parents had decided to buy a condo in Florida five years ago, she'd cashed in her teacher's retirement fund, made a down payment on the farm and taken over with their blessing.

In the lonely hours of the night, she admitted the proximity to H & H Cattle Company influenced her career change. But she didn't regret her decision. She plain flat liked raising pigs.

Unreeling a long hose from its wall mount, she surveyed the row of stalls in amusement. Hogs scrambled forward and bunched against the front concrete wall, their snouts thrust upward and every one of them grunting expectantly. They looked like a class of first graders at the teacher's desk, waiting for suckers to be handed out. She walked beside the pens and doused each group with a spray of water, laughing at their delighted squeals. Having no sweat glands, they craved moisture however they could get it.

At the end of the line, she sighed and faced facts. "Okay, kiddos, looks like it's just you and me. Everybody cooperate and I'll give you a treat later."

Herding the porkers into a separate holding pen, she aimed a high-pressure water jet at the leavings fastidiously deposited at the opposite end from the feeders. Hogs were surprisingly clean animals if given the opportunity. Even so, twenty pigs in a ten-by-fifteen foot space could make a serious mess.

By the last stall, Ada was spattered with droplets of water. The humid air had undoubtedly turned her wavy hair into the Orphan Annie corkscrews she detested. And she'd broken one of the fingernails she'd felt compelled to grow longer during the past few weeks. The sound of Clive's pickup truck gave her irritation a target.

Crouched with scraper in hand on the concrete floor, she heard the sound of boot steps and narrowed her eyes. Come to make his excuses, had he? He'd timed his appearance perfectly, the good-for-nothing slug. How convenient to show up when the job was almost finished. Pure devilment seized her.

Grabbing the hose she'd laid aside, Ada jumped up and aimed a high-pressure stream of water at the tall man standing just inside the entrance. He dropped a paper bag and threw up his hands in self-defense, staggering a bit at the water pummeling his chest.

Recognition dawned. Ada released the washer-gun trigger and stared in horror at the sight of Grant standing with a bemused expression on his face, water dripping from his chin and puddling at his boots.

He lowered his hands. "Was it something I said?"

Ada dropped the hose and rushed forward, kicking over a bucket of disinfectant in her haste. She splashed through the suds and pulled out her shirttail as she went. "Oh m'gosh, Grant—" she dabbed at his face with the damp cotton hem "—I'm so sorry. I thought you were Clive, and I was so angry I didn't stop to make sure...." She wrung out the cotton and dabbed some more. "And then I couldn't stop the water fast enough, and...I'm so sorry." Lowering her shirttail, she felt absurdly like crying.

His eyes twinkled. "It's okay, Ada. I feel kinda...refreshed." He stooped to pick up something by his feet. "I stopped by to bring you this. Clive said you needed them."

She took the soggy paper bag he handed her and peeked inside. "My nozzles. But how...?"

"His truck wouldn't start outside Luling Feed and Hardware. He and Ben were fiddling with the engine when I left. I said I'd tell you what happened when I brought the nozzles."

She studied his carefully bland expression with rising hope. The nozzles could've waited. Clive could've called her from the store and explained what happened. Grant had wanted to see her. Oh, glory be, he'd created a really lame excuse to see her!

Her gaze roved lovingly over the shirt clinging to his chest, the jeans plastered to his legs. He'd gained weight during the past few weeks. His rangy strength was evident, and she sent up a prayer of thanks that his health was returning. She pressed timid fingertips against his shirt.

"You're soaked," she said stupidly, helpless to stop the circular motion of her hand. The skin beneath the saturated fabric felt firm and surprisingly hot. Wiry chest hair tickled the pads of her fingers. Sometime during her exploration, awareness of his tension penetrated her senses.

She breathed it first in the musky, humid air. She saw it next under tight, wet denim. She felt it finally in her own body's softening response, a feminine counterpoint to Grant's obvious arousal. For her? Dazed, she tilted her head back.

Under dark lashes, the shifting green and gold of his eyes glittered with desire. For her.

Happiness expanded in her chest. She gazed into his beautiful eyes with all the love she'd suppressed for years. Let him see how she felt. She was tired of hiding.

A strangled sound escaped his throat. "You really should be careful how you look at a man, Ada. He might get the wrong idea."

"Or the right one, Grant. He might get the right idea at last."

His eyes darkened. He reached out and threaded his fingers through her damp curls, the heels of his palms cupping her ears like warm and gentle conch shells. A roaring surf of blood filled her head.

"Ada, my friend, my neighbor. What am I gonna do with you?"

Unable to speak, she told him with her eyes what she ached for him to do.

His fingers pressed into her scalp. "You're sure?"

In answer, she turned her face and kissed his palm.

Tossing her paper bag aside, Grant clasped her wrist and towed her out into the sunlight. She stumbled along behind his lengthier strides past the farrowing barn, past the water well, past the fenced plot containing five young boars. Heat rushed to her cheeks and other select spots. Grant's fingers tightened around her wrist.

He reached her house. She tripped on the second step of the porch. His steel grip prevented her from falling, then he hauled her up the remaining steps. Shouldering through the front door, he pulled her inside.

Over the years, Grant had been in her home maybe half-a-dozen times. She blinked as he headed unerringly for her bedroom. At the huge four-poster bed, he stopped and released her wrist. They faced each other, their breathing heavy.

Ada had no idea what to do. Grant watched her from under lowered lids, his eyes glinting emerald fire.

"I don't want to embarrass you Ada, but I've got to know." He drew a deep breath. "Do we need protection?"

Whatever she'd expected him to say, it wasn't that. She hadn't been seeing anyone seriously to warrant her seeking birth control. She was still menstruating, as he knew with embarrassing certainty. Oh, dammit all, he was going to stop and she couldn't bear it.

"Yes, Grant," she said, wishing she could lie. "But I'm . . . not prepared."

Nodding grimly, he dug in his pocket, pulled out a foil-wrapped package and tossed it onto the bed. "Good thing I am. I sure as hell can't wait."

The evidence that he'd been hoping for this encounter was a heady aphrodisiac for Ada. Closing the gap between them, Grant backed her against the fluted bedpost and crushed her mouth with his. She looped her arms around his neck and kissed him with equal greediness.

What followed was bold and lush; the passion of two mature adults who realized their mortality and savored their pumping hearts, their fevered blood and their heightened senses. Prolonging the inevitable, they took a shower together, laughing like children until Ada kissed the vivid scar running down the center of his chest and then continued on down past its end. She found herself in bed soon after, receiving his lavish attention.

Every woman should experience loving like this once in her life, Ada thought while she could still think. Tender, playful and masterly by turns, Grant made her feel beautiful and cherished. Her heart was simply not big enough to contain her swelling emotions.

When he entered her body at last, she smiled in exultation. When he increased his tempo, she gasped in pleasure. When they climaxed together, she cried quietly with joy.

Much later Grant gathered her close under the covers and nuzzled her neck. "I almost forgot the main reason I came over today. Margaret's making a special birthday supper for me on Friday, and I'd like you to be my guest."

Ada, who'd thought a person couldn't get much happier, discovered she'd been wrong. She smiled against his chest. "I don't know, Grant. I'm not the kind of woman who jumps into a kitchen with just any man."

He didn't laugh. "Are... are you sorry we did this, Ada?"

She pulled back and cupped his jaw with her hand. "Oh, Grant, I thought we'd never get around to *this*. Thank goodness I sent Clive for those nozzles."

A wicked gleam entered his eyes, sparking the banked embers of her desire. He waggled his brows and rolled to cover her body with his long length.

"You want a nozzle, ma'am? I've got just the one you need."

MARGARET INSPECTED the kitchen counter and worried her lower lip. She wanted Grant's birthday celebration tonight to be perfect, that was the problem. Perfection wasn't her forte.

Spice jars, plastic bags filled with vegetables, cans of broth, eggs, flour, beef tenderloin wrapped in butcher's paper, a carton of buttermilk... The ingredients grew larger before her eyes and tightened her throat with fear.

Calm down, Margaret. You can do this. Organize your thoughts, take a deep breath... Now take one step at a time.

The ingredients shrank back to normal size on the counter. Weak with relief, she pushed the long sleeves of her shirt up to her elbows and washed her hands at the sink. Close call there. She'd almost let her ambitious task overwhelm her. Thank heavens her past tutoring had come to the rescue.

Her gaze strayed to the clock. She had... five hours—yes, that was right, five—to prepare the meal she'd been cornered into cooking. After all, she'd been the one to suggest the celebration a week ago. Appearing delighted with the plan, Grant had given her an affectionate kiss on the cheek and asked if he could invite Ada. Pete was coming, as well. And Scott.

She paused, her stomach fluttering like a treeful of starlings. Scott couldn't avoid her tonight. He would have to withstand her company for at least the duration of a meal, which was more than he'd done for nearly two weeks. He'd been getting up before dawn, packing food to take with him, and not returning until late. First the water pump had broken down. Then the herd had needed spraying for insects. And so on and so forth. Ever since she'd almost killed his prize heifer, he hadn't been able to stand the sight of her.

The memory depressed her. She'd apologized over and over at the time, had even gone with Doc Chalmers and Scott and watched while they tended Lady Love's wound. The cow would be fine. Margaret wasn't so sure about herself. She couldn't take much more of Scott's silent treatment.

Drying her hands, she moved all the ingredients for Burgundy Beef with Parsleyed Fettuccine to the kitchen table. She would bake Grant's birthday cake first and free up the oven for the entrée. In spite of Scott's feelings, or more likely because of them, she wanted plenty of time to change from her shorts into something dressier for dinner. Something that wouldn't be so... invisible.

Opening Grant's cookbook to a recipe for low-fat carrot cake, Margaret ran her finger beneath the type. "Combine first five ingredients in a medium bowl, stirring well," she read, then set to work.

Two cups of flour poofed into the bowl. One teaspoon of baking soda topped the mound. One-half teaspoon of salt—ridiculous measurement, but who was she to question?—sprinkled into the white heap and disappeared. One cup sugar cascaded over the peak. One teaspoon—

Knock, knock!

Margaret set down the baking powder and opened the back door.

"Since when do you have to knock? Come on in."

Behind the screen, Pete shook his head, hat in hand. "No thanks. I, um, just wanted you t'know I changed Twister's beddin' straw."

"Why, thank you, Pete! That was very thoughtful."

"No problem. I figured you'd be busy here and all." He toed the cement step with one boot. His leathery cheeks reddened.

"Is there something I can get you? Some iced tea maybe?"

"No, ma'am. But I was kinda wonderin' what time you want me here for Grant's shindig."

"Oh, didn't Scott tell you?"

Pete scowled fiercely. "That boy's head ain't been screwed on straight since y—" He stopped, his hands turning the frayed straw brim around and around. "He just ain't been hisself, that's all."

"Hmm, well, I hope you can join us at six-thirty. Is that too early?"

"No, ma'am, it surely ain't. Is there somethin' you'd like me t'bring?" His light blue eyes were bright with pleasure. Although he insisted on eating most meals in his trailer behind the barn, he obviously welcomed a break in his routine.

She smiled warmly. "Only your appetite. And make sure it's a big one." She gestured behind her to the table loaded with food. "I've got enough here to satisfy even Orca. I swear every time I see him he's gained another pound. How much do you feed him, anyway?"

Pete cackled and backed down two steps. "As much as that killer pig wants. Keeps him from goin' after my hide." Putting on his hat, he tipped the brim. "See you tonight, Margaret."

"I'm looking forward to it, Pete."

And she was. More eager to sit at a rickety kitchen table with two ranchers, a pig farmer and a bow-legged wrangler, in fact, than she'd ever been to dine with Jim's associates at the country club. She closed the door with a smile and returned to the mixing bowl.

Now, where was she? Margaret scanned the open cookbook, tension slowly tightening her muscles. Idiot. Why hadn't she marked off the steps as they were completed? She'd lost her place, of course. The bowl contained a mound of dry, white ingredients, so anything wet or colored was safe to add. But when she turned back to the instructions, words became blurry, chopped pieces. She read each letter aloud separately to bring them back into focus.

The eggs needed to be divided, a task she'd seen done but had never attempted herself. Half a dozen eggs later, she dumped two questionably pure egg whites into a separate bowl and happened to look down at her chest. Orange yolk smeared the front of her light pink T-shirt. Scrubbing it with a wet rag produced a beautiful, puckered sunset. Groaning, she threw down the rag and checked the clock. More than an hour had passed!

Suddenly all the time in the world had changed to just enough time—if everything went right. *Focus your thoughts, Margaret. Take it step by step.*

She tried. She went back to the recipe and labored through it with increasing panic. The ticking clock became her enemy, mocking her slowness every time she checked. Her organization habits slipped, so that she quit cleaning her mess as she went. By the time she'd poured the batter, the pressure squeezing her chest made it hard to breathe. She set the oven at 350 degrees, slid the cake pan inside and mentally formed a picture of the clock face thirty-five minutes from now. *Don't forget, don't forget, don't forget.*

If only she'd thought to buy a kitchen timer! Grant had said the oven's hadn't worked in years.

As she headed back to the sink, her foot skidded on something slick. Her knee slammed into the metal handle of a lower cabinet. She inspected the throbbing scrape, then searched for the culprit. An oozing eggshell. The floor was littered with several. Gaping, she noted the kitchen's condition as if seeing it for the first time. Dirty bowls, spoons and measuring cups cluttered the countertop, along with shreds of grated carrot, spatters of oil and dollops of batter.

She hadn't even begun marinating the meat. Cleanup would have to wait.

Piling everything into the sink to wash later, she transferred what she needed from the table to the countertop. Once turned, the tenderloin revealed a lot of hidden fat. Trimming it off took valuable time. Cutting the beef into cubes took longer. She checked the clock. Another five minutes until the cake was done. Why, oh why, had she picked such a complicated meal to prepare? She should have learned by now not to overestimate her abilities.

The marinade itself was a complex recipe. After combining the final ingredients, her eyes and brain felt strained to the limit. "Pour over beef and marinate in refrigerator for at least four hours," she read aloud.

Four hours? Her gaze flew to the clock. She only had two and a half hours left. Oh, God, in two and a half hours, Grant would expect the gourmet meal she'd foolishly promised. He'd been so nice to her, never pointing out her weaknesses, always praising her strengths. She'd wanted so much to show him her appreciation. To show Scott she could bring one of the finer offerings of city living to this very kitchen.

What a loser she was. What a pitiful, miserable failure. At this rate, all she'd be serving for dinner was...*the cake!*

Spinning around, she gasped at the smoke curling from the seams of the closed oven door. She grabbed a dish towel and yanked it open.

"My ca-a-ake," Margaret wailed.

Fanning the air, she pulled out the aluminum pan and set it on the rim of a glass bowl in the sink. Metal sizzled. Charred cake steamed. The new smoke alarm kicked into a shrill buzz.

And Scott walked in the back door.

CHAPTER NINE

SCOTT SWEPT off his hat and waved smoke aside, frantically searching the kitchen for flames. He took in the open oven door, the steaming cake pan and Maggie's devastated expression at a glance, then dragged a chair to the far wall. Damn, that smoke alarm was harder on his nerves than a cattle prod.

He climbed onto the chair and shut off the angry buzz. His heartbeat instantly calmed. Better. At least he could think now. He'd been cleaning the hayloft with Pete and his dad when the urge for a Coke had hit strong. Good thing he'd given in.

Turning, Scott tossed his hat onto the table and slowly scanned the mess. Unbelievable. It looked like a garbage-disposal unit had exploded in the sink. His gaze moved to Maggie.

She stood unnaturally still, staring at her hands clasped in front of her white shorts. Strands of baby fine hair escaped her ponytail and straggled about her ears. A finger pad of flour stamped her nose. Orange stains smeared her T-shirt. Her cheeks were flushed and dewy, her bare legs pale and skinned on one knee.

She reminded him of a little girl caught playing in her mama's kitchen. He started to smile, but some instinct made him stop and inspect her more closely.

Her white-knuckled hands trembled. Her stained T-shirt rose and fell in quick, staccato movements. Her bare legs were locked at the knees.

He walked forward as if approaching a wounded doe. "Maggie?"

"I burned the cake," she said in a small, fearful voice.

Did she think he'd get mad like the time she'd ruined the frying pan? Shame heated his face. He'd done a lot of thinking since his father had accused him of punishing Maggie. He could begin making amends right now.

"You torched it," he agreed. "But hey, it's no big deal. Nothing to get upset about."

She shook her head, her eyes still lowered. "It was Grant's birthday cake, and I ruined it. I should've known I would. I always ruin everything."

He stopped in front of her, puzzled at the depth of her distress. "Don't be ridiculous."

She jerked her head up with a bitter laugh. "Don't be *stupid,* isn't that what you mean? It's a more accurate description, or so I've been told . . . and told."

He felt a tweak of conscience. "C'mon, Maggie. Nobody thinks you're stupid."

"Oh, no? What did you think when I fed Lady Love an apple?" Her challenging look dared him to lie.

"I thought you didn't know anything about cattle. And that you handled yourself well in a cris—"

"What did you think when I forced Matt to take a joyride in your old car? Did you think I was *smart?*" Her voice held the shrill edge of hysteria.

She was hurting, yet handing him a weapon sure to inflict fresh wounds. He had no stomach for it anymore.

"I thought...no, I think, you made a mistake, Maggie. A mistake with cruel consequences, but a mistake just the same. Like the one I made warning your father you were about to elope." An immediate calm filled him, as if he'd been waiting a long time to say the words.

"No, I was stupid," she said with conviction. "But when I saw Daddy pull up, something inside me...snapped. I knew if I let him take me, I'd never be strong enough to defy him again. If I hadn't panicked..." Her haunted gray eyes shimmered with misery.

Scott reached out and cupped her elbows, rubbing her forearms with his thumbs. "You made an error in judgment. Everybody in the world's done that. You're no different."

"But I am. I've always been different! Look at the cake, Scott. I didn't just burn it. The thing's flat as a horseshoe. I must've left out something important from the recipe. And now we can't light birthday candles."

"Give yourself a break. Are you worried about disappointing Dad? Hell, I'll run into town and buy another cake if it means that much to you."

"Can you pick up some Burgundy Beef with Parsleyed Fettuccini while you're there? Because that's the only way we'll eat it for dinner. I certainly can't f-follow the recipe." Her lower lip began to quiver.

"Aw, sure you can, Maggie."

"No, I c-can't." She squeezed her eyes shut, drawing a deep breath through flared nostrils. Her golden lashes fluttered, lifted and revealed a soul-deep sorrow that wasn't about a recipe. "I wanted everything to be p-perfect, you know? It was supposed to b-be perfect. But I'm so *stupid* I can't even bake a c-cake."

Her choked voice and tear-brimmed eyes broke his heart. She looked utterly forlorn, so unlike the gutsy woman who'd saved his heifer, that a fierce surge of protectiveness swept through him.

"Don't cry, Maggie darlin'. I'll help you make that burgundy-beef stuff for dinner."

To Scott's dismay, her face crumpled. He stepped closer and gathered her into his arms, pressing her head to his chest.

"Okay, I won't help you. How 'bout I stop by the café and pick up something to go?"

She began weeping in earnest, and he decided to shut up.

He'd never seen a woman cry like this, with deep, shuddering sobs that racked her body and vibrated through his. There was nothing dainty or pretty about Maggie's tears. She snuffled and shook and wadded his soaked shirt between curled fingers.

He felt her pain like a tangible thing. It buffeted him in waves. Uncertain what to do, he simply stroked her hair and waited out the storm, absorbing as much of her anguish as she would allow.

"It'll be all right, Maggie. Whatever it is, it'll be all right." He murmured the chant over and over, noting with relief the decreasing intensity of her sobs.

When her crying finally stopped and all that remained was an occasional hiccup, he guided her like a sleepwalker to a chair. She stared at it dully and swayed on her feet. With a soft curse, Scott sat and pulled her onto his lap, draping her arm around his neck. She curled against his body without protest, as boneless as a cat.

He anchored his hand behind the shapely legs he'd dreamed about and scarcely noticed their feel. Poor thing was completely wiped out. She fit perfectly beneath his chin. Her cheek and palm rested against his chest with trusting vulnerability. There was no trace of the haughty princess in the woman he held now. He wondered if there ever had been.

Smoothing her silky hair back from her face, he cleared his throat. "Are you ready to talk now, Maggie?"

She grew very still.

"C'mon, darlin', what's all this fuss about? Not a burned cake, that's for damn sure."

The whine of the screen door snared Scott's attention. Maggie buried her face in his shoulder.

His father took one step into the kitchen and drew up short. Sweeping the room and the situation with a penetrating gaze, he turned around and walked back out the door, closing it gently behind him.

Maggie stirred. "Who was that?"

Her voice sounded muffled and embarrassed. Scott gently turned her head so she could breathe.

"It was Dad. He'll keep anyone else from interrupting. You were about to tell me what's wrong."

She sighed heavily, as if resigned to the inevitable. *"I'm* what's wrong, Scott. At least, the way my brain processes signals is wrong—different from everybody else." Her muscles tensed. "I have dyslexia. It's a learning disability."

Snippets of information flashed in Scott's mind. Problems with reading, confusion with numbers... His brain made a vital connection and called up relevant memories: a young princess staring at his napkin and refusing to write down her phone number; an elegant socialite rushing to the pharmacy, rather than writing down the name of an arthritis cream; a warm, generous woman reduced to tears by a simple recipe.

The puzzle pieces of her personality fell into place with sickening results. He closed his eyes. *Oh, Maggie girl, what have I done?*

"I've—" He stopped and cleared his throat. "I've heard of it."

Her body remained tense and expectant.

"I read an article on Olympic gold medalists," Scott offered lamely. "Bruce Jenner talked about having dyslexia. He was pretty frank about his frustrations."

She relaxed slightly. "Celebrities have done a lot to inform the public. Some of their stories are amazing."

"This article said Bruce's disability helped make him a decathlon champion."

"That's because when you can't do things that are simple for most people, you make the most of what you *can* do."

"Like your riding?"

She nodded. "It was the one thing I was good at, that my parents took pride in. So I worked hard to be a winner. I thought, if I could just become a champion, maybe they would love..." Her hand made a dismissive little movement against his chest. "Anyway, it wasn't enough. Nothing I ever did was enough."

Sliding his palm up and down her thigh, Scott rested his cheek on her peach-scented hair. For all her material wealth, Maggie had been deprived of the love and security he'd taken for granted during his childhood. He remembered Donald's chilling contempt and his own belittling sarcasm, and felt a volatile mixture of anger and shame.

"I'm sorry, Maggie."

"Don't be. I got used to it. And once I was tested and diagnosed, boarding school was a lot better. I had special tutoring to help me with my problems."

She'd always intrigued him. He seized the opportunity to learn more. "Tell me what school was like."

In brief, halting sentences, she described a list of difficulties that would've seemed insurmountable to him. Yet her soft, melodious voice held no hint of self-pity. If anything, she seemed contemptuous of her so-called failures. By the time her words trailed into silence, his image of her had shifted once again and locked into place.

He'd misjudged her completely. Attending school, hell, attending *life,* had challenged her at every turn. Her courage humbled him.

"Why didn't you tell me this before, Maggie? It would've explained so many things."

She toyed with a button on his shirt. "My first summer at Riverbend, the other kids thought I was different enough as it was. Admitting I couldn't write down a phone number would've made me a freak." Her fingers stilled against his chest. "I wanted you to have my number, Scott. I even wrote it down in private and kept it in my pocket for weeks, but I never saw you again."

Because he'd avoided any places he thought she might go. The following summers, he'd trolled for women in more worldly waters than the local high school hangouts. Remembering his bruised ego and immature reaction, Scott experienced a choking sense of regret.

"I was busy workin' the ranch," he finally managed to say. "But you could've told me when you first came here. I wouldn't've been such an ass if I'd known."

She curled her hand into a fist. "Or you wouldn't have agreed to my plan in the first place."

"I'm not that narrow-minded, I hope." He winced at her long silence.

"I couldn't take the chance. Besides, I wanted to prove I didn't need a man's help. Pretty stupid, huh?"

He covered her fist with his hand and squeezed. "No. I'd say it was pretty brave. And I'm the stupid one around here, for being so blind." Sighing, he massaged her knuckles and spoke from his heart. "I'm sorry about the way I treated you, Maggie."

She shifted her body and looked up through swollen eyelids. "You don't hate me?"

Her patrician nose was red, her flawless complexion blotchy. She'd chewed off her lipstick, and he tensed against a violent surge of desire as unexpected as it was inappropriate. His timing really stank.

"No, I don't hate you."

"You don't?" Her sweet little bottom shifted again.

"No," he said through his teeth.

Her smile started slowly, gaining warmth and momentum until it took Scott's breath away.

"I don't hate you, either," she said, still smiling.

"You don't?"

"No." Her dimple deepened.

For the life of him, he couldn't keep from smiling back.

MARGARET CLIMBED out of the tub on jellied legs and hastily dried off. Scott had insisted she take first shift in the bathroom, despite the state of the kitchen. Everything would work out tonight, he'd assured her, and a hot bath would make her feel better about the situation.

She did feel better. Relaxed and happy and... reborn. But she couldn't give credit to her bath.

Scott's healing words had lifted a crushing burden from her spirit. He didn't blame her for Matt's death! She would never be free of regret and sorrow, but maybe she could begin to forgive herself.

His compassion had stunned her, enfolding her as tenderly as his arms. Thus protected, she'd revealed past humiliations never shared with anyone else. He'd listened and offered sympathy, not pity. She wondered now why hiding her dyslexia had seemed so important. Pride, no doubt. She was her father's daughter, after all.

Slipping into a robe, she braced herself and faced the mirror. No red splotches left. If anything, her skin seemed abnormally pale. The cold rag on her eyes had reduced the swelling a little. But not enough.

Memory of Scott looking down at her tear-ravaged face brought color to her cheeks. His unmistakable arousal must have been an automatic response. Any woman cuddled on his lap would have caused the same reaction. She wished she didn't care.

As little as two hours ago, Margaret would have gratefully accepted Scott's kindness and counted herself lucky. She stared at the face in the mirror now as if at a stranger. This woman didn't look grateful. This woman looked self-assured and determined to earn respect, instead of sympathy—a new and improved version of The Mule. As Margaret smiled, The Mule smiled back in approval. Unzipping a makeup bag, they both set to work in perfect accord.

Fifteen minutes later, Margaret walked into her room thanking hot rollers and Estée Lauder with equal fervor. The large, cherry armoire bulged with clothes. Shopping had been one of the few pastimes Jim had encouraged. He'd considered a well-dressed wife essential to his career.

Pulling out a one-piece black knit jumpsuit, she stepped into the legs and shimmied into the long sleeves. Dome-shaped gold buttons ran from the scooped neck to below the elasticized waist. She fastened them all and craned to see as much of herself as possible in the silver-spotted mirror above the dresser.

Black suited her, she admitted. Her sleek blond waves seemed brighter, her skin creamier than usual. She inserted gold loop earrings and added a delicate gold chain and pendant, settling the small heart just so above her breasts. Only the faintest hint of cleavage showed, of course. Tasteful, but not totally demure. Spritzing on her favorite light cologne, she slipped into black skimmer flats and headed for the kitchen with a pounding heart.

At the doorway, she froze.

Scott stood facing the sink in the final stages of an effort that was nothing short of miraculous. The floor had been mopped, the counters cleaned and dishes washed. The square table had been cleared and covered with a pristine white cloth. She gazed from the white fabric to the tall man responsible and felt tears sting her nose.

Don't you dare ruin your makeup, Margaret Winston.

Regaining control, she admired the flex and shift of his broad shoulders, the mesmerizing twist of his rear pockets as he scrubbed the porcelain sink. Suddenly he grew still.

"Have a nice bath?" he asked without turning around.

"Yes, thank you. I feel much better."

"Good."

He rinsed out the dishrag, draped it across the faucet and rolled down the sleeve of one arm as he turned. His eyes widened. His fingers stopped fussing with his shirt. His Adam's apple bobbed. And Margaret felt the purely feminine thrill of flustering a confident man.

She gestured widely at the kitchen. "I don't know what to say. 'Thank you' seems so inadequate."

Avoiding her eyes, he buttoned his cuff and started on the other sleeve. "Don't thank me too much. I'm about to put you to work. Dad went over to Ada's to shower and change, but they'll be back soon."

Startled, she moved from the doorway and checked the clock. Ten after six! Grant must have gathered his things and left while she was in the tub.

"I—I didn't mean to take so long in the bathroom. Oh, Scott, nothing's ready. What will I serve?" Her newfound confidence cratered in the face of hostessing a dinner party with no dinner.

He met her eyes then, his gaze steady and calm. "The meat's marinating in the refrigerator. The vegetables are washed. And the cake's being taken care of. Trust me, Maggie. Everything will be fine."

Her chest loosened. She released a shaky breath. "All right, oh, wise and great one. How can I help?"

"Set the table."

She nodded, warming under his obvious approval.

His lids lowered, his leonine gaze sliding to her feet, then climbing leisurely back up to her hair. Heat of another kind spilled through her veins as he stared at the dainty gold heart trembling on her chest.

"I'm gonna take a shower," he said gruffly, striding out of the kitchen as if the hounds of hell yapped at his boot heels.

Margaret blinked at the empty doorway. Alone with her thoughts, she didn't try to restrain her silly grin. It stayed with her as she bustled into action, pulling china and glasses from the cabinet. It refused to leave as she folded napkins and set out flatware. It remained plastered while she dragged in an extra chair from the porch. And when Ada and Grant burst in through the kitchen door, it grew to face-cracking proportions. They looked fabulous.

Grant's black jeans and royal blue Western shirt complemented his graying auburn hair perfectly. Ada's long denim skirt and red blouse set with silver studs flattered her dark coloring and trim figure. Together, they could turn heads in a posh city nightclub or a country dance hall.

If Grant was surprised at Margaret's transformation, he hid it well. "*Another* gorgeous woman. Pinch me, Ada, so I'll know I haven't died and gone to heaven."

Ada closed the door with one hip and set two bottles of Chablis on the counter. "I'll pinch you, all right, if you don't keep your eyes where they belong. Why steal the egg when the hen is nice and plump?" Her teasing glance included Margaret in the fun.

"That all depends—" Grant plopped a three-layer chocolate cake beside the wine "—on how nice and plump the hen is."

"Nicer than an old fox deserves and plumper than the hen would like."

"Ah, but old foxes prefer their hens with a little meat on them. There's more to sink their teeth into, don't you know?"

Watching the exchange, Margaret empathized with Ada's sudden flush. When the Hayes men turned on that singularly intense, masculine look, no woman under ninety could remain unaffected. Judging from the melting gaze Ada returned, she was no exception.

Feeling voyeuristic, Margaret turned away and gaped, helpless to do otherwise.

"Why do I get the feeling I missed something here?" Scott asked from the hall doorway.

He wore casual dark blue slacks and a matching blue knit sports shirt with forest green collar and sleeve bands. His black loafers and belt gleamed dully, as did the silver watch on his wrist. He'd combed his wet hair back from his forehead, but already it slid forward in varying lengths and colors of brown. His square jaw had a shiny, just-shaved look, and he smelled of some wonderful, outdoorsy cologne.

The members of her Junior League would've collectively swooned at the sight of him.

"You've got the wrong party, mister," Grant said, his eyes belying his stern tone. "The nearest country club's twenty miles east of—" he clapped a hand to his chest "—good Lord, it's Scott. For a minute I thought a stockbroker had made a wrong turn into our gate."

Ada pushed Grant's shoulder. "Behave yourself." She smiled warmly at Scott. "You look very handsome, doesn't he, Margaret?"

Handsome. Urbane. Intimidating. She couldn't stop staring.

Scott flicked his eyes her way, then gazed stonily ahead.

He was nervous! And embarrassed, if the red stain creeping up his tanned throat was any indication. She knew that awful, squirmy sensation well.

"If that's what a stockbroker looks like, remind me to call Merrill Lynch in the morning," Margaret said with feeling.

Scott's startled gaze met her admiring one. Suddenly the man who'd held her while she cried was visible. *Thank you,* his eyes said.

She smiled, happiness spreading giddily through her system.

Walking briskly into the room, Scott took command. "Okay, people, we've got a small kitchen here and everybody's got to cooperate to make this work." He pulled Grant's cookbook off the top of the refrigerator and opened it to a marked page. "Maggie and I will handle the—" he peered down at the recipe and read slowly "—Burgundy Beef with Parsleyed Fettuccine. Dad, you and Ada are in charge of the salad. Nothing fancy. The stuff in the fridge is already washed."

He answered a sharp knock on the door and Pete walked in, spiffed and shined in stiff new jeans and a crisp white Western-yoked shirt. Scott pointed a finger at the wrangler. "You've got bartender duty, Pete, and I need a beer. Pronto. You'll have to ask what everybody else wants."

Scott scanned each face in turn. "Anybody have any questions?"

Margaret cringed. Her dinner guests were being ordered to prepare their own meal. Yet Scott must have warned them in advance. The sight of their kind, willing expressions misted her eyes.

"No? Okay then, let's get this party on the road." Scott snapped his fingers above his head. "Bartender, I'm waiting."

"I'm comin', I'm comin'," Pete grumbled without rancor, pushing past Scott and opening the refrigerator. "S'long as I'm here, who else wants a beer?"

"I do," Margaret piped up, earning several double takes. She lifted her chin and sniffed. "In the bottle, not a glass."

Grins broke out all around, and everybody moved into action.

It should've been a disaster. There was a lot to do and very little space in which to do it. But somehow, they'd all caught the same festive mood, and even the jostling and collisions became part of the fun.

Working as a team in such close quarters afforded intriguing opportunities. Like arms and hips brushing. Fingers fumbling for the same knife. A small hand placed on a brawny shoulder, a large hand splayed on a delicate back—all for the common cause of course.

To her astonishment, Pete could handle a corkscrew as deftly as a pitchfork. He lifted the wet half of the cork to his knobby nose, haughtily pronounced the wine fit for consumption and proceeded to do more than his share of consuming. His rusty cackle punctuated the general chaos at regular intervals.

Margaret didn't even try to read the cookbook recipe, but followed Scott's instructions like a willing slave. She would be strong and independent tomorrow. Tonight she would be happy.

"Make way, comin' through," Scott finally bellowed, lifting a pot of boiling water off the stove and heading for the sink.

Margaret dropped in a collander seconds before a torrent of water and pasta poured into the strainer. Billows of steam forced her back. She touched Scott's arm, her fingers lingering on taut biceps.

He bent his head solicitously, his eyes worried. "Did I splash you?"

She shook her head, but didn't lift her fingers. Some inner demon made her gently massage his muscle, instead. It hardened to steel. His eyes smoldered.

She couldn't breathe, looking into those eyes. They promised her things she couldn't put a name to, but yearned for just the same. Her ears buzzed. Everything ceased to exist but his slow, knowing smile.

"Watch out, Maggie. You're askin' to get burned."

"What if I'm careful?"

Their gazes locked, hers shyly curious, his threatening to consume her in its sudden blaze.

"Salad's on!" Grant called from the table, drawing Scott's attention.

Margaret sighed, whether with relief or disappointment she couldn't have said.

Joining the bustle of people settling around the table, she decided relief was the wiser emotion. Scott was a natural leader, charismatic and authoritative. Just look at how they'd all accepted his direction without protest. But the same vitality that attracted her would eventually swallow her personality whole. And the warm sense of family she'd experienced tonight was equally dangerous to her need to stand alone.

She was a fool to play with fire, no matter how tempting the flames.

"A toast," Grant said, raising his wineglass and looking around the table. "To Margaret. For making this one of the nicest birthdays I've had in years."

"Here, here!" the others chorused.

Margaret forced a wobbly smile, wishing the thought of standing alone didn't make her feel so very, very lonely.

CHAPTER TEN

SCOTT LEANED AGAINST the Cryopreservation Mobile Unit door and grinned in satisfaction. Chalk up another winning idea for Maggie. In the week since his dad's birthday celebration, she'd plunged into ranch life with tireless enthusiasm. The house was cleaner than it'd been in years. The vegetable garden was making a comeback. Hell, she'd even started making new kitchen curtains out of some old sheets.

Not that she'd asked *him* for permission to play Suzy Homemaker. Scott jammed his boot toe into the dirt and shoveled a furrow. The only time Maggie had come near was when she'd recommended the cryopreservation service. He'd been grumpy and resistant—even though her reluctance to be around him suited his purposes just fine. But she'd insisted he couldn't afford *not* to utilize modern technology.

Now Bandolero was getting "plugged into" a frozen-semen distribution network that opened up a worldwide market for his bloodline. Who'd've thought?

"Daydreaming about all the money you're gonna make on that lusty SOB?"

Scott jerked and twisted around. Dr. Lawson smiled from the other side of the van.

"Promises, promises," Scott mumbled under his breath.

"Hop in and I'll give you a ride to the house."

"Thanks." He'd just as soon avoid his dad and Pete, who'd griped about his foul mood during the entire extraction procedure.

Climbing into the passenger seat, Scott waited for the portly, middle-aged veterinarian to settle behind the wheel before speaking. "So you think Bandolero has potential?"

"There's no thinking about it. That's as fine a Santa Gertrudis bull as any I've seen. When he's plugged into the international network, he'll make you a pretty penny," Dr. Lawson assured him, pulling away from the H & H holding pens. Dad and Pete trailed behind in the pickup.

Scott checked the side mirror and frowned at the billowing dust. Damn, they needed some rain. The biggest water tank was dangerously low—almost as drained as his operating capital. He'd have to pen the herd close to the house and its supply of artesian-well water soon. And that meant higher feed bills.

Shoving aside the troublesome thoughts, he turned to the vet. "I should be able to haul Bandolero to your San Antonio clinic on Wednesday if that works for you." Collection was much easier and more reliable in a controlled environment.

"Fine. Ten days at the clinic should yield enough doses to put you in business. I'll be happy to lend my endorsement to Bandolero's electronic file if you'd like."

Scott cocked one eyebrow.

Dr. Lawson chuckled. "Margaret's very persuasive. When I closed my general practice and started specializing in cryopreservation, I wouldn't have made it without referrals from Riverbend Arabian Farm. She thought I might enjoy helping out a newcomer."

Maggie had asked this man a favor on his behalf? "Look, you're not obligated to—"

"Don't worry. I wouldn't risk my reputation on a bull that couldn't cut it." Pulling a handkerchief from his shirt pocket, Dr. Lawson blotted his receding hairline, leaned forward and adjusted the air-conditioning temperature. "A van full of liquid nitrogen, and I can't get cool," he grumbled, sitting back with a huff.

"How long have you known Mag—er, Margaret?"

"Since she was a teenager. Shyest little thing I ever saw, but that didn't keep her from dogging my heels and asking a million questions. She knows more about Arabians than a lot of the top trainers I deal with."

"More than Liz Howarth?"

There was a beat of silence. "Liz can make a horse perform, no doubt about it."

"But?"

Shrewd hazel eyes glanced at Scott consideringly. The van hit a rut and jerked Dr. Lawson's gaze back to the road. He seemed to make a decision.

"I once saw Margaret arguing with Liz over a gelding scheduled to show the next day. Margaret insisted the horse was in pain and should be withdrawn from competition. She was in tears, so I offered to check him over.

"Liz wouldn't let me in the stall. Said she'd get the staff vet to examine him. Still, I managed to swing by his stall later and take a closer look." His expression grew pensive.

Scott waited. The house and barn loomed into sight. "Dr. Lawson?"

"Huh? Oh, yes. Well, damned if I could find anything wrong with that animal. But on my next visit, his stall was empty. Margaret had gone back to school, and Liz said the gelding's owners had decided to get rid of a loser."

"They sold him?"

"That's what Liz implied. But actually he collapsed right after an English Pleasure class. Died within twenty-four hours, a groom told me."

Dr. Lawson pulled up in front of the house, cut the engine and draped an arm over the seat back. "The diagnosis was serum hepatitis from a contaminated tetanus shot. The symptoms hadn't appeared yet when I examined the gelding or when Liz kept him in the show. But Margaret knew something was wrong." His gaze sharpened. "You tell me who knows more about horses."

The ranch pickup rattled to a stop beside the van, diverting Dr. Lawson's attention. His story only confirmed what Scott had known for weeks. Maggie was special. Her uncanny gift with animals, combined with her practical experience, would ensure her success when she left the H & H.

As if on cue, Maggie emerged from the barn and smiled, each strand of her blond hair reflecting sunlight. Ignoring the sudden ache in his chest, Scott slid out of the van amid slamming doors all around. He lagged behind the other men as they walked toward the barn.

She faced them eagerly. "So how did it go? Was Liberty Bell cooperative? Did you get a good sample?"

Scott felt his face heat. His dad studied a thumbnail. Pete looked toward his trailer longingly.

She made a sound of disgust. "Oh, for heaven's sake. Dr. Lawson?"

The veterinarian chuckled. "We could've used a breeding rack to support Bandolero's weight, but Liberty Bell's a big girl. She's fine, and we got a good sample."

"What about his sperm motility?"

"His pre- and post-freezing evaluations are excellent."

"That's fantastic!" She turned to Scott with a smile. "When are you taking him to the clinic?"

Her clear gray eyes shone. It took him a moment to find his voice. "Wednesday, if you don't need the truck."

"Not me. Grant, Pete?"

They shook their heads, obviously as uncomfortable in front of Maggie with the subject matter as Scott.

"I'd best be gettin' back t'work now," Pete mumbled.

"I think I'll go get lunch started," Grant added, shaking Dr. Lawson's hand. "Thanks for coming out. It was...an education."

"Thank Margaret for calling me. I'm always happy to add a bull of Bandolero's caliber to the network." As Grant and Pete headed off in opposite directions, the doctor cocked his head at Margaret. "So where's this wonderful stallion of yours you told me about?"

"In the barn. But he's not really, um, *my* stallion. Scott and I, um, share ownership."

Now she blushes, Scott thought in amazement.

"Whatever. If he's out of Aladdin's Girl and Peichur, you'll be needing my services for him, too." Dr. Lawson glanced at the van speculatively. "You know...the unit's not usually set up for both cattle and horses, but I've got an appointment at Shamrock Stables this afternoon. I could get a test sample from your stallion now if you'd like."

Scott exchanged a hesitant look with Maggie.

"Wouldn't cost you anything," Dr. Lawson added, sweetening the offer. "Equine cryopreservation is years behind the cattle industry. Until the success ratio catches up, I don't charge for the first collection. If the sperm can withstand the stress of freezing and thawing, the straws are yours free and clear."

"Straws?" Scott asked weakly.

"Breeding doses," Margaret supplied. "But Dr. Lawson, we don't have a mare."

"I have a breeding dummy in the van."

"Breeding dummy?" A ludicrous image flashed in Scott's mind. "You don't mean...?"

Dr. Lawson's eyes twinkled. " 'Fraid so."

Scott bristled with masculine indignation. "Twister wouldn't be fooled."

"Right." Maggie folded her arms, her condescending expression as old as Eve. "And men buy *Playboy* for the articles. Care to place a little bet that Twister won't be fooled?"

Behind her back, Dr. Lawson made a negative chopping motion with his hand.

Scott swallowed his first response and shook his head.

She grinned. "Smart move. Those dummies all look alike in the dark."

Watching Maggie saunter toward the van, Scott almost wished the princess would come back. At least she'd been quiet.

TWISTER TOSSED his head playfully, sensing freedom just ahead in the south pasture. During the two weeks since Dr. Lawson's visit, Margaret had intensified the stallion's workouts. The stallion looked forward to his daily turnout, especially since she'd begun letting Orca into the pasture, as well. If only the pig would cooperate.

Holding Twister by a lead rope, Margaret glared down at the eighty-pound culprit who had blocked her shins one too many times. "That's it, Orca! If you can't walk straight, I'm taking you back to the barn."

The pig looked up with a "Who, me?" expression that made Margaret's lips twitch. If she gave in to laughter, he'd never behave. Eventually he broke under the pressure and sidled out of her way.

"Good boy," she praised him, her brief pat stirring his tail like wind on a whirligig.

Half a mile up the dirt track, she stopped at one of the few slatted aluminum gates on the ranch and eased it open. Orca squirmed through and trotted off. Twister nickered anxiously, not wanting to be left behind.

"All right, all right, let me get this open all the way." She gave the lead shank a sharp jerk. "Hey, quit pushing! Have I ever left you behind?"

Ignoring Margaret completely, Twister gazed at the pig rooting happily beneath a live oak in the center of the field. Why did she bother? It was like trying to restrain a little boy at the gate of an amusement park while his best friend boarded the roller coaster. She unlatched the frayed halter, slipped it off and turned her face aside.

Clods of dirt sprayed her cheek as Twister thrust into a hard gallop. She brushed off her face and watched him slide to a stop beside Orca. The barrel-shaped pig looked homely and graceless next to the majestic stallion. Yet, as sculptured gray muzzle touched uplifted snout, she felt her heart contract.

Unconcerned with physical differences, the two animals had established an odd-couple friendship baffling to everyone but Margaret.

Twister had lived in isolation since Scott had sold all his animals but the cattle more than a year ago. Orca had been ripped from his mother and deposited in the same environment. She'd sensed their loneliness and suggested they be introduced. From that day on, they seemed much happier in each other's company than when alone.

At some silent cue, the two animals broke apart and resumed separate activities. She closed the gate and stacked her hands on top.

It was already the second week of June. The Armand Hammer Classic was in late August. So much depended on Twister's talent. Since he'd never started a race, he had to show two officially timed works and be gate-approved in order to enter the Classic. Bandera Downs was the nearest racing facility, about ninety miles away. But Twister desperately needed experience on a track before he was officially clocked for the record.

Riverbend had a practice track. Within easy riding distance, too. Much as she hated to use anything connected with her father or put Liz in an awkward position, Margaret was prepared to do both for her future's sake. Besides, Donald Winston rarely visited Riverbend. He preferred escorting his friends to the racetrack paddock before post time and playing the grand owner there. When he did visit the farm, he always alerted his general manager in advance.

What he didn't know wouldn't hurt him *or* Liz.

Margaret had phoned and invited her mentor to stop by today for a cup of coffee and a chat. If all went well, Twister would soon get the experience he needed.

Chin planted on her hands, she drifted into her favorite daydream. The one where Twister pounded across the finish line in first place and Scott wrapped her in his arms. The one where Scott continued the devastating kiss he'd started in the barn so many weeks ago. The one where, this time, he didn't stop, and the kiss went on and on and on....

Margaret blinked. Something about Twister grazing in the distance—a stillness perhaps—sharpened her gaze. His head swept up and turned to the west. Grass fell from his mouth unheeded. He pricked his ears forward and sniffed the air.

Suddenly his top lip curled up over his nostrils in a strange, almost laughlike gesture. Margaret wasn't amused. The special *flehmen* action, which trapped air inside the stallion's nasal cavities, spelled trouble.

Sure enough, Twister uncurled his lip and arched his neck in a bulging display of macho power. He galloped to the barbed-wire fence and veered at the last second, racing parallel for twenty yards before wheeling to gallop against the wire in the opposite direction.

Margaret shuddered. Each Riverbend pasture was fenced with solid oak boards. Gates were custommade of two-inch steel pipe. Hinges and latches were free of protruding bolts or edges. Every feasible hazard had been eliminated for the safety of the horses. In contrast, this ranch was a veritable booby trap.

She turned in the direction Twister was gazing. Nothing there. Maybe the whiff he'd caught was far away. Stallions could detect certain smells up to half a mile from the source.

Her hopes plummeted at the sight of a dark-haired woman trotting into sight astride a dainty blood-bay horse. Margaret lifted her hand and motioned urgently for the rider to turn back. Liz smiled, rose in her stirrups and waved.

Twister emitted a forceful nicker. With a look of startled awareness, Liz settled back into the saddle, turned her horse around and cantered back the way she'd come.

Margaret spared no time watching her leave. Slipping through the fence, she headed for the stallion racing away from her up the fence line. Barbs snagged his tender flesh as he went. In his state of high arousal, he obviously didn't feel them.

At the far corner of the field he stopped, his head held high, his gaze fixed on the point where the mare had disappeared. He let out a high, extended whinny. *Come here!* he commanded.

When he got no response, Twister turned and galloped back toward the gate, his silver tail streaming behind him like smoke from a locomotive.

He was going to charge the barbed wire. Maybe try to jump it! Yelling wouldn't stop him. He'd tear himself to shreds in his frenzy to get to the mare.

With a curious sense of weightlessness, Margaret moved into his direct path. Her mind blocked out the drumming hoofbeats, the hot sun on her skin, the gritty dust in her mouth, the sight of eleven hundred pounds of runaway muscle and bone charging closer and closer to where she stood. She focused solely on the wild spirit filled with raging frustration.

Easy, friend, I am here, her thoughts warned. *Twister, stop!*

Twister's head snapped forward. He dug in his hooves and rode his haunches to a skidding stop that sprayed her with dirt.

Her arms trembling, Margaret quickly slipped the halter over his head and fastened the buckle. His ribs heaved. Trickles of blood marred his beautiful pearl gray coat on both sides. If she hadn't broken through to him ...

Still holding the lead rope, Margaret threw her arms around his neck and hugged. She barely registered the sound of pounding feet. Twister fidgeted, his attention still focused on the unseen mare.

"You little fool!"

Hands gripped her shoulders and spun her around.

Scott glowered down at her, looking more furious than she'd ever seen him. "Just what on God's green earth were you trying to do a minute ago? Get yourself *killed?*"

Stung at his lack of faith, she tilted her jaw. "He was about to charge the fence. I had to stop him."

His fingers tightened on her shoulders. "What if he hadn't stopped? What if he'd run you over? My God, do you know how I felt running down that road knowing I was too far away to reach you?" He shook her hard enough to snap her head back, then released her abruptly.

She rubbed her shoulders, noting with a mixture of chagrin and pleasure the pallor underneath his tan. "I'm sorry I worried you. But Twister stopped, didn't he? I *knew* he would hear me."

Scott looked at her oddly. "You never opened your mouth, Maggie."

The implication hovered between them. She turned wondering eyes on the stallion. Already the incident seemed unreal, as if she'd been dreaming. Whatever connection she and Twister had shared was broken now. He danced in place, gazing anxiously at the horizon.

"Where's Liz?" she asked, sidestepping further discussion.

"Waiting for you up at the house. I was heading in for lunch when she rode up asking where you were. She took off before I could stop her, came back a little while later and I...had this feeling. Dad has the truck, or I would've gotten here sooner."

"Don't blame yourself. Liz *knows* better than to bring a mare anywhere near Twister." Margaret thrust the lead shank into Scott's hands. "How about doing a little male bonding with your old buddy and taking Twister for a walk? A long walk, in the opposite direction of the house."

"What about these cuts?" Frowning, he gently probed several gouges in the gray coat.

She hid a smile. Big, bad Scott Hayes was a fraud. "They're superficial, thank goodness. He'll be fine. Give me at least thirty minutes, okay?"

"Yeah, sure. But I've got a better idea than walking." In one fluid motion, he grabbed a fistful of mane and vaulted up onto Twister's back. "Open the gate, would you?"

For a minute she couldn't move. During the entire time she'd lived on the ranch, she'd never seen Scott ride the stallion. The sight of two such perfect male specimens together was magnificent.

She opened the gate, squelching a pang of jealousy as the stallion trotted through and continued on up the dirt track without balking. Scott rode with the natural, athletic grace he exhibited in all things.

Sensing he had control of Twister despite his lack of a bridle, she started to close the gate. Orca squealed indignantly from across the field. Margaret waited while he trotted toward her on stubby legs, his ears flapping rhythmically. He reached the gate and snapped at a metal slat in passing.

"Don't get mad at the gate for shutting you in. It's your fault for not paying closer attention. I have other things on my mind." *Like giving Liz a piece of it when I see her.* Fastening the latch, Margaret headed for the house with Orca grunting at her heels.

Five minutes later, she watched Liz rise from a chair on the front porch and walk down the steps. Her tweed jodhpurs, wheat-colored blouse and glossy black chignon were mannequin perfect. "I've been so worried. Are you all right?" Liz asked, her concerned blue gaze doing a lot to soothe Margaret's irritation.

Orca chose that moment to plop his rump on Margaret's left boot and sit doggy-style, his forelegs braced. He yawned widely and smacked his lips.

Resisting the urge to giggle, she bent down and scratched a floppy ear. "Twister's a little nicked up, but he'll be okay with some antiseptic." She nodded toward the dozing bay whose reins were looped over the porch rail. "I can't believe you brought a mare that's in heat onto this ranch."

"In heat?" Liz shook her head slowly, as if unable to credit her ears. "Margaret Winston, I did no such thing! You of all people should know that."

Memory of Liz's patient instruction in the ring sent heat to Margaret's cheeks. She owed her first taste of winning, as well as much of what she knew about Arabians, to this woman's guidance.

"You're right, I do know."

Liz sniffed, obviously still wounded. "Dancing Flame was teased just this morning and nearly kicked poor Nova's face in. I wouldn't have ridden her otherwise."

"Nova's still in action?" The gentle standardbred stallion used to gauge Riverbend mares' heat cycles had been a favorite of Margaret's. "He must be, what? Twenty-two, at least."

"Twenty-three. And I trust a mare's reaction to him over a veterinarian's opinion any day. If your stallion cut himself up over Dancing Flame, he must be extremely excitable."

"I can handle him."

Liz looked as if she wanted to object, then shrugged. "Maybe so, but what about his jockey? What about the strangers he encounters at the racetrack. How are his manners there?"

"He, um, hasn't run on a racetrack yet. I've been conditioning him here on the ranch."

In the eloquent silence, Margaret felt sixteen years old again, her horsemanship skills reduced to amateur status next to an acknowledged master's.

Suddenly Liz smiled. "Don't look so glum. It's not that bad. I'd say it's time we saw what your Twister can do on a real track." She draped her arm around Margaret's shoulders and squeezed. "Why don't you make that cup of coffee you promised me, and we'll talk some more?"

"WHOA, TWISTER, hold up." Scott shifted his weight and grimaced as steamy denim clung to his buttocks and thighs.

Ah, yes, the joys of riding bareback. How could he have forgotten? Not that remembering would've changed his impulsive action. His need to reach the highest point on the H & H ranch had been too strong.

He gazed at the sweeping view of cleared fields and dense brush below. Clouds skudded across a bluebonnet sky, trailing shadows over the land.

His land.

He knew every sandstone rock, every clump of cactus, every gully and tree and precious blade of grass on the place. He'd dreamed of improving and expanding it into something grand. He'd settled for keeping it, period. The land was all-important. His reason for living.

Yet for the first time since he was twelve, the panoramic vista ahead failed to soothe him. He couldn't shake the image of Maggie standing directly in Twister's path.

She'd looked so small and fragile. She would've been crushed like a sprig of clover beneath Twister's hooves if he hadn't stopped. Watching the scene unfold had been . . . Scott drew in a strangled breath. He never wanted to feel that way again as long as he lived.

Ever since his father's birthday celebration, his feelings toward Maggie had changed. Become something that involved his heart, as well as hormones. He actually looked forward now to each new day. Hell, he even thought Twister might be the answer to the H & H's financial problems, after all.

A lazy horsefly circled Twister's ears. The stallion shook his head. His long tail swished, slapping Scott's leg and jolting him back to the present.

Bandolero wouldn't bring in appreciable income for months. Scott would have to sell some of the herd to cover expenses through the summer. He would make an appointment with the bank and ask for another extension. And he would damn well keep his hands off Maggie until he knew which way the wind blew.

She deserved better than a bankrupt cowboy.

For two weeks he'd managed to treat her as a big brother would, truly believing he could keep his banked attraction under control. But today's episode proved he'd been fooling himself as much as her.

Big brothers did *not* shake their sisters silly to keep from kissing them senseless.

CHAPTER ELEVEN

ANOTHER POLE flashed by. Twister hugged the inside rail as Margaret crouched low over his withers. Air whistled in her ears. Her hands pumped back and forth. His thudding hooves vibrated through the stirrup irons, up her legs and into her very bones.

Two days ago Liz had offered the use of Riverbend's track to an unproved six-year-old. Margaret grinned behind the stallion's whipping mane. He'd proved himself all right. The courage of desert ancestors fed his spirit. The blood of champions fueled his heart.

The dirt track ahead beckoned dry and smooth. *Safe,* her conscience assured her. The desire to show Scott exactly what they owned got the best of her.

She loosened the reins a notch.

Twister flattened his ears and lengthened his neck, converting the extra inch of rein into pure undiluted speed—wind across sand. Margaret laughed aloud.

This was more than talent. This was greatness of a kind horsemen hungered for, spent lifetimes and fortunes breeding for in the hopes of producing an athlete like Twister.

He swept past the eighth pole for the second time, completing one and one-eighth miles—the same dis-

tance as the Armand Hammer Classic. Margaret
pulled back firmly on the reins. Twister shook his head
but didn't slow. Setting her teeth, she stood in the
stirrups and hauled back using her full weight.

"Stop, you stubborn mule," she commanded.

Although comparable in size to male jockeys, she
lacked their upper-body strength. Twister strained
against the bit. Now what? Just when she thought her
arms would wrench from their sockets, he slowed to an
easy gallop.

As he rounded the far curve of the track and headed
into the homestretch, Margaret settled down in the flat
racing saddle. Two figures hung over the outside rail
near the eighth pole. Her gaze fastened on the one
wearing a cowboy hat. His grin flashed white in the
distance. She raised her arm and waved—and heard a
muffled pop.

Twister jerked.

Then clamped his teeth on the bit and surged forward, ripping one rein from her loosened grip. She
teetered. Recovered. Hung on grimly during his erratic flight down the track. He was out of control. And
so was she.

The loose rein writhed in the air. She grabbed for it,
bumping perilously against his neck before scrab-
bling upright. If he stepped on the rein...

She'd once seen a mare's neck snap in a similar situation.

"Jump!" Scott shouted in the distance.

Kicking free of the irons, she gripped Twister's
heaving ribs with her thighs. Balance. That was the

key. Native Americans had done this kind of thing without killing themselves.

Lower and lower she leaned, watching for her chance. The rein hit the dirt and rebounded wildly in her direction. She stretched her torso to the limit, caught the rein with the tip of her fingers and groaned when it slithered away. Her weakening legs slipped. With a last surge of energy, she swung herself upright. And gasped.

There was no time to think, no time to do anything but gather the one pitiful rein she held and feel Twister's powerful hindquarters bunch.

Then they were flying over the outside railing at the far curve of the track. The landing jarred Margaret's teeth and propelled her halfway up Twister's neck. Somehow she managed to get back in the saddle.

Twister, stop! her mind commanded.

No connection. She was too unfocused.

Twister pounded over a manicured lawn, his hooves kicking up huge divots of turf. He streaked past a bed of rosebushes, his dangling rein snagging through the thorns.

Her strength was almost gone, but she couldn't give up. This was *Twister*. She clamped her legs and started the heart-catching slide downward.

The pounding in her ears grew thunderous. Flashing forelegs inched into sight. Her fuzzy brain noted they were black, not gray. She felt herself slipping and briefly wished she could've been stronger.

"Hold on," Scott's steely voice ordered seconds before his arm banded her waist.

Airborne for a dizzying instant, Margaret landed stomach-down over the withers of his galloping horse.

Hold on to what? she thought wildly, bouncing like Orca's ears at a fast trot. Blood rushed to her hanging head and arms. She clutched a denim-covered leg ending in a boot far below. Her own legs bumped between the two horses. Scott strained forward, reached for Twister's bridle and pulled.

The jerky transition from full gallop to a trembling stop almost sent her tumbling. Exhausted and bruised, she hung limp and waited for the inevitable outburst.

"Dammit, Maggie!" Scott dismounted and pulled her off the horse.

The minute her riding boots touched the ground, her legs crumpled. He caught her under the armpits and spun her around, crushing her to his chest.

She clung hard, then reared back. "Twister. I've got to—"

"Settle down." Scott's arms tightened, caging her with insulting ease. "He's worn-out, but he'll be fine."

With a grateful sigh, she slid her arms around his waist and let him support most of her weight. Both horses breathed heavily. Scott's heartbeat drummed beneath her ear. His arms felt strong and safe and overwhelmingly *right*.

"Thank you, Scott." Her lips curved up at the thought of this rangy cowboy playing white knight to her damsel in distress. "How'd you manage to find a horse?"

"He was coming on to the track for a workout."

"You kidnapped one of Liz's racehorses to follow me?"

"I just...borrowed him. Damn near didn't reach you in time, either." His voice sounded strained. "Do you have a death wish, Maggie?"

"N-no."

"Then why the hell didn't you jump when I yelled?"

She tilted her head back in astonishment. "Twister needed me."

His gaze raked her face a long moment, his expression a peculiar blend of emotions she found difficult to read.

"Something happened to spook him, didn't it?" he said finally.

She worried her lower lip, struggling to reconstruct the event. "There was a noise, I think. And I felt him jerk. Then he went berserk."

"What kind of noise?"

"A...pop." She replayed the sound in her mind and couldn't place it.

Scott's eyes hardened. The breeze stirred his hatless hair, giving him the appearance of a dangerous stranger. Margaret realized he was looking over her shoulder. She pushed away from his comforting embrace and turned, wanting more than anything to stay buried against his hard chest.

Liz, Dr. Morley, an exercise boy and a tall, silver-haired man were hurrying toward them. Margaret moved to Twister's side and inspected him for bleeding. *Something* had spurred him into madness. She was almost disappointed to find no visible evidence. Weariness weighed his drooping head. Foamy sweat lathered his coat. She prayed soreness was all he would suffer from the experience.

The contingent had reached them. Dr. Morley exchanged Scott's cowboy hat for the gelding's reins and began running his hands over the horse.

"My God, are you okay, Margaret?" Liz asked.

"Just a little shaky."

"I almost had heart failure when you jumped that rail. And then to see Gambler running hell-for-leather across uneven ground..." Liz walked toward Dr. Morley. "How does he look? Will he be okay?"

"I'm fine, but thanks for askin'," Scott drawled.

Liz spun around, her eyes flashing. "Excuse me for being a little upset. Gambler is a valuable animal. Any deviation from his training schedule could make him peak early or late. He's my responsibility—"

"But I own him," the distinguished older man interrupted firmly, stepping forward and extending his hand to Scott. "Daniel Brady. I operate Oasis Arabians, outside Houston. Perhaps you've heard of it?"

Scott pumped the man's hand once. "Scott Hayes. And no, I'm afraid I'm pretty new to the Arabian-racing industry. Cattle ranching is more my thing." He seemed to take Mr. Brady's measure, and for the first time looked a bit sheepish. "I'm sorry for takin' your horse like that, Mr. Brady, but it was an emergency."

Daniel chuckled. "So I gathered. And call me Daniel. You are one helluva rider, Scott." He turned to Margaret. "You, too, young lady. I thought I was watching Buffalo Bill's Wild West Show there for a minute." His lively blue eyes conveyed a mixture of concern and admiration.

Margaret liked him immediately.

Liz's dark winged brows drew together. "I didn't teach you to be a stunt rider, Margaret. Sloppy riding lost you that rein." She gestured at the exercise boy. "It wouldn't have happened with Billy in the saddle."

The men glanced uneasily at Liz. Margaret blushed miserably.

She *had* been careless. And selfish. A stronger rider might have regained control with one rein. But she'd pleaded to ride Twister during his first track workout, wanting to show off the results of her training.

"No harm done," Daniel said, turning to Dr. Morley. "Gambler looks just fine to me. But just to be on the safe side, would you mind looking him over more thoroughly at the stables? I'll check on him before I leave."

"Of course not, Mr. Brady." Dr. Morley sought Margaret's eyes. "Bring Twister by when he's cooled down, and I'll take a look at him, too."

She nodded gratefully as he led the gelding away.

"Would you like me to walk Twister for you, Miss Winston?" Billy asked, his voice startlingly deep. The wiry exercise "boy" was probably in his late twenties.

"Margaret has legs," Liz said. "Apparently she's forgotten the first rule of horsemanship—always see to your horse's needs before your own."

Scott took a step forward, his expression thunderous. "Maggie risked her neck to save Twister's. I'd say that's seeing to his needs before—"

"No, Scott, Liz is right," Margaret interrupted, ashamed she'd had to be reminded. She'd neglected

Twister too long already. Gathering his reins, she sent Liz a silent apology.

Liz's stern gaze softened. "You do look a bit shaky, dear. I suppose Billy could cool him out for you—just this once." Her smile took the sting out of her words. She glanced at Billy and nodded. "Go ahead. But keep that stallion away from the barns."

"Yes, ma'am."

"Thanks, Billy," Margaret whispered, handing him the reins.

He grinned, giving Twister an admiring once-over. "I ain't never seen a horse run like this one. You gonna enter him in a race soon? I wanna be sure and place a bet—"

"Billy?" Liz's warning tone wiped the grin from his face.

He shrugged at Margaret and led Twister in the opposite direction of the barns.

"I caught the last of his workout, too," Daniel said, a speculative gleam in his eyes. "Anybody get a time on him?"

Liz moved closer and tucked her arm through his. "He's raw, Daniel. Hasn't even been gate-trained yet." She gave him a dazzling smile. "Why don't we go back to my office and review Gambler's progress? He picked up a half second in the last week."

But Daniel's attention was riveted on something else. Margaret turned and spotted the stopwatch Scott cradled in his palm. She hurried to his side and read the digital numbers.

Impossible. Her dyslexia must be confusing her perception again.

"What distance did you time?" she asked Scott sharply.

"A mile and an eighth."

"Read the time out loud please."

He did, drawing a whistle from Daniel.

"Is that good?" Scott asked.

Liz looked as if she'd been slapped. "Manual timing is never accurate."

Scott made a wry face. "It must be good."

"Even if it's off a couple of seconds, that's still a record!" Daniel's excitement was infectious.

Margaret met Scott's eyes, relishing his dawning awareness. *Yes,* she told him silently. *It's true. We have a real shot at winning.*

His wondering expression evolved into a thousand-watt smile, boyish and full of hope. She smiled back so broadly her face hurt.

Daniel bent his head to Liz. "Why don't you go on about your business, and I'll stop by your office in a little while?" He gently disengaged her hand from his arm, his manner turning brisk. "I have a few questions I'd like to ask these two."

THE NEXT DAY Scott walked quickly toward his truck, aware he'd kept Maggie waiting in the hot sun. "Sorry, but I couldn't find my..." His steps faltered and stopped. "Do I have mustard on my tie or something?"

Maggie closed her dropped jaw too late. "No."

"Then why were you staring at it?"

"It...threw me for a minute, okay? I've never seen you wear one."

He felt like a total hayseed. "I'll try not blow my nose on it in front of the bank officer." Striding to her passenger door, he swung it open and held out his hand. Her sleeveless white dress looked expensive, elegant and restrictively narrow at the knees.

Tossing her purse and portfolio on the seat, she accepted his supporting boost into the pickup. Her dress hitched high for mouth-drying seconds before she settled and tugged at the hem.

Scowling, he slammed the door and jogged to his side of the truck. He would've gone to the bank by himself, but without her expert testimony and backing, he wouldn't have a prayer of getting the capital he needed to see H & H Cattle Company through August. Sliding behind the wheel, he started the engine and adjusted the rearview mirror.

"Scott?"

"Hmm?" He fiddled with the air-conditioning controls, hoping the Freon would hold until they got to Gonzales.

"You look very handsome. I *like* your tie."

His head snapped around. She studied it through a fringe of long lashes, her eyes sultry with approval. His relief changed to hot pleasure, and he willed her not to admire his belt.

Shifting gears, he pulled away from the house. "Thanks. You look nice, too."

Nice? Scott's mouth twisted. Grandmothers looked nice. Not gorgeous blondes with creamy "touch me" skin and legs fashioned to torment a man's dreams. As Maggie smoothed her dress in a self-conscious movement, he fought a rush of tenderness.

He'd once thought her spoiled, unworthy of meeting the challenge of living on a ranch. But now he knew *he* was the one lacking.

Maggie was brave and kind and deserving of the best things in life—things he certainly couldn't provide. Her father would relent and open his purse strings eventually. Scott refused to encourage a personal relationship that would force her to give up so much.

One hour and a deliberately sparse conversation later, Scott parked in front of what everyone in the county referred to as The Bank. Generations of farmers and ranchers had done business at the Gonzales Bank and Trust, and the Hayes family was no exception.

"Ready to face the wolves?" he asked.

"Just a minute."

Margaret pawed through her purse, pulled out a compact and checked whatever it was women checked in the small mirror. She looked damn good to him.

Dabbing her nose, she smoothed a fingertip beneath one eye and bared her teeth before snapping the compact shut. "Okay, let's go."

The bank lobby hadn't changed since Scott, nineteen and eager to take the world by storm, had asked J. D. Cameron for a loan to buy old man Perkin's place. J.D. was president of the bank now, but the lobby still smelled like money. Rich walnut paneling and original Western oil paintings graced the walls. The chairs were solid, covered in subdued fabrics and built to hold a large man without threatening to collapse. Nothing flashed or glinted in the place, unlike the chrome-and-marble lobbies of newer banks.

Ken Moller, the loan officer, had moved here two years ago from Dallas after a nasty divorce. They'd immediately developed a bond of bachelorhood that Scott hoped would benefit his cause today. He headed for the corner office guarded by a helmet-haired secretary in a vivid lime green dress.

She looked up over the rim of half glasses, her gaze moving from Scott to Maggie and back without expression.

"H'lo, Miss Harrison." Scott offered her the shameless smile that had served him well over the years. "You look glowing today."

Her flushing cheeks clashed with her dress.

"We've got an appointment to see Ken at two o'clock. Scott Hayes and Margaret Winston," he added helpfully, knowing the secretary knew exactly who he was. He'd managed to make her smile during his last visit, and Ken swore no one had ever done that before.

Miss Harrison's nut brown eyes softened. "One moment, Mr. Hayes." She bypassed the intercom and knocked once on the door behind her, then slipped through and closed it quietly.

Maggie looked at Scott and raised one brow.

He shoved his hands into the pockets of his navy dress slacks. "What?"

"Glowing?"

He grinned. "I've seen lightning bugs glow less than that dress."

She tsked and shook her head, but her eyes danced. When he continued to stare, her amusement dissolved into awareness. She lowered her chin and looked up through those long lashes the way she had in the truck earlier. His body responded no less strongly the second time around.

The office door suddenly opened. Miss Harrison marched out and nodded stiffly. "Mr. Moller will see you now."

Scott walked inside, introduced Maggie and took the second guest chair opposite a massive desk. As she crossed her legs, he watched his bank officer watch her and felt his gut clench.

The bank's youngest vice president was handsome, pleasant and prosperous—an exceedingly suitable match for a woman like Maggie. Ken's dazed expression said she'd knocked him on his ass, but Scott predicted a fast recovery. He was right.

For the next ten minutes, Ken and Maggie discussed personal backgrounds, the city of Dallas and mutual friends and interests. They seemed to have met all the same people, to have eaten at all the same restaurants, to have *thought* all the same thoughts, for God's sake.

He charmed. She graced. And Scott stewed.

Ken finally noticed something was amiss. "Sorry we got carried away, Scott. You didn't make an appointment and drive sixty miles to talk about this stuff, did you?"

"I haven't talked since I sat down." Scott ignored Maggie's startled glance.

"Right." Ken chuckled uneasily. "Sorry again. It's just that Margaret and I have so much in common. You understand."

"Yeah, I think I do."

They exchanged a man-to-man look, Ken testing the boundaries of Scott's claim on Maggie. It was a decent thing to do before making a move. Scott should consider what was best for her. Hell, he should consider what was best for the loan he needed. Ken smiled. "Then you'll forgive me for monopolizing Margaret's time?"

"Oh, sure. 'Course, I wouldn't want you to make a habit of it." Scott held the other man's gaze. "You understand."

The flare of challenge in Ken's pale blue eyes slowly faded to resignation. "Yeah, I think I do."

Scott started to relax, then saw the toe of Maggie's leather pump twitching up and down. There'd be hell to pay later.

Ken tapped a manila folder on his desk, then opened it briskly. "Okay then, let's get down to business. I reviewed H & H's file after your phone call, Scott, and frankly I'm surprised you're asking for another loan. If Mr. Cameron wasn't sentimental about old ranching families in the county, we would've already foreclosed on your property. You were lucky to get an extension on the note until September."

Scott strove to keep his expression blank while his stomach burned. "I realize that and I'm grateful. But you and I both know Mr. Cameron doesn't want to be in the real-estate business. Help me get through the summer, and the bank can stick to banking."

"How much do you need?"

"Fifteen thousand." Peanuts, in the scheme of life. But to Scott, the continuation of life as he knew it.

"We'd require collateral, and everything you own is secured with the first note."

"Not everything," Maggie said coolly, drawing both men's attention. She picked up her portfolio from the floor, pulled out a long sheet of paper and slid it toward Ken.

He glanced at it briefly and looked up. "What's this?"

"Collateral." She smiled at his skeptical expression. "That pedigree is worth ten times the amount Scott wants to borrow. Allow me to explain..."

MARGARET BURST from the bank into the sunlight and marched to the parked truck. Scott followed warily. How long would he have before the dung hit the fan?

At the passenger door, she whirled around. "Are you crazy?"

Not very long, he thought ruefully. "Excuse me?"

"Oh, please. Spare me the innocent act." Deepening her voice, she mimicked, "I wouldn't want you to make a habit of monopolizing Margaret's time."

"Oh, that."

"Yes, that. Besides antagonizing the man you were about to hit up for money, that's the kind of macho BS Jim used to pull. I hated it! From now on, *I'll* decide who I spend my time with, thank you very much." Her eyes flashed silver.

Scott's own temper flared. "Fine. Ken's a great guy. You sure as hell seemed to like him. Y'all have a nice life." He inserted the key in her door and jerked it open.

She threw in her purse and portfolio with a sound of disgust. "Don't be ridiculous. I have no personal interest in the man. But a little schmoozing never hurts when you've got a tough sell ahead." Accepting his hand for a boost up, she paused and worried her lip. "I hope I left him enough information for the loan-committee meeting."

She started to climb. His hand clamped her wrist. "You have no personal interest in Ken?"

Their gazes met and held. Her pulse accelerated beneath his thumb. Her body seemed to soften along with her expression.

"No, Scott. None at all," she said with quiet conviction.

A fierce thrill tightened his hand. She leaned forward infinitesimally. He yanked her the rest of the way home and tightened his arms.

She fit him as he knew she would. Perfectly. Laying her cheek against his chest, she sighed. He breathed in the scent of peaches and instantly grew hard.

"You were terrific in there, Maggie. Ken was really impressed."

"You think so? I didn't read the numbers wrong? I get so nervous under pressure."

"No, I was ready to jump in, but you didn't need me once."

"Practicing my spiel on Grant last night must've helped."

Scott gave her a brief squeeze. "You were great." He broke into a smile. "Did you see Ken's face when you gave him the stud-fee projections? He looked like he'd swallowed a wasp."

Her bubble of laughter lifted his heart. "Kind of like you did when you saw that breeding dummy."

"Watch yourself, smarty. It's a long way back to the ranch, and I've got the keys."

"I could always rough it in a hotel. A hot shower and room service doesn't sound too bad right now."

A half-dozen images involving water, food and Maggie on a king-size bed flashed in Scott's mind. From her sudden stillness, he figured she was doing some picturing of her own. He almost groaned aloud. God, what he would give to lock out the rest of the world and discover the sweetness of Maggie.

She pressed into his erection and lifted her face, her eyes slumberous. He did groan then, and slowly lowered his head.

A car horn blasted ten feet away.

Scott and Maggie jumped apart. Four teenage boys jeered and whistled loudly out the windows of a Jeep trolling the parking lot. Cursing under his breath, Scott forced a sheepish wave to acknowledge their prank. They sped off with a squeal of tires.

Maggie had already scrambled into the truck. He slammed the door and rounded the bumper. It was probably for the best, he consoled himself. All his noble plans to save her from himself would have dissolved at the first touch of her lips. Those kids had been a blessing in disguise.

But if he ever saw the little punks again, they were dead meat.

CHAPTER TWELVE

ADA POPPED OPEN the lid of a rusting paint can and set it on a bed of newspaper. She'd bought the paint a year ago for her own kitchen, then switched her color scheme from yellow to ivory. Staring now at a layer of oily gunk concealing the paint beneath, she congratulated herself on a wise decision.

Margaret crowded close and peered over the rim. "Maybe the other cans are better."

"It just needs a good stirring," Ada said, forcing the doubt from her voice. Why hadn't she checked the cans before donating them to the cause?

A week had passed since Scott and Margaret had traveled to Gonzales. They were expecting a call from their bank officer "sometime this afternoon" after the loan-committee meeting. Margaret had suggested painting the kitchen to keep them occupied and near the phone. Grant had mentioned the plan to Ada— and here they were.

Ada popped open another can and looked inside. "Don't panic."

"Panic?" Margaret gestured to the room as a whole and made a face. "Any color would be an improvement over grunge."

"Good point."

The steady rasp of sandpaper abruptly ceased.

"Grunge?" Grant cleared his throat with mock offense from a ladder by the upper cabinets. "I do believe we're being insulted, Scott. What do you say we go on strike and see if their manners improve?"

"Sounds like a good idea to me. My arm's about to fall off." Kneeling on the floor, Scott lowered his sandpaper and rubbed his shoulder. "How many times have these cabinets been painted, Dad?"

"Two...no, three times. I repainted them after your mother died."

"They used to be blue, right?"

"As a field of bluebonnets." A reminiscent smile lit Grant's eyes. He propped one elbow on a rung and stared into space. "Patricia nagged and nagged me the spring Laura was due until I painted the kitchen to match the bluebonnets outside. This was the heart of the house, she used to say, and it oughtta be as beautiful as her family. Remember that? She rocked Laura to sleep in here every day."

"I'd forgotten." Scott's voice sounded husky. "How could I have forgotten?"

Ada's throat thickened. She met Margaret's eyes and they exchanged a misty look.

Scott leaned forward, blew a puff of chalky substance from a cabinet door and scratched the sanded area with his fingernail. "Damn, I don't remember it being *this* blue. It practically glows. Miss Harrison at the bank would've loved it." He slanted an intimate smile up at Margaret as if they shared a private joke.

Watching the younger woman's melting response, Ada experienced a rush of empathy. No doubt she got that same sappy expression whenever Grant smiled at her. Frustration welled in her breast.

"Better get back to work," she told the men more harshly than intended. "We'll be ready to paint soon." She shoved the second can of paint across the table, along with a wooden stick. "Here you are, Margaret. Go to town."

As the rasping sound of sandpaper started up again, Ada plunged another wooden stick deep into her paint can and stirred. Pigs were a whole lot smarter than people sometimes. Anyone could see that Margaret was crazy about Scott—and good for his soul. He'd gentled around the edges since she'd arrived, and looked years younger.

Instinct told Ada they hadn't made the critical transition from friends to lovers. With a sensual man like Scott, that could only mean he felt more for Margaret than mere physical attraction.

Yet like his father, he was letting male pride interfere with happiness. Ada churned the paint more vigorously.

Men. Did they think all women judged a man by his bank account and what he could provide materially? Maybe some women did. But not her. And she'd bet the farm that Margaret didn't, either.

"You tryin' to make butter over there, Ada?" Grant's perceptive gaze belied his teasing tone.

She released the stick as if burned. He was always sensitive to her moods. That was one of the reasons she wanted to marry him, whether the bank foreclosed on the ranch or not. She didn't care if he had a pot to pee in, as long as she had him.

Margaret cocked her head thoughtfully. "Actually it does look like butter now that it's mixed. It's pretty, Ada." She scraped off excess paint from the stir stick and held it up. "Grant, Scott? What do you think?"

They looked at the painted strip of wood, then at each other, then back at the strip.

"It's fine," Scott said.

"Fine," Grant agreed.

Margaret frowned. "But do you *like* it? You'll be living with this color a long time."

Their eyes glazed.

"Yeah, it's fine," Scott said.

"Like butter," Grant elaborated, looking pleased with himself.

Margaret tossed the stick on the newspaper and rolled her eyes at Ada. "Why did I ask?"

"You had to try. But remember, they've been happy as hogs in a potato patch living with grunge."

"Good point."

Waiting out two indignant groans, Ada suggested the women tackle the walls while the men finished sanding. Margaret had never done this before, and latex wall paint was much easier to apply than the thicker enamel paint the cabinets required.

As Ada organized the supplies and studied the room with a critical eye, her gaze kept detouring to Grant's broad back. Silver-threaded auburn hair curled slightly over the collar of his blue work shirt. Her fingers itched to rub his back, to smooth the goose-down softness of his hair. She jumped at a gentle touch on her arm.

Margaret dimpled knowingly. "What do you want me to do? You're the boss."

"How about I take the ceiling trim and you edge the baseboards, then we'll use the roller to fill in. Is that okay?"

"Sure. Let's do it."

Ada climbed the ladder she'd brought from home and dipped her brush. The first stroke of bright, sunny paint made the existing wall color intolerable.

"Oh, Ada, it's going to be beautiful," Margaret murmured from the floor. "I'm so glad we're doing this."

"Me, too." Obviously Margaret shared her warm satisfaction in creating a cozier environment for these special men.

The next two hours passed peacefully, broken by deceptively casual requests for the time or an occasional muttered expletive. Grant and Scott completed the sanding and cleaned the powdery mess as best they could. Margaret and Ada finished the trimwork just as the men started painting the cabinets.

Ada climbed down the ladder and dropped her brush in a bucket of water. "Hand me that roller tray, would you, Mar—"

The ringing phone jerked four pair of eyes to the wall between the refrigerator and hall door. Ada put a hand over her laboring heart, knowing the others must be feeling the same anxiety or worse. Survival of the ranch would give them all a chance at a future together.

Scott carefully set down his brush and walked to the phone. He picked up the receiver on the third ring. "Hello."

Oh, please, let him get the loan.

"Yes, hold on." He turned to Margaret, his expression a mixture of relief and disappointment. "It's for you."

She moved forward hesitantly and took the receiver. "Hello? Yes, this is she. Yes, of course I remember you, Mr. Brady." She listened and held Scott's gaze, excitement building in her expressive eyes. "I'm glad you feel that way. You're smart to get a jump on other breeders while his fee is relatively low."

Her thumbs-up signal and brilliant smile had them all grinning. She listened for several minutes. "I'm flattered. I don't think that'll be a problem, but let me discuss it with Scott and call you back, if I may. What's your phone number?" Snapping her fingers, she made a frantic scribbling motion with her hands.

Grant yanked open a drawer and rushed over with a pencil and pad.

Her distressed gaze sought Scott. "Area code 713," she pronounced distinctly, relief flooding her face when Scott took the pad and began writing. She finished stating the phone number, promised to call back as soon as possible and hung up.

"Yes!" Slamming down an imaginary football, she raised her fists and did a little victory dance. It was so out of character they all gaped. Scott was the first to recover.

"Spill it out, Maggie."

"You'll never believe what Mr. Brady wanted."

"Not if you don't ever tell me," he said.

"He was impressed enough after seeing Twister's workout to want to breed a couple of Oasis mares to him. And Mr. Brady wants *me* to recommend which mares to cross for the best results."

Scott looked as if he wanted to do more than smile at her. "That's great! I could tell you blew him away when he asked you about Twister's pedigree. But does this mean you'll have to go to Houston?"

She nodded. "Just overnight. I have to see the mares in person, look at them in motion, in order to make an accurate judgment. He wants us day after tomorrow if possible. But he said he'll pay our expenses."

"*Our* expenses?"

"Well . . . yes. We billed ourselves as a team last Friday. He specifically asked you to come, too."

Scott's face grew shuttered. "I can't leave the ranch."

They were talking as if they were alone in the room. As if no one else existed, which Ada suspected was true for them at the moment. She met Grant's eyes with a silent plea. These two young people belonged together.

"Of course you can leave the ranch," Grant said, resting a hand on Scott's shoulder. "It'll be a nice break for both of you."

"But—"

"No buts. You can see Laura and Alec. They've invited us to visit for the past four months. Besides, if you don't go, I'll think you can't trust me to run things here for two lousy days.''

Ada knew Grant meant what he'd said. He'd confessed his guilt about taking a back seat in ranch affairs in the past and had made a dedicated effort recently to become more active. She prayed Scott would give the right answer.

The phone rang shrilly, making them all jump.

''Damn, I'm glad I had heart surgery,'' Grant muttered, glaring at the instrument.

Scott picked up the receiver. ''Hello.'' He quickly turned his back to the room. ''Yeah, hi, Ken. What's up?''

Holding her breath, Ada listened shamelessly through a series of ''uh-huhs'' and ''yeahs.'' Where was the whoop of excitement?

''I know. It was a long shot.''

Ada suddenly felt as sick as Margaret looked.

''Listen, Ken, I appreciate your calling and telling me. You bet. Thanks again. Bye.''

When Scott turned, he looked as if he'd been whacked in the stomach with a two-by-four.

''You didn't get it,'' Margaret whispered, her eyes stricken.

Grant studiously avoided Ada's gaze. ''That's all right, son. We'll tighten the belt another notch and make it through. You'll see.''

Scott shook his head.

Grant's mouth thinned. ''I'm not saying it'll be easy. We might have to sell a few of the cows—''

''We got the loan,'' Scott interrupted. ''Ken's depositing the money in our company account today.''

There was a moment of stunned silence. Maggie stood on tiptoe and thumped Scott on the head with a flick of her thumb and middle finger. He clutched his skull and stared.

"What the hell was that for?"

"For scaring us half to death, Scott Hayes. Why didn't you tell us right away you'd been approved?"

"I dunno. I was too surprised, I guess. Ken said it was a close call, but your income forecast made the difference." He gave her a lopsided grin. "C'mon, Maggie, don't be mad."

Ada would've handed him a cookie if she'd had one.

Margaret only glared.

His grin faded. "I'm sorry I scared you."

"Then prove it." Her eyes gleamed with challenge.

His glinted with wariness. "How?"

"Take me to Houston."

"No."

"Yes."

"*No.*"

"*Yes.* You might as well get used to dealing with the Mr. Bradys of the horse industry, Scott. You'll be handling a lot of breeder requests once Twister's made a name for himself. Don't be chicken."

Scott visibly stiffened, then expelled a peeved breath.

Margaret's taunt had nothing to do with horses, Ada sensed intuitively. Her affection and admiration for Margaret increased.

"I'll think about it," he muttered, massaging his neck.

Margaret inclined her head like royalty. "Thank you."

Ada turned away to hide her smile. She'd been worried for nothing. Scott didn't stand a chance of resisting this young woman. If only she felt as sure of her own effect on Grant.

THREE DAYS LATER Scott draped his forearms over the Oasis paddock fence and watched the last of the mares being led in. Hell, they'd all looked good to him. But Daniel and Margaret had talked about length of shoulder and correctness of legs, subtleties of type and bloodlines, until Scott had given up trying to figure out what it all meant. He'd left them to their business and strolled the grounds, winding up here with nothing to do but hold up the fence.

It'd been a pleasant drive from Riverbend—once Maggie'd recovered from leaving Twister there. She'd accepted Liz's offer to supervise his gate training, but Lord, had she regretted it this morning.

Between Orca's distressed squeals as they pulled away from the H & H and Maggie's welling eyes the first fifty miles on the road, Scott had been tempted to turn around and cancel the whole trip. He was damn glad now that he hadn't.

Stretching mightily, he adjusted his hat and scanned the surrounding complex. He'd be busting butt right now if he was home. The knowledge heightened his appreciation of the view.

Located on the rural outskirts of Houston, Oasis Arabians' paddocks, pastures, barns and two-story brick home were impressive, but not as showy as Riverbend. Of course, what was? Scott waited for the familiar sour envy to burn away his pleasure.

Nothing. His gut stayed calm.

He probed his new contentment experimentally, expecting residual pain. Instead, his sense of well-being spread. Deepened.

Healed.

He lifted his gaze heavenward. The sky seemed bluer, the air sweeter, the possibilities greater than since he'd learned ten years ago that Donald Winston had bought Andrew Perkin's ranch. His gaze snapped to Maggie. Lovely, gifted, tenderhearted Maggie, who'd borne the brunt of his scorn and vengefulness with courage and grace. She'd forced him to take risks and fight for his future. Somewhere along the way, he'd stopped regretting his past. Could he dare put it behind him for good?

He believed in Twister now as much as Maggie always had. After the bank note was paid off, after the necessary improvements were made, the H & H could be a prosperous and comfortable homestead. Never a showplace, but hadn't Maggie proved that wasn't important to her? Scott's heart thrummed crazily.

She'd known that the thought of being alone with her on this trip terrified him, because his self-control was already strained to the limit. Yet she'd pushed for him to join her, anyway. *Don't be chicken,* she'd said.

Doubt clashed with hope. Excitement warred with fear. *Don't be chicken.*

Maggie finished examining the last mare, a bay with black points, and handed her over to a groom. She and Daniel appeared to compare notes. Scott couldn't read the expression in her eyes, but her animated gestures and dazzling smile said the mare was a winner. Finally she gave the bay's neck an admiring pat and scanned the surrounding area.

The moment she spotted him, he could feel the signals crackling between them. She wanted him, too.

He pushed off the fence and dragged his gaze from hers. So be it. They hadn't had many breaks, he and Maggie. They both were due for a little happiness. If the future turned sour and they ended up with only tonight...well, he would make damn sure it was a night worth remembering.

MARGARET WALKED beside Scott on the thick hallway carpet, her card key digging into her palm. The hotel's hushed atmosphere added to her nervousness. "Do you think I should call Liz and see how Twister's doing?"

"Billy's a pro," Scott said reassuringly. "Besides, he won't let anything happen to a horse he plans to bet money on."

"I guess you're right." His hip brushed hers, sending a shock wave down her leg. "Mr. Brady says if the mares I pick produce winning foals, Twister's reputation is set."

"I heard him."

"He's president of the Arabian Jockey Club, you know."

"I know."

"Mr. Brady says—"

"Whoa, Maggie." Scott clamped Margaret's upper arm with one hand and pulled her to a stop. He

loomed tall and rugged under the dim lights, his hat
casting a shadow over his face.

She looked down at the fingers on her arm, and her
mouth went dry.

"You passed your room," he explained, amusement lacing his deep voice.

"M-my room. Of course." Struggling for composure, she backed up to the correct door. "What time
are we meeting Alec and Laura at the restaurant?"

"Seven. I'll stop by your room at six-thirty. Will
that give you enough time?"

Margaret smiled ruefully. She must look as wind-
blown as she felt. "I can't make any promises on the
results, but I'll be ready. What should I wear?"

He started to say something, then stopped himself.

"Will you be wearing a tie?" she prodded, trying
another tack.

"No."

"Then I'll wear slacks." As she turned to open her
door, his fingers caught her shoulder. She looked up.
His expression was curiously intent.

"Wear a dress."

The thought of panty hose and heels was definitely
not appealing. "They're *nice* slacks," she assured him.

His fingers rubbed her shoulder in a small, caressing motion. "You look great in a dress, Maggie."

She stared into his eyes and suddenly couldn't
breathe, much less move. He took the card key from
her limp fingers, ran it through the lock and gently
pushed her through the doorway.

"See you at six-thirty." His cocky smirk said he
knew exactly how she felt.

Nodding, she closed the door, spun around and leaned back before her knees collapsed. Something was happening to their relationship. Something pivotal. Every look, every touch since he'd watched her from the paddock fence added to the delicious anticipation.

Not long ago Margaret would have feared the coming storm, wondered if it would flatten her to the nonentity she used to be. But she didn't feel like Margaret anymore. She didn't even feel like The Mule. She was Maggie now. Stronger. More confident. Aware and yet forgiving of her many failings. She would remain standing, whatever the future held.

One hour later she applied deep rose lipstick, spritzed on cologne and stepped back from the full-length mirror. She'd packed the light gray jersey dress for its wrinkle-free properties, but she had to admit it was flattering. Her weeks of intense riding had firmed and toned a body not given to excess flesh anyway. Cowl-necked, sleeveless, and two inches above the knee, the designer label earned its outrageous cost by whispering sexiness.

The color matched her eyes and gave her hair a silvery cast. She'd already toned down her sunburn and curled and fluffed her hair. As a final touch, she slipped sterling-silver loops through her ears and strappy silver sandals on her feet.

A sharp rap on the door jolted her heart. She threw a last despairing glance at her reflection. This was as good as she got. Please let it be good enough to set off the storm.

Grabbing her purse from the bed, she flung open the door and stared.

Scott's jeans looked new. A bold geometric design in blue, black and teal slashed across the top of his "brush popper" shirt, the lower half tapered in solid blue. The pattern emphasized his broad shoulders and lean waist. A black hat dipped low on his forehead, and shiny black boots were planted wide on the carpet.

He was the most gorgeous cowboy she'd ever seen, and she wanted to kill him.

"I'm changing," she snapped, whirling around and heading for the closet.

He caught up with her in two strides, passed her in three. She rammed against his chest and sputtered furiously.

"You don't have time to change, Maggie."

"I'm overdressed, Scott. I'll look ridiculous next to you."

"We're going to Apollo One, and people wear everything from tuxedos to jeans, Laura says. You look fine, Maggie."

"I look fine," she said in a deadpan voice. "As good as butter maybe?" She tried to maneuver around his body, but he blocked every attempt. Damn, she hated being small.

He reached out and clamped her shoulders. "Look at me, Maggie."

She pouted at his fourth snap button, then glared up.

"Have you ever seen moonlight break through the mist?"

Wary, she shook her head.

"Your eyes are like that, Maggie, only a thousand times finer. And your skin—" he lifted one hand and stroked a knuckle gently down her cheek "—I've never felt anything as soft and fine as your skin, not even the fur of a newborn calf. You wanna know what your hair makes me think of, darlin'?"

Thoroughly entranced now, she nodded. When he lowered his head, she slowly raised her lips. He pressed a kiss on the top of her head and inhaled deeply.

"Peaches," he mumbled reverently. "Fine, downy peaches just plucked off the tree." She felt him shudder. He pulled back, his heated gaze searing a path down her flushed body, then swiftly back up to her face. His laugh was half groan.

"Ah, Maggie, you're so fine I want to forget my pregnant sister who thinks I don't love her anymore and toss you down on that bed here and now. But I'm not going to. When it happens, I want plenty of time and no interruptions. I want to take off that pretty dress slow and easy, and kiss every inch of that soft skin, and breathe in peaches till I—"

Maggie launched herself forward and flung her arms around his neck. Their lips connected in an openmouthed, tongue-thrusting kiss. Lightning sizzled down her spine. She pressed closer and tried to crawl inside his skin. As he rubbed her aching breasts against him, a strangled sound was wrenched from his throat. He thrust his hips once as if unable to stop himself, then gently unpeeled her arms and set her away from his body.

The separation physically hurt. The sound of their harsh breathing filled the room. She blinked, her disorientation rapidly dissolving to embarrassment.

Scott lifted his hat and combed unsteady fingers through his hair. "My mistake, Maggie. I should never've started this—*now*." He settled his hat, flicked a meaningful glance at the king-size bed and backed up to the door. "I'm gonna step into the hallway while you go fix your lipstick. Make it quick. We're runnin' late." He slipped through the door and left her staring blankly at the hotel's list of checkout procedures.

Still dazed, Margaret walked into the bathroom and peered in the mirror. Yes, she looked mussed and thoroughly aroused. If she'd had any doubts about Scott's intentions tonight, he'd erased them with his words. Asking herself how she felt about his arrogant presumption, she leaned forward to repair her smudged lipstick.

It was hard to do while she smiled.

CHAPTER THIRTEEN

"MOTHERHOOD AGREES with you. Corny as it sounds, you really do glow," Scott said, taking advantage of Alec and Maggie's absorbed conversation on marketing Arabians to speak with Laura. "Are you happy, runt?"

She caressed the rounded belly grazing the dinner table's edge and laughed. "That nickname hardly applies right now, but yes. I didn't think it was possible to be this happy." Her golden eyes, so like his own, strayed to her dark-haired husband and softened. As if feeling her gaze, Alec glanced up.

The look he sent his wife was loving and possessive and intensely private. Feeling restless and hollow, Scott searched out Maggie. Her eyes were fixed on Laura's stomach with a wistful expression.

She wants a baby.

The knowledge kicked the air from Scott's lungs. He pictured Maggie's belly swollen with a child—and knew with savage certainty he wanted to be the father.

"I like her, Scott," Laura murmured in his ear, regaining his attention. She squeezed his arm with sisterly affection. "I like what she's doing for the ranch, I like how she looks at you, and I sure as hell like how she's brought my cocky brother to his knees. She deserves the dozen roses.''

He started to pop off a flippant remark, then met her amused eyes. They'd never been able to fool each other. "Wish me luck, runt. I need all of it I can get.''

Her expression grew gentle and serious. "I do, Scott. Somebody once told me not to sacrifice my happiness for the sake of the ranch. It was good advice. I hope you'll take it.''

Recognizing his own words, Scott smiled. "If everything works out, I won't have to sacrifice anything.''

The rest of the meal was sweet torture for Scott. Maggie was so beautiful he had to ration his glances in order to stay coherent. She, on the other hand, was articulate and animated—able to discuss marketing strategy and garden manure with equal authority. His sister and brother-in-law kept sending him "hold on to this one'' looks across the table.

Pride swelled his chest. Try as he might, he couldn't imagine any of his previous dates earning such wholehearted approval.

When their waiter arrived with the bill, Scott made a grab for it. He wasn't fast enough.

Folding his arms, he cocked his head at Alec. "All right, hotshot. But the next time you visit the ranch, Sunday lunch at Lucy's Café is my treat.''

Laura groaned. "Say it ain't so.''

"Don't listen to her. She likes *tofu*. I'm tellin' ya, Alec, the chicken fried steaks are as big as Frisbees. The cream gravy and biscuits keep comin'. And the coconut cream pie..." Scott rolled his eyes and sighed reverently. "Men have *proposed* to Lucy for her coconut cream pie."

Alec grinned. "So has she married any of them?"

"They all died of heart attacks before the wedding," Laura muttered.

Maggie's peal of laughter played hell with Scott's pulse. For that matter, so did her moon-spun hair and dainty sandals and everything in between he'd avoided ogling all night. A man had his limits.

He threw down his napkin and scraped back his chair. "Alec, Laura, thanks for the great dinner. Sorry to eat and run, but Maggie and I are trying to make a late feature."

Alec perked up. "Oh, yeah? What movie are you go—" He jerked and grimaced.

Beside him, Laura smiled brightly. "Don't worry about us. Actually I'm feeling kind of tired," she said, initiating the general scramble for purses, last sips of water and credit-card receipt.

Scott had never loved his sister more.

At last they wove single file through the packed tables, the women drawing interested glances. Scott followed Maggie's curvy backside and resisted the urge to hustle her through the restaurant faster.

"What are you scowling at?" Laura asked him once they stood outside under the awning.

He relaxed his face. "Nothing."

"Mmm. Right. Well, c'mere liar, and tell your fat sister goodbye." She opened her arms.

He wrapped her in a bear hug and closed his eyes. The feel of her extended abdomen brought a lump to his throat.

She tightened her arms. "Tell Dad I love him. And y'all come see this baby when it's born, you hear?"

"Yeah, runt, we'll do that. Take care of yourself." He squeezed her briefly and stepped back.

Laura turned to Maggie with a warm smile. Simultaneously they moved forward and hugged. Again Scott had trouble swallowing.

Maggie pulled away shyly. "I'm so glad I met you, Laura. You're as special as Scott said." Her dimple flashed. "And your husband is a downright hunk."

"I know. I can't take Alec anywhere without guarding his cute little—"

"Hey!" Alec splayed a hand on his brawny chest and sniffed. "I'm not just some piece of meat, you know."

Laura smiled and patted his fanny. "That's right. You're *my* piece of meat, and don't you forget it. Now give the valet your ticket, beefcake, so I can go home and get off my feet." She glanced at Scott and Maggie. "Y'all want a ride to the truck?"

Scott grabbed Maggie's hand. "No, that's okay, we'll walk. It's a nice night." He lifted their joined fingers in a mutual wave and headed for the truck parked two blocks away.

By consciously squelching memory of Maggie's earlier passion, he'd managed to make it through the meal without tenting his napkin more than twice. Soon he would have her behind locked doors.

Maggie stumbled. "Scott, please. I can't keep up."

He glanced down in chagrin and stopped. He'd been dragging her by the hair to his cave, forgetting she had to take two steps for his every one. "I'm sorry, Maggie. Are you all right?"

She balanced on one foot and massaged the other. "I thought I'd twisted my ankle, but it seems to be okay. Are . . . are we really going to a movie?"

The sight of her small fingers rubbing that delicate ankle mesmerized him. She lowered her foot to the sidewalk, and he dragged his gaze up.

"Do you want to go to a movie?" he managed hoarsely.

Her cautious gray eyes searched his while he cursed himself for asking. If she said yes, he'd put a gun to his head and finish the job quickly.

"I'd like to go back to the hotel," she whispered finally.

Praise God and country! Scott's body saluted the sentiment.

THE FRONT-DESK CLERK looked up as Margaret and Scott passed by. "Good night, folks."

Margaret summoned a vague smile, her focus centered on the man guiding her firmly by the elbow. So tall. So commanding. So very much a cowboy in the finest sense of the word.

Unlike her father's or Jim's possessiveness, Scott's wasn't motivated by self-interest, but by masculine instinct. He made her feel safe and cherished—a trait far sexier than his handsome face. Little wonder her legs threatened to buckle.

She stepped into the elevator and leaned against the mirrored wall. Scott followed, shrinking the space with his presence.

"Quite a day, wasn't it?" he asked.

"The best," she answered.

Their gazes met and held, both of them thinking of the night ahead. Her heart rate tripled. He reached out and threaded his fingers through hers, the action more erotic than anything she'd ever experienced. And he was just holding her *hand*.

The elevator doors opened. Her stomach dipped. They walked in charged silence to the door to her room and stopped.

She released his fingers and fumbled in her purse for the plastic card key. "I hope it didn't fall out when— Ah! Here it is," she babbled, slipping in the card and pulling it quickly out of the lock.

Green light. This was it. All the waiting, all the curiosity and yearning was about to end. She cracked the door open and turned, not quite meeting his eyes.

"Well . . . thank you for a lovely dinner." God, she sounded like Doris Day.

"Thank Alec, not me."

He moved closer, to that prickly zone inches from body contact. She could feel his heat, smell his after-shave, hear his quickened breathing. He reached up and braced one palm on the doorjamb above her head, blocking her view of the hall. A dominating pose. Overwhelmingly masculine.

"Well," she repeated in a strangled whisper.

"Tell me what you want, Maggie."

Heat flooded her cheeks at the images crowding her mind.

"C'mon, tell me," he prompted, his husky baritone snapping the taut band of desire holding her still.

She flung up her chin and stared. "What do I want, cowboy? I want *everything*. All of it. Everything your eyes have promised since the day we first met, with nothing held back!"

Her outburst faded to absolute silence. Oh, God, had she really said that? Spinning around, she pushed through the door and slammed it on Scott's boot. He shouldered his way in with ease.

She took one look at his face and began backing up. He watched her with the wild, unguarded gaze of a man pushed to the limits of his sexual control. Her legs hit the bed and she sat hard.

"You're not goin' anywhere, darlin'." He shot the dead bolt home.

A shocked thrill raced through her. She scrambled to the middle of the mattress.

He tossed his hat onto a side chair, his gaze never wavering from hers. "We can do this like friends or like animals. But nothing short of death will stop me now, you understand, Maggie?"

She nodded slowly, his words priming her body for his possession. He stood unmoving, letting the wondrous sexual tension build. She moistened her lips and watched his hungry gaze fasten on her mouth.

He moved then, a sound of agonized pleasure escaping his throat. The mattress sank beneath the weight of his knees. They collided chest, stomach and thigh in the middle of the bed, their arms wrapping each other tight.

Ah, to be held like this. To be wanted like this by a man she'd loved since she was sixteen. Admitting her feelings was cathartic. She wanted to laugh and cry and shout, "Look, Matt, I love him, too!"

She tilted her head back and smiled.

Scott ran a single fingertip from her hairline, down her nose and over her bottom lip, misshaping it while his eyes grew tender. "Your smile could make flowers grow, Maggie."

He lowered his head slowly, bypassing her mouth to strike random, petal-soft kisses over her face. She sought his lips blindly. Impatiently.

With a capitulating growl, he locked his mouth over hers and ravished her with his tongue.

She ravished him back, reveling in the freedom to express herself with such complete abandon.

His hands played her vertebrae like the keys of a clarinet, sweeping down to cup her bottom and press her against the promise of ecstasy.

It wasn't enough. She was tired of promises.

When she moved to reach between them, he broke their kiss and thrust her away with a choked laugh.

"If you don't slow down, I'm gonna disgrace myself like I haven't since I was fourteen."

She sat back on her heels and looked up through her lashes.

"You're a drug in my bloodstream," she said. "A fever. I can't control myself when I touch you."

He squeezed his lids shut as if in pain. When they opened, his eyes were smoldering amber, hot and bright beneath the rim of sable lashes. "Then I guess you'll have to let me do the touchin' from now on." He scooted to the edge of the bed.

Her heart thumped as loudly as his boots hitting the floor.

"Give me your foot," he commanded.

"M-my foot?"

He nodded. "Left or right. Your choice."

Flustered, she offered her right foot.

He worked the tiny buckle at her heel and slipped off her sandal. It looked feminine and frivolous dangling from his tanned finger by a single strap. Flipping the shoe over his shoulder, he took her foot in both hands and kissed her instep.

Heat liquified her bones, her organs, her brain. She'd fantasized a hundred scenarios with Scott, but not one of them had involved her feet. Dropping back on propped elbows, she felt her lids drift shut.

He lowered her foot and reached for its mate, repeating the process and adding a love bite for good measure. She opened her eyes to see his gaze rising from the inside of her thigh. Arousal flushed her face. Her lids fluttered down.

"Take off your panty hose, darlin'."

Her eyes popped open.

Scott chuckled. "I'll be happy to do it for you if you're shy."

She swung her legs off the bed, stood and peeled down her hose as discreetly as possible. Now what?

He curled his forefinger. "C'mere."

The exquisite torment of sexual foreplay was new to her. She found his deliberate game exciting and intriguing. She crawled on hands and knees to the middle of the bed and sat primly.

"Now, what was it I was supposed to do? Oh, yeah, take off your dress slow and easy, then kiss every inch of your skin."

He failed the first part of his instructions miserably. In seconds Margaret shivered in the champagne silk panties and bra she'd worn for just this moment.

And then he was nibbling, kissing—devouring her shoulders, neck and arms until she was dazed with the feel of his lips. He fumbled with the clasp of her bra and slipped it off, replacing the scrap of silk with his callused palms.

"Look at you, Maggie. Look at you."

His reverent tone made her obey. She watched him take a stiff pink nipple into his mouth, felt him warm it with his tongue. Saw his tanned jaw work against her white flesh, felt him suckle greedily. Tendrils of sensation spiraled downward as she watched and experienced at the same time.

He lifted his head to watch her face, his eyes smoky. "Ah, that's it, darlin', don't hold back."

He gave her no choice. Spinning her around so that she leaned back against his chest and thighs, he banded one arm across her ribs and slipped his free hand inside her panties. When her head lolled back against his shoulder, he whispered in her ear.

Words of praise, words of encouragement, dark erotic words she'd never heard before but responded to nonetheless. She moaned his name, clutching his forearm to anchor herself against the swell of sensation lifting her heavenward.

She stiffened and caught her breath.

Her climax splintered through her, ripping a cry from her throat. Scott twisted her around and trapped the last vibration with his mouth, bending her over his arm and tangling his hand in her hair.

All the pent-up hunger of months was in his savage kiss. It swept away every vestige of intelligent thought and left only quivering sensations. She clung to his neck even as he lowered her to the bed and stripped off her panties.

Yanking out his shirttail, he fought his way free of the garment and flung it aside. She curled her fingers in his chest hair while he dug in his pocket for a foil-wrapped packet, wrestled his jeans down and kicked them away.

As long as she lived, Margaret would never forget the sight of Scott magnificently aroused. He turned for a moment, then slid naked up her body for the first time. Hard against soft. Rough against smooth. Mate against mate. She gasped as he plunged deep with a force that lifted her hips off the bed. He held himself still with obvious effort, allowing her body to adjust.

"Did I hurt you?" he said through his teeth.

She was a small woman who hadn't made love in a year. But she was fully aroused and joined with the man she loved. Tilting her hips, she accepted him fully, wringing a groan from deep in his chest.

"No, darlin'," she said, mimicking his drawl perfectly. "I want everything, remember? Nothing held back."

He raised up on his elbows and grinned, the wild promise in his eyes burning bright. "My pleasure, ma'am."

And the warm sensations began anew. Itching, building, stabbing her with previews of the release awaiting her any second . . . any second . . .

The explosion took the top off her head. She wrapped her legs around his waist, triggering Scott's release and extending her pleasure for exquisite seconds.

Reality returned by slow degrees. Her body felt drained, her mind stunned by the enormity of her experience.

How had she ever thought this man would overpower her identity? Because of him, she was no longer haunted by Matt's death. Because of him, she'd gained confidence in her ability to stand alone. Because of him, she no longer felt compelled to prove she could.

She wanted everything. His problems. His joys. His children. His heart. Nothing held back.

Scott brushed a strand of hair from her face. "What are you thinkin' that's got you so serious?"

Margaret smiled tremulously. "I'm thinking that I love you."

His pupils dilated with strong emotion, but he remained silent. Margaret tried not to be hurt. If he didn't love her, he'd shown her he cared in a hundred ways. She would build on that.

Striving to lighten his somber expression, she forced a smile. "I'm also wondering if I set myself up for disappointment. How can I possibly top that experience, cowboy?''

Amazingly she felt him stir inside her. His grin was slow. Arrogant. Vintage Scott Hayes. "Stick around and find out, darlin'. The night's still young."

SCOTT SURFACED from sleep reluctantly, his body clinging to warmth and sated relaxation. He hugged his pillow closer and breathed in the scent of peaches.

Maggie.

She lay spooned against him, her head beneath his chin, her rounded bottom snugged tight against his groin. His morning erection grew painful, and he wondered if he'd ever get enough of this woman. He didn't think so, but he was more than willing to spend a lifetime trying.

What a revelation his princess had been!

Being deprived of love while growing up could easily have made her sexually repressed. Instead, it was as if she'd stored a lifetime of tender emotion deep inside and had released it at long last. On him. A small-time rancher who'd given up his big-time dreams—until she came along.

God knew he wasn't worthy. And he loved her enough not to declare his own feelings. Yet. His prospects were definitely improving, but far from secure. After the big race, he promised himself, he would ask her to be his wife. August wasn't so very long to wait.

Maggie shifted, filling his palm with an indescribably soft mound of flesh. His fingers stirred and made an interesting discovery. So she was awake, was she?

Burying his smile in her silken hair, he caressed her lightly. Her thighs tensed. Her breathing quickened. But still she feigned sleep.

He skimmed his hand south and confirmed her readiness, then flipped her over and drove himself deep with a single stroke. They both sighed.

Scott raised up and looked down into her eyes. What a damn fine way to start the morning!

"H'lo, Maggie," he said with a spreading grin.

"Hello, Scott." Her eyes were drowsy and tender. She placed her palms against his chest and kneaded like a kitten. "You're looking awfully chipper this morning."

He ground his hips and leered. "I'm feelin' mighty chipper. How 'bout you?"

She lifted a hand and stroked his jaw, his neck, the hair at his nape. "I'm feeling you inside me and loving it. I love *you*."

Her breathy words were bellows on his burning libido. Every trace of playfulness vanished, replaced by a turbulent mixture of love and lust and wonder and fear he couldn't verbally express. So he let his body do the talking.

With hands that worshiped her beautiful rosy-tipped breasts. With lips that roamed and tasted and adored wherever they touched. With long, smooth strokes angled to give her the most pleasure possible.

Maggie's gratification increased his own a thousandfold, so that when she cried out his name, her climax fueled his in a blissful release that went on and on.

As his breathing slowly returned to normal, Scott rolled off and pulled Maggie close. The nightstand clock read seven-fifteen, slothfully late by his normal standards. But hell, they could leave at nine and still make it home for lunch. Another hour of sleep with Maggie in his arms was too tempting to resist.

Mmm, this was nice. Maybe he wouldn't wait until August, after all. His eyes drifted shut, contentment blanketing his heart....

Something was dragging him up toward wakefulness. Something insistent and shrill. The phone. He cracked his eyelids at the considerably brighter room. Maggie remained comatose beneath his arm. With a muttered curse, he flung himself over to the nightstand and snatched up the receiver.

"Yeah?" he said rudely.

A beat of silence. "Scott?"

A beat of silence. "Dad?"

"Yes, son, it's me. I'm sorry to bother you, but I'm afraid it's an emergency."

Scott scrambled upright, his heart pounding. Maggie mumbled and stirred beside him. "Are you all right, Dad?"

"Yes, yes, I'm fine. It's not me. It's Twister. He's been in an accident of some kind at Riverbend. Dr. Morley said it's pretty serious."

Maggie sat up beside Scott, wide-eyed and clutching the sheet to her chest. He avoided her eyes.

"Scott?" His father sounded odd.

"Yeah, Dad, I'm here. Did Dr. Morley say what happened?"

"He was very vague. Wouldn't say any more than that Twister hit his head somehow. And that...well, that you and Margaret should get to Riverbend as soon as possible."

Oh God, no. Not this. Not now. "We're on our way."

CHAPTER FOURTEEN

MARGARET STOLE a peek at Scott's implacable face. She longed to nestle close and absorb his strength, but he gripped the steering wheel with both hands, his eyes never leaving the road.

Not knowing Twister's condition frayed her sanity. Yet what she might learn frightened her more.

For all their strength, or perhaps because of it, horses were notorious for injuring themselves in a variety of bizarre ways. She never should've left Twister in another's care. She should've supervised his gate-training herself.

Guilt curled her shoulders. She hugged her stomach against the bitterly familiar sensation. What would this mean for the future? Her mind refused to speculate.

The old pickup rattled and whined, pushed to the limits of its capacity for speed. She concentrated on the passing miles.

"We're almost there," Scott said, not sparing her a glance.

The man who'd shown her such tender passion hours ago had disappeared, replaced by a grim stranger. Scott was worried sick, too, Margaret rationalized. Wanting him to comfort her was selfish.

Straightening, she tensed as the truck turned onto the gravel county road that led to Riverbend Arabian Farm.

She had to be brave enough to face the worst, and flexible enough to develop a contingency plan. If Twister couldn't run in the Armand Hammer Classic, then there were several other prestigious races later in the year that would serve the same purpose. His health was the main priority now.

An elaborate wrought-iron archway incorporating Riverbend's logo loomed ahead. The pickup rolled through the entrance gate and onto a paved road much nicer than the one the county maintained. Towering oaks dappled the windshield with shade. A majestic white-columned house crowned a sloping hill in the distance. They passed the racetrack, and Margaret noted the mechanized starting gate stretching across the dirt. One of two horses being led into the gate balked violently, and her stomach lurched. Is that how Twister had been hurt?

She scanned the grounds as Scott pulled up in front of the stallion facility. The absence of man or beast was odd. Her uneasiness increased. Just then a short, wiry man emerged from the building and stood near the dark entrance. Margaret was out of the truck before Scott had cut the engine.

"Billy!" She jogged over, her welcome fading to sickened dread at the expression on his homely face. He wouldn't look her in the eye. Her hands lifted involuntarily to her cheeks. "Oh, my God."

"Dr. Morley and Miss Howarth wanted me to tell them when you got here. I'll just run up to the office while you— Hey!'' Billy grabbed her shoulder as she walked past. "Don't go in there, Miss Winston, please. Wait for Dr. Morley."

Margaret shrugged aside his hand and ran into the barn. Denial raged in her brain. Everything would be fine. Twister was in perfect physical condition. She would nurse him through whatever injury he'd received. If he could *never* race, then that was fine, too. He could have a happy, productive life standing stud. But please God, don't let him... She couldn't finish the thought.

Walking slowly up the long corridor, she glanced into each stall. Swiveling ears pricked forward as she passed. Beautiful dish-shaped faces turned her way, none of them the one she sought. Her finely tuned inner radar—the sixth sense she'd always possessed— slowed her feet as she neared the second-to-last stall. She approached it cautiously. Stumbled to a stop. Stuffed her knuckles into her mouth and stifled a cry of anguish.

The stall door was open, but there was no danger of Twister escaping.

He stood with his muzzle almost touching the ground, his eyes closed and ears drooping. His powerful body listed drunkenly to one side. Margaret's mind rejected the physical clues.

"Twister?"

His delicate ears twitched. He tried valiantly to lift his head. The effort made him stagger. He recovered his precarious balance and resumed his former position. She dropped on her knees before him and sandwiched his face with her palms. He whuffled softly in response.

"Oh, Twister, what have I done to you?" she whispered brokenly.

He opened his eyes for the space of a heartbeat, revealing dark, vacant corneas rimmed with red vessels. It was then she saw the blood trickling from his nostrils.

Margaret pressed his magnificent head to her breaking heart and keened. When a masculine hand tried to pull her away, she hugged tighter.

"Maggie, let go. Dr. Morley and Liz are here," Scott said gruffly.

Her overwhelming agony found outlet in fury. Still holding Twister tightly, she glared over her shoulder at the two Riverbend employees. "How could this have happened? How could you have *let* this happen?"

Liz's nostrils flared. She bristled with defensiveness. "That's not fair, Margaret. You know how careful we are with the horses here."

"Was it the starting gate? Did he spook during training?"

"No. Twister did fine during his schooling this morning. But he pitched a fit when Billy led him back into the barn."

"Into the barn?" The irony twisted Margaret's heart. This splendid specimen had survived ranch hazards and training hardships only to be defeated by a *barn?*

Liz crouched down, gently pried Margaret's hands from Twister, then squeezed them with her own. "Oh, honey, I'd give anything to change things. It was a freak accident. He reared up and hit his head on the entrance overhang. Caught him right on the poll. There was no way we could have foreseen it, right, Thomas?'' She looked up at the tall man standing behind Scott.

Dr. Morley's dark eyes held compassion and regret. ''She's right, Margaret. We got him to his stall, but I'm afraid there's not much we can do in cases of cerebral hemorrhage. Frankly I'm surprised... Well, I'm glad you got here so quickly.''

Twister's legs suddenly buckled. He fell heavily, without any trace of the fluid coordination Margaret had come to expect from him. Dr. Morley swept past the two women and raised the stallion's eyelids. He looked from Margaret to Scott with an expression of helpless frustration.

Liz patted Margaret on the shoulder.

It can't be true. It can't be! She sent Scott a look of wild appeal.

Shaken and pale, Scott ground the heel of his palm into one temple. When he lowered his hand, he seemed to have aged ten years. ''What about an operation? A shot? *Something,* for God's sake. We can't just let him suffer.''

''I agree,'' Dr. Morley said gently. ''But I need your signature for permission to put him down. Otherwise, the insurance company won't pay your claim.'' He was talking about euthanasia.

Margaret met Scott's shocked eyes. ''There has to be another solution,'' she choked out.

Dr. Morley stood up and sighed. "Twister is start-ing to convulse. He's already totally blind. Theory has it he's not in pain at this point, but we can't be abso-lutely sure. Is it kind to leave him like this?"

Margaret forced herself to look at Twister closely. He lay on his side with his eyes closed, his ribs rising and falling in a shallow, quick cadence. When his legs jerked spasmodically, she groped blindly for Scott's hand. He moved to her side and laced his fingers through hers, sharing her wretchedness and provid-ing stability in this waking nightmare.

"We don't have any choice, Maggie." His voice sounded unnaturally thick, but resolute.

She knew the admission cost him dearly, not only in lost dreams, but companionship, as well. Scott had raised Twister from a foal, and a lasting bond had been formed in the process. Intellectually she ac-knowledged that Scott was right. But, oh...how would she bear the loss?

Dropping her head, she noted with detachment the blood saturating the front of her white shirt and trail-ing into her navy slacks. The sound of Twister's la-bored breathing filled her head. Was he in pain? What was he feeling? Once before, when he'd tried to reach Liz's mare, Dancing Flame, Margaret had entered a realm of mental communication with Twister. Could she reach him that way again?

She looked up into Scott's tormented eyes. "Why don't you go sign whatever it is Dr. Morley needs for permission and give me a minute alone with Twister?"

"I've got the medical forms in my office," Liz vol-unteered from behind.

Scott squeezed Margaret's hand. He swallowed twice in rapid succession, then nodded bleakly and rose to walk with Liz and Dr. Morley down the corridor.

Sitting inside the stall, Margaret lifted Twister's head and cradled it in her lap. He'd withdrawn to an inner world, oblivious to his surroundings. Still, she stroked his neck and scratched his favorite spot beneath his chin, untangled his mane with her fingers and crooned loving nonsense.

The actions comforted her. Soothed and relaxed the part of her mind she desperately wanted to function beyond what she'd ever attempted in the past. Drawing a deep breath, she lapsed into silence and closed her eyes. Channeled her mental energy into probing an invisible and mysterious barrier. Pushed hard... harder...harder still...and it dissolved like mist.

FEAR. SUFFOCATING, paralyzing. Swallowing Margaret whole and snuffing out all light. She struggled to break free, then stopped.

He was alone. So alone.

Twister, I am here.

Confusion. Flickering, wary. Circling her tentatively, then swelling with wonder. Strengthening with hope. She smiled in the darkness.

Yes. Friend is here.

Joy. Dazzling, blinding. Prancing and cavorting, then racing beyond the fear. Higher and higher. Faster and faster. Fainter and fainter.

Twister, stop!

Love. Infinite, humbling. Filling her heart to bursting, then vanishing into nothingness.

She was alone. So alone.

MARGARET GASPED and opened her eyes. Scott was leaning down, gripping her shoulders hard enough to bruise. His frightened expression melted into relief.

He lifted one hand and brushed beneath her eyes with his knuckle. For the first time, Margaret realized she was crying.

"Scott..." Awe closed her throat. She couldn't seem to stop her tears.

"I know darlin', I know. You can get up now. Twister's...gone."

She looked down at the head she still cradled. No tortured breath stirred Twister's velvety nostrils. He lay utterly still. Yet she couldn't mourn him. Not after what she'd just experienced.

"C'mon, Maggie. It's better this way. Twister's out of pain now." Scott's own pain showed in his slow speech, his carefully controlled expression, the tremor in his hand that reached out to help her up.

She placed her palm in his, but resisted his pull. "I was with him at the end, Scott."

He squeezed her hand briefly. "I'm glad. Twister loved you."

Platitudes, spoken to ease her heartache when it was his own that needed soothing. She tugged Scott's hand for attention, recalling Twister's joy and lack of fear.

"You don't understand. I was with him in his *mind*. He wasn't in pain, Scott." Margaret stared into Scott's skeptical eyes and willed him to believe. "Remember the day Twister almost ran me over? I was with him then, too. I stopped him with my mind. And just now... Oh, Scott."

She saw him struggle with the concept and search her face intently. When she smiled, his eyes widened. Something of her wonder and tranquillity must have shown, because the terrible rigidity of his features relaxed.

He rubbed her palm with his thumb. "I'm glad." No platitude this time, she sensed, but sincerely felt. "Let's go home now, Maggie."

THE SMALL GRANITE headstone sparkled in the early August sunlight. Maggie's doing. She'd driven into Gonzales and ordered it the day after Twister's death. Hat in hand, he glanced at the inscription he'd memorized long ago.

Twist of Fate, aka Twister. May his spirit run free forever.

The red mound of dirt had settled a bit, but no grass had rooted. Maggie's roses lay wedged against the headstone. The dozen long-stemmed beauties, tied with a vivid red ribbon, were brown and brittle now. The attached card stirred in the breeze. Scott had memorized that, too.

Congratulations to the woman who finally brought Scott to his knees. Love, Laura.

Maggie'd received the extravagant delivery the day Twister died, before Laura had known of the tragedy.

Scott hadn't explained that his sister was making good on a personal vow. Nor had he given Maggie any reason since then to believe the card's sentiment. He'd stared at those damn roses in the center of his kitchen table for more than a week, then one day they'd disappeared. And that'd been even worse.

Scott put on his hat and snugged it down. The dry, windy hill supported little but cactus, a stunted mesquite tree and now a lonely grave. It'd seemed fitting to bury the stallion here, the place where Scott had planned and dreamed. He snorted and kicked the mounded dirt.

The bank would foreclose on the ranch in two weeks. Maggie'd sent résumés to all the top breeding farms. One of them would pan out soon. Grant had insisted she stay this long to save what meager funds she had left until she found a position. As for father and son...

Twister's insurance settlement had covered about half the balance due on Scott's most recent bank loan. Much as he hated to sell the herd, he and his father needed the money to tide them over until Scott found a job. He had a strong back and a good brain, marketable commodities in this area. He would find work—as long as no employer expected him to have a heart, too. That had died with Twister.

The proof lay before him, in the panoramic view that failed to stir his emotions. He scrubbed his face with both hands and muttered a curse. Maggie would marry him if he asked. The knowledge tortured him day and night. Maintaining his facade of cold indifference was a living hell in the presence of her constant loving support.

He could start over, she insisted. This was a setback, nothing more. She would help. She *wanted* to help, if he would only let her.

When the temptation to agree became unbearable, he made himself picture her living in an apartment inferior to the maid's quarters at Riverbend. Or driving his disreputable pickup truck another five years. Or replacing her designer wardrobe piece by piece with discount-store specials. It didn't matter that her values weren't that shallow, that she didn't seem to care about such things.

He cared. Desperately. Deeply. With everything that made him who he was and allowed him a small measure of masculine pride. It was the Texas way.

Sighing, he headed for the truck at the bottom of the hill and vowed not to weaken. Hurting Maggie now would save her a lifetime of drudgery. She would thank him for his kindness one day.

Ten minutes later Scott drove up to the yellow farmhouse and narrowed his eyes at the Lexus parked in front. Donald Winston had phoned once after Twister's accident and surprised them all. Instead of ranting over the use of Riverbend without Donald's knowledge, he'd expressed sympathy and repeated his offer for Maggie to live at her childhood home. She'd turned him down, against Scott's protests. Cutting the engine, he wondered now if Donald was here to bully her in person.

Scott opened the kitchen door to the sound of voices in the parlor. He walked up the hall and stopped in the doorway. Maggie and Donald sat on the sofa, oblivious to anyone but themselves.

"I'm offering you exactly what you said you wanted, Margaret. How can you turn me down?"

"For one thing, Daddy, it's not *exactly* what I said I wanted. And what I wanted then isn't what I want now, anyway."

Donald looked thoroughly confused.

"For another thing, I could never take Liz's job away from her. She taught me everything I know. Riverbend is her home. It would devastate her to leave."

"She's already left, dammit. That's what I've been trying to tell you. I fired her yesterday."

Maggie's eyes widened, then flashed. "Liz has devoted ten years to making Riverbend the best—"

"Liz Howarth has been stealing Riverbend blind for at least seven years! She's been in cahoots with Thomas Morley for the last three, trumping up fake injuries and splitting his overcharges."

Maggie grew very still. "H-how do you know?"

"You remember Harold and Jean Canning? They've dabbled in Arabians now for several years. Harold brought in his Lexus for servicing and stopped by my office with an invoice from Riverbend. It included treatment charges for a laceration on his gelding. Harold said his daughter had just seen the horse and there hadn't been any sign of a wound."

Maggie shook her head as if trying to absorb the news.

"I sent my accountant down for a look-see. The deeper my man got into the books, the lower Liz sank.

I still don't have the total figure, but if you had all the money she skimmed over the years, you'd have your own breeding operation now, I can tell you that."

Leaning against the doorframe, Scott watched Maggie's face grow pale. She looked dazed and a little lost and a lot vulnerable. It took all his control to stay where he was.

She drew a shaky breath. "What's going to happen to her and Dr. Morley?"

"I'm pressing full charges."

"They could go to prison?"

"Very likely. We all have to pay for our mistakes sometime. At least we should. I'm certainly paying for not keeping a closer eye on Riverbend." Donald reached out as if to stroke Maggie's hair, then let his hand fall awkwardly to his lap. "And I . . . I've made a lot of mistakes with you, Margaret. I know that. But I've kept tabs on what you've been doing recently, and it's damn impressive. If you'd accept my offer to manage Riverbend, I'd be very proud."

Maggie looked as shocked as if he'd slapped her. Pink tinged her cheeks. "But all the paperwork . . . I'm so slow . . ."

"I'd hire an office manager for the clerical stuff. I need someone with an overall working knowledge of Arabians to manage the farm. Someone I can trust. I can't think of anyone more qualified than you."

She smiled tremulously, her eyes glistening. "Oh, Daddy."

Scott was torn between gratitude for Donald's words and anger that they'd come so late. He pushed off the doorframe and entered the room.

"She's qualified all right. You'd better snatch her up before someone else does."

Maggie's smile dimmed.

Donald rose and started to extend his hand, then seemed to think better of it. "I know you told me not to come back without an invitation, Scott, but I had to make Margaret see the sense in this. She can't stay here, with the bank about to..." He reddened beneath Scott's level stare. "I—I mean, she needs to relocate. And I need a manager for Riverbend. It's a perfect solution."

Scott schooled his expression to blandness. "I agree."

"You do?" Donald smiled broadly. "That's wonderful! See, Margaret? Scott thinks it's the right decision, too."

"Is that what you think, Scott? That my future is at Riverbend? That I should accept the job?" Her mist gray eyes beseeched. Adored. Condemned.

She was willing to sacrifice everything for him. He could do no less for her.

Scott chose his words carefully. "I think you'd be *stupid* to wait for another offer to come along."

MARGARET HEARD the distant whine of an engine and held her breath. A surprising number of vehicles visited Riverbend every day. She waited for the sputter and rattle that would announce the ranch truck, then wilted in her tufted leather executive chair. It wasn't Scott. If he hadn't come in a week, he wasn't coming at all. He didn't want to see her. When would she get that through her *stupid* head?

She glared around her plush office as if it were a prison cell. She'd accepted this job for lack of the one she really wanted: wife and helpmate to a hardheaded cowboy. Her father's offer for her to manage River-bend had shocked her, thrilled her, soothed her old wounds. But it hadn't tempted her. Not in the least. She no longer needed Donald Winston's approval or respect, because at last she respected herself.

What she did need was Scott.

Telling herself his masculine pride was the cause of his rejection didn't wash. After all, Grant was every bit as stubborn as his son, yet Ada had convinced *him* to move in with her after the foreclosure next week.

Margaret fought the sting of tears and admitted the truth. Scott didn't love her. At least, not enough to share his adversity or to consider her a partner in their relationship.

Suddenly she missed Twister with aching intensity. He would have settled his chin on her shoulder and provided silent, unconditional comfort.

Blinking to clear her blurred vision, she tried to concentrate on the detailed medical charts spread out on the desk. She was interviewing new veterinarians this week and wanted to get a handle on the farm's re-quirements and history.

From what she'd learned, Liz and Dr. Morley had taken excellent care of the eighty-some-odd horses at Riverbend, about a third of which were boarded by long-distance owners. It was this last group of ani-mals the two conspirators had selected for their scam. Claiming minor injuries or illnesses that never actu-ally occurred, they billed treatments through River-bend.

The recent police investigation had revealed Thomas Morley's motivation. Oh, he loved racehorses, all right. But not nearly as much as he liked to bet on them at the track. Apparently Liz had exploited his gambling weakness to gain his cooperation.

According to one detective on the case, Dr. Morley was devastated at the destruction of his career, yet relieved the truth was out. Whatever his legal punishment, therapy for his addiction would no doubt be included. Margaret was glad.

The office door opened and a groom's head popped through. "The feed truck is here, Miss Winston. You want me to show 'm where to unload?"

"No, that's all right...Dan, isn't it?" She smiled at the groom's obvious surprise. "I'll be there in a minute."

He nodded shyly and ducked out of the room.

Margaret stared at the door and sighed. The feed truck. Another shocking deception revealed. For years Riverbend had been paying for deliveries of hay and grain that had never arrived. Not every month—that would've been too obvious. But often enough to clothe Liz in the fashionable styles she loved.

Liz's accomplice, an old flame who worked at a large feed store in San Antonio, had falsified the invoices. It might've continued indefinitely if Harold Canning hadn't confronted Margaret's father with his suspicions. Margaret was still reeling from the extent of her mentor's greed and deceit.

Why, Liz? Why?

She'd been paid a generous salary. She'd lived in the guest quarters and used the main house freely when

Margaret's parents weren't in residence, which was most of the time. So why had she risked destroying the life she'd built?

Shaking her head, Margaret walked to the door and threw it open. Chances were she would never learn the full truth. Liz had holed up in a motel and communicated now only through her lawyer.

Blazing sunlight dispelled some of Margaret's gloom as she headed for the storage shed. The pickup and trailer parked in the visitors' lot boasted a newly painted logo: Luling Feed & Hardware. Margaret smiled, knowing she was partially responsible for the pride it revealed.

Funneling Riverbend funds back into the local economy dulled some of her pain over the loss of Twister and Scott. At least something good had come of her personal tragedy. She motioned the driver toward the storage shed and watched as he carefully backed up to the large metal building where grain and hay were stored.

Pudge Webster opened the truck door and stretched down his stocky legs as if testing the temperature of a swimming pool. He slipped the last few inches and landed heavily, his round face flushing to his dark curly roots.

Margaret walked forward and extended her hand. "Martin, how nice of you to deliver the order in person." At her use of his given name, his neck grew even pinker against his aqua-and-beige plaid collar.

He wiped his palm on his khaki slacks and grasped her hand. "I wanted to make sure you're pleased with the first order. And to thank you again for opening an account with us. You won't be sorry." His black eyes shone with gratitude.

She patted his plump hand once before releasing it and studying the bales of hay piled high in the trailer bed. "I didn't expect you to bring the timothy so soon."

Pudge's chest expanded, straining the buttons curving over his belly. "Not a musty bale in the lot. Bill Taylor harvested his fields last week. We worked out a deal, and he's going to put in more timothy acreage. I'll beat your last supplier's price, Margaret."

"Call me Maggie. And I never doubted it for a minute. Any problem with the rest of the list I faxed you?" Pudge had computerized his business after she'd guaranteed him a standing monthly order. He should be able to handle other sizable accounts as a result.

He pulled a printout from his pocket and scanned it briefly. "Everything's here. You want to check it as I unload?"

"Let me call my maintenance manager. You'll need help with the bales, anyway." She entered the dim storage shed and headed for a wall-mounted phone. There were five barns scattered over the property, each with its own phone extension. She dialed quickly.

"Stallion barn, José speaking."

"José, this is Mar... Maggie. Is Charlie still there working on the automatic waterers?"

"*Sí.* You wish to speak with him, no?"

"No. I mean, would you ask him to come to the feed storage shed? Mr. Webster's here with the delivery."

"*Sí, señorita.* Right away."

She hung up and turned, jumping when the phone immediately jangled. "Maggie Winston," she answered.

"Miss Winston, glad I found you. This is Riley at the brood-mare barn. We've moved Aladdin's Girl to the foaling stall. You said to let you know when her time came."

Maggie gripped the phone tighter. "How long now?"

"Her teats have waxed. She's having contractions. But it could be hours yet."

"Thanks for letting me know, Riley. When her water breaks, have someone find me, will you? I'd really like to be there."

"You got it, Miss Winston. She'll be glad to have a friend with her."

Maggie hung up smiling. During her apprenticeship at Riverbend, she'd made many friends, both human and equine. Riley had helped deliver Twister and knew the fondness she felt for his dam, Aladdin's Girl. Watching a new foal enter the world—especially one distantly related to Twister—would boost Maggie's morale as nothing else could.

Pudge had unlatched the trailer gate and begun hoisting bales to the ground. Already his face glistened with sweat. Margaret frowned.

"Charlie will be here any minute, Martin. Why don't you wait—" Maggie cocked her head at the sound of an engine. Its distinctive sputter and rattle accelerated her heartbeat.

"You okay, Mar...Maggie?" Pudge watched her quizzically.

"Mmm? Oh, yes, thank you." Her leaden feet moved past his trailer toward the main driveway. "Stop by the office before you leave, Martin, and I'll cut you a check," she said over her shoulder, picking up speed.

He might have answered, but she didn't hear him. Her ears roared with the blood surging through her reawakened body. She broke into a trot. Spotting the battered pickup, she wondered how she'd functioned during the past week. The truck grew closer. She stopped in front of her office and shaded her eyes with one hand.

Tall, broad-shouldered and handsome, the driver grinned and waved. Maggie felt the blood drain from her face and locked her knees to keep from swooning.

Grant's smile faded as he pulled to a stop in front of the office. He slammed out of the truck and rounded the front fender at a lope. Draping an arm around her shoulders, he guided her underneath the awning jutting above the office door.

"Take a deep breath—that's right. Aw, honey, I should've called first. I didn't even consider you might think I was Scott."

Maggie laughed shakily. "That obvious, huh?"

Grant made a wry face. "Let's just say I'm glad my ego's not fragile." He stepped away, sliding his palm from her shoulder to her wrist.

She clasped his hand gratefully. "I'm sorry, Grant. I really am glad to see you, it's just..." To her horror, a single tear spilled free.

Grant brushed it away, his expression a mixture of tenderness and frustration. "I swear I'm ready to take a belt to that son of mine. But he's miserable enough as it is."

She studied the yellow marigolds planted beside the office entrance. "Miserable?"

"He isn't sleeping to speak of, and he growls at me and Pete like a bobcat in a cactus patch."

She sniffed, her spirits lifting a bit.

"His appetite's lousy, he's lost interest in the herd and he looks like hell."

She forced a weak smile. "You're just saying that to make me feel better."

Grant's chuckle was enough like Scott's to pierce her heart. She blinked rapidly and turned her head toward the truck, her jaw slackening at what she'd failed to see before.

"Orca?" She rushed back into the sunlight and gripped the sides of the truck bed, smiling genuinely for the first time in weeks. At two hundred pounds, the Hampshire hog was actually underweight for five months old, but his growth amazed Margaret. "Orca!"

Grunting an excited hello, he lumbered over to be petted.

"How are you, sweetie? I've missed you so much." She scratched up his spine and beneath one drooping ear.

He tilted his head and pressed against her fingers, his stubby lashes drifting shut, then plonked down as if unable to support his ecstasy.

Grant leaned on the tailgate and snorted. "That hog has been meaner'n a two-headed rattler since you left. I could take him with me to Ada's, but...well, I don't really like pork all that much." He averted his gaze, looking distinctly embarrassed.

"You're not going to slaughter him?" Maggie's smile broadened. "Are you saying I can keep him?"

"Only if you want to, Margaret. Scott thought maybe you'd like to have a killer pig to protect the place, since dogs upset the horses too much."

Scott had known she'd find comfort in Orca's presence. It was a kind and thoughtful gift—but he'd sent his father to deliver it. She stroked the hog's bristly black-and-white coat and looked up through her lashes.

"I don't go by the name Margaret anymore. I'd be honored if you'd call me Maggie." She ignored his obvious surprise. "And I'd love to keep Orca, Grant. Thank you for bringing him. Be sure and tell Scott how much I appreciate it, would you?"

Grant's expression softened. "Sure, Maggie, I'll tell him."

"And Grant?" She held his gaze a long moment. "Tell him something else for me, too. Tell him I said, don't be chicken."

CHAPTER FIFTEEN

"*DON'T BE CHICKEN?*" Scott scraped back his chair and snatched up his dinner plate and glass. Stalking to the sink, he opened the cabinet door below and dumped his half-eaten turkey meatloaf into the trash.

The last time he'd responded to those words, he'd found heaven in Maggie's arms. But that was before his life had gone to hell.

"That's what she said, son." Grant picked up his own dishes and carried them to the counter. "And I think it's good advice."

Scott turned on the faucet with enough force to send water splashing over the front of his shirt. He didn't need this.

"She thought I was you at first—drivin' the truck, that is. 'Bout near broke my heart when she recognized my face. She looks tired and pale, like she hasn't been sleepin'."

Reaching for a dishcloth, Scott scrubbed blindly at his plate. He really didn't need this.

"I think you should talk to her, son. You're both makin' yourselves sick—"

"I think you should stay the hell out of my business! I am *not* gonna ride Maggie's apron strings like you're doin' with Ada." Scott stopped scrubbing, appalled at his cruel outburst.

Grant reached over and turned off the faucet. "Is that how you see me, son? As a parasite livin' off a woman's charity?"

Scott threw down the dishrag and rubbed his neck. He didn't know what he felt anymore, his emotions were so tangled. All he knew was he'd done what he had to do—for Maggie and his self-respect. "No, Dad. I'm sorry I blew up. But you need to stop houndin' me about Maggie. I have nothin' to offer her, and that's that."

"Sit down, son."

He didn't need this now. He goddamn didn't need this at all. "I'm goin' out to the barn," Scott said grimly, heading for the door.

"Travis Scott Hayes, sit your tail down!"

Shock as much as anything else dropped Scott into a chair. His dad hadn't yelled his full name since he'd taken the pickup at age thirteen without permission and totaled it in a ditch. He watched warily as Grant pulled out another chair and slowly sat, his expression solemn.

"I've stayed outta your business for eighteen years now, so you can just sit still and listen to me a minute. I...I know I failed you when your mother died—" he held up his palm as Scott started to protest "—and I'll regret it for the rest of my life. But you grew into a fine man without my help. A strong and honorable man. I'm damn proud to be your father."

Scott's chest tightened until he couldn't speak, couldn't do anything but stare into the loving green gaze that seemed to understand his battered pride. He hadn't realized how much he'd longed to know his father didn't blame him for losing the ranch.

"You know I'm moving in with Ada next week, but what you don't know is she asked me to marry her. And I said yes."

At first Scott thought he'd heard wrong. He noted the mischief gleaming in Grant's eyes and felt his own mouth twitch. "Th-that's good, Dad. Really. Ada's great."

"Yes, she is. But I had to nearly die in order to see it. To realize that God had put her under my nose and waited for me to gain the strength to love again, to risk breaking my heart again." Grant reached out and twirled a glass pepper shaker on the Formica table. "It takes a lot of courage to give a woman that kind of power over you."

Scott shifted in his chair, not liking where this was headed.

The pepper shaker wobbled to a stop. "You've faced every problem alone since you were twelve, and it's my fault you don't know any different. But buildin' a life with the right woman, trustin' and respectin' her enough to let her share the bad times, as well as the good, well, there's no greater adventure in the world, Scott."

Grant's gaze intensified. "I have a second chance with Ada, but you might not be so lucky. Don't look back in eighteen years and regret what might've been."

Scott couldn't think of a thing to say. Fortunately his dad didn't seem to expect an answer.

Grant rose, his expression sheepish. "I expect that's about all the wisdom you can stomach for now. I think I'll go do some packin' and let you think in peace."

Scott didn't notice his father leave. Arms folded, legs stretched out and crossed at the ankles, he was oblivious to everything but the memories surfacing in rapid succession.

Maggie replacing a ruined skillet and struggling to expand his father's diet. Maggie plunging her hand down a choking cow's throat and stretching for a dangling rein as Twister galloped wildly. Maggie painting the kitchen and raising her awed, tear-streaked face from Twister's still form. Maggie demanding everything he had to give before they made love and giving him her soul in return.

Within her delicate body beat the heart of a lioness. He'd long ago stopped thinking her too frail to withstand honest, hard work. So why was he pushing her away? Why wasn't he respecting her strength of spirit and giving her the option of forging a new life with him?

Because I'm chicken.

Maggie'd pegged him right. She had more guts in one painted pink toenail than he had in his whole sorry carcass. Letting her go hadn't been a noble act of self-sacrifice; it had been a craven act of self-defense.

What had his father said about loving a woman? Oh, yeah, that it takes a lot of courage to give a woman that kind of power over you.

The alternative loomed before him, familiar and safe and terrifyingly lonely.

Scott drew in his boots and straightened his spine. The butter yellow kitchen came slowly back into focus. For the first time in weeks, his world righted itself. Without knowing how he got there, he stood in the hallway.

"I'm gonna take the truck for a little while, Dad," he called loudly. "There's somethin' I need to do." He turned and headed for the back door, his father's "Hallelujah" echoing behind him.

MAGGIE CLUTCHED the heavy wire mesh door and stared, mesmerized, into the stall. Aladdin's Girl stood calmly munching hay as if she hadn't given birth a mere four hours ago. Her sculptured gray head, a smaller replica of Twister's, turned every few minutes to nuzzle the newborn at her side. Maggie's heart contracted.

The dark filly suckled greedily, her long spindly legs spread wide, her frizzy tail bobbing up and down with each tug on the teat. She was a beautiful foal, all the more so to Maggie because she'd witnessed the birth.

Riley moved up beside her and admired his handiwork. "Glad to see her finally going at it. Another hour, and I would've started to worry."

If the filly hadn't nursed within five hours, she could have weakened drastically. A mare's first milky secretion, colostrum, was high in protein and filled with antibodies that protected a foal from serious infection. Maggie dragged her gaze away from the pair and slanted a teasing glance at Riverbend's foaling man.

"You were wonderful, Riley. So calm and efficient. If I ever remarry, will you promise to deliver my children?"

He guffawed and pushed her shoulder, at ease with her after their shared experience. "Three's my limit, missy. After that, you'll have to get some quack obstetrician to help you."

Although Maggie laughed, the sound was strained. She wouldn't remarry, wouldn't bear the children she'd dreamed about raising. Tawny-eyed, chocolate-haired boys with lopsided grins to die for, who would love her because she would never give them reasons not to. No, she was destined always to stand at stall doors or hospital windows and coo at others' babies.

Sighing, she watched the filly release a teat and lower knobby knees to the straw. Within minutes, the newborn was stretched out and napping soundly.

Riley scratched his silver head. Rolled one shoulder as if it ached. Yawned widely.

He looked beat, poor man. Maggie had gone back to her office while he and an assistant dealt with the critical delivery of afterbirth and the cleanup of mother and baby. She checked her watch. The grooms had left for the day, and there was still another hour before Steve came on duty.

"Why don't you go home now and take it easy? I'll stay here and fill Steve in on the birth. Doc Chalmers will be here at seven tomorrow to examine the filly. Everything's under control."

Riley looked surprised. "I couldn't let you do that, Miss Winston."

She made a face. "Call me Maggie, please. And why can't you leave? I'll just stand here and watch these two like TV even if you do stay. Take advantage of it."

"Well..." He looked down the corridor wistfully. "If you're really sure..."

"I'm *really* sure. Now go." She pulled him away from the stall and gave him a light shove. "I'll see you in the morning. Don't be late."

"No, Miss...Maggie, I won't. And thank you kindly." The warmth of his gap-toothed smile stayed with her long after he'd left the barn. She breathed in deeply, savoring the varied smells she preferred over the two-hundred-dollar-an-ounce perfume Jim had given her every Valentine Day. Wheat straw. Healthy horses. Antiseptic. New-mown hay.

Real smells, of an occupation she loved and felt competent handling. Thank God she had this to get her through the days ahead. The nights...well, she wouldn't think about those now. Pushing away from the wire mesh, she strolled down the corridor and checked each stall, pausing several times to greet a favorite mare or admire a gangly foal. The tack-room door stood open. She walked forward to close it and stopped, riveted by the sight of someone rummaging through a large trunk in the corner.

"Liz?" Maggie whispered.

The woman went still, then straightened and spun around. Maggie controlled her shock with effort.

Liz's black trousers and red silk blouse looked as if they'd been worn round-the-clock for several days. Her normally glossy black hair hung dull and unkempt about her shoulders. The skin beneath her eyes looked sunken and bruised, as if she'd slept less than Maggie during the past week. Such disregard for appearance was disturbing. Liz was *always* impeccably groomed.

After a tense moment, the woman turned back around and continued pawing frantically through the trunk.

"Liz, what are you looking for?"

Liniment, bandages, currycombs, brushes—all went flying one after the other over Liz's shoulder. Maggie frowned and glanced at her watch. Steve wasn't due for another thirty minutes. José was still on duty at the stallion barn. Maybe she should call him.

Suddenly Liz froze. Reaching deep into the trunk, she lifted out something and pivoted on one foot. A crumpled and stained blue ribbon dangled from her fingers.

"You remember when I won this, Margaret? It was one of the last classes I entered before the demands of Riverbend kept me from competing."

Maggie opened and closed her mouth. Liz had already divested Riverbend's trophy case of her personal silver cups, huge rosette ribbons and Olympic gold medal. What could she possibly want with a scruffy ribbon from a minor horse show?

"What are you staring at?" Liz asked.

"I . . . nothing. You startled me, that's all. I didn't expect to see you here."

Liz's upper lip curled. "I'm sure you didn't. You expected to live happily ever after with *my job* and your daddy's money. So are you Winstons happy now,

Margaret? Now that you've made a public spectacle of
me, now that you've stripped me of everything I
own—including my dignity?''

Maggie refrained from saying Liz had done that to
herself.

"Well, you can take everything else away, but
this—" she lifted her chin and shook the ribbon
"—belongs to me. *Me*, do you understand?"

Pity swelled in Maggie's chest. Liz would lose all her
assets before the wheels of justice stopped turning. She
was clinging to the only possessions that couldn't be
legally seized or sold. Maggie walked forward and
gently touched the distraught woman's shoulder.

Liz flung up her arm and strode to the doorway.
Pausing there, she spoke without turning. "You must
be feeling pretty smug right now."

Seeing her idol crash down from the pedestal
wrenched Maggie's heart. "No. I don't feel smug at
all."

The older woman whirled, her dark blue gaze nar-
rowing, then flashing with outrage. "Don't you *dare*
pity me, you stupid little moron. You won't last two
weeks as manager of this farm. God, do you know
how much I despised standing in the ring hour after
hour while you screwed up your left and right leads? I
used to knock back two shots of bourbon before each
of your lessons to get through them."

Maggie shook her head, feeling slightly sick.

"You never knew, did you? Always so quiet. Always so worshipful. At first it was flattering to be
adored. But puppies grow up fast, Margaret, and stop
being cute. Even then I could've forgiven you, if you

hadn't started . . .'' The venomous gleam in Liz's eyes made Maggie recoil.

The tack-room walls closed in on her. The door seemed miles away. "Started what? What did I do to make you hate me so?" She inched forward, nearer the doorway.

"So innocent. So protected. You've never gone hungry a day in your life, have you? You've never seen the inside of a women's shelter or flipped hamburgers to buy decent clothes for a date. Daddy paid for everything, didn't he? Including a world-class trainer to make his little loser into a winner. And all the credit for winning went to *you.*"

Liz's altered face was as horrifying—as fascinating—as Medusa's. Maggie couldn't look away even as she edged closer to the door.

"I was an Olympic Gold medalist, for God's sake. But the *Arabian Times* called you the most gifted dressage rider of our day." Liz stopped, appearing to notice Maggie's proximity for the first time.

Maggie backed up a step, her heart hammering painfully. "I always gave you credit, Liz. Those articles talked about you, too."

Liz rolled her eyes dismissively. "Token lines. *Crumbs,* Margaret, when you got the whole cake. I started with nothing and became a respected trainer and manager. But no one wanted to tell my story. No one bothered to learn that I was the brain behind your talent. And I had to smile and keep my mouth shut or lose my job."

She tossed her lank hair. Cast a nervous glance over her shoulder. Turned back and froze Maggie in mid-step with a cunning smile. "But I found a way to get even, to get what I deserve and make sure I'd never die in a charity ward like my mother. When Matt died, things got even better. You tucked tail and ran just like I told you to. Donald never suspected a thing—until you came back." Her smile faded into a hostile glare. "Everything started falling apart then."

Liz needed professional help. Maggie needed out of the tack room—and preferably miles away from Liz. "Let's go somewhere and talk about this calmly. Maybe get a bite to eat."

Liz braced her hands on opposite sides of the doorframe. "You couldn't leave it alone, could you? You just had to come back and create a stir with your wonder horse. What was I supposed to do, Margaret? It was happening all over again, and you ignored all my warnings. Daniel Brady thought you were—"

"Warnings?" The word echoed in Maggie's head.

Liz smiled, and Maggie backed up another step. "You were right about the mare I rode to the H & H, dear—she *was* in heat. And that little Wild West show you put on for Daniel? A BB gun and fifty bucks goes a long way in the hands of a groom making minimum wage."

Maggie hugged her stomach and curled over at the next logical thought. *Please, no. Please let me be wrong.* She lifted her gaze.

Liz clucked sympathetically, an obscene parody of the woman Maggie had thought she'd known. "So you've finally figured it out? Such a waste of fine horseflesh, Margaret, but all your fault. If only you hadn't been so ambitious, Twister would still be rounding up little dogies today.''

Maggie squeezed her lids shut and swallowed a bitter surge of bile. *Twister, my friend. I'm so sorry.* She drew in a shaky breath. "How could you?" she choked out.

"With a straight pin actually. I must admit he cooperated beautifully, rearing up at just the right angle like that. A true champion to the end, he was."

Hot, murderous fury rose from the center of Maggie's soul and escaped her throat in an animalistic snarl. She opened her eyes, and this time it was Liz who backed up, staggering into the corridor as Maggie lunged forward, her fingers curled into claws.

The door slammed shut. Maggie's hands crashed into wood. She yowled in frustration and pain, then pushed with her shoulder. Locked. Stepping back, she threw her full weight against the door. The simple rod-and-pin latch held tight. Damn!

She spun around and kicked a nearby bag of grain. She'd actually felt sorry at first for Liz. Dropping her head back, Maggie laughed bitterly. She was trapped like a rat while the sick monster who'd killed Twister was getting away. *Damn!*

She scanned the tack room and resigned herself to the obvious. Steve was due in thirty minutes. Liz wouldn't have time to get far.

The fury drained from Maggie in a weakening rush. She walked to the trunk like an old woman, closed the lid and sat facing the door. Her spirit felt bruised and weary. If she could misjudge Liz so completely, how could she trust her instincts regarding Scott?

Up until now, despite everything, she'd secretly hoped he would come to his senses and declare his love for her. But perhaps she'd been as naive as ever, seeing emotions in him he simply didn't feel. Perhaps she should quit issuing challenges and let the poor man alone.

A mare whinnied. Another answered. Maggie frowned and looked up. Something in their tone stiffened her spine. A muffled bump made her cock her head. Another whinny rang out, this one clearly frightened. Oh, God, what was going on?

She ran to the door and pounded with her fist. "Steve?" She pounded some more. "Steve, is that you?" she yelled.

The mares on the east side of the barn were in an uproar now. Their fear spread quickly, until the sound of shrill neighing reverberated throughout the barn. Maggie rammed against the door and rebounded in pain.

Pressing her ear to the wood, she listened in helpless frustration. What was that other noise? That sound filtering through the terrified cacophony? That...crackle.

Icy dread chilled her blood and numbed her mind. She closed her eyes in denial. Forced herself to take a deep breath. Registered the smell that confirmed her horrified suspicion.

Fire!

THE MARES' TERROR flipped a switch in Maggie's brain. Her knees buckled. Gritting her teeth, she ruthlessly shut down her sixth sense. She couldn't afford distraction. Already smoke oozed beneath the door.

She whirled and searched the room, looking for something—anything—to use as a battering ram. The fire extinguisher! She jerked the canister from its wall mount. Good heft. Nice solid feel.

Don't think about puncturing the metal.

She rocked it back, then swung it forward to crash against the wood. Rocked it back and swung it forward over and over. The door shook. Then splintered. Then exploded open into the bowels of hell.

Smoke billowed in, forcing her backward. Coughing, she snatched up a cleaning rag. Tied it bandit-style over her nose. Tucked the fire extinguisher under one arm and faced the open doorway. One...two...*three!*

Plunging into the corridor, she turned toward the source of smoke. A stack of baled hay—a bonfire at the end of the aisle. Flames licked up the concrete block wall like a snake's tongue. Tasting. Searching for flammable materials to devour. Feasting on the wooden ceiling beams her mother had thought quaint. Thank heaven the roof was steel. The mare nearest the fire screamed. Maggie ran forward.

Oh, God, the straw. She yanked the spring-loaded latch chain and opened the door. The bedding crackled and curled. *Oh, God.*

The trapped mare slammed into a wall. Staggered. Slammed into another and miraculously lurched through the doorway. The smell of charred hair and flesh made Maggie gag. She slapped the trembling hindquarters and hoped the mare would find her way out.

Don't think about it. Stop the fire.

Hoisting up the extinguisher, Maggie triggered a blast of smothering foam over the bedding. The chemical stench fueled her nausea.

Don't think about it. Stop the fire.

Holding the extinguisher like an Uzi, she attacked the baled hay. Then the treated beams. Too high. Damn! They burned slowly, but spit red embers just the same. Three more stalls ignited. She stopped and sent three more crazed mares galloping toward the entrance.

When the last of the foam sputtered weakly, Maggie had sprayed everything within reach to the center of the barn. The beam fire had crept forward a few feet. She'd bought some time—not victory.

Tossing the now-empty canister aside, she fanned her way through the smoke to the main entrance. An ember hit her forearm and sizzled. Her eyes streamed. Her lungs burned. She groped for the wall phone mounted by the double doors and lifted the receiver. No dial tone. Her fingers walked up the long cord and met air. Cut.

Liz.

The woman had killed Twister. Maggie had let it happen. But by God, these mares *would not die.* Not while there was breath left in her body.

Turning back to the aisle, she set to work grimly, methodically. Most of the mares bolted through the open door. A few wouldn't budge. She threw a saddle blanket over their eyes and led them out, the foals at their heels. So new to the world, so frightened by its ugliness.

The smoke was horrible. Painful. It filled her hair, her eyes, her lungs. It filled her brain. Distorted her perception. Formed the shape of a man.

"Steve?" Was that croak coming from her?

"M-Miss Winston?" His forearm covered his nose.

She could just make out his worried eyes. "Break office window... Call 911—" she fought for breath between words "—Come back... help get hor—" Hacking coughs ripped through her lungs. Steve supported her until she stopped.

"Come out, Miss Winston, and wait for help."

"Go!" Maggie shoved him toward the door. She was in no shape to run.

He looked torn, then determined. "I'll hurry."

She nodded and headed back down the aisle.

Time stopped. The world narrowed to a smoke-filled corridor and the encroaching enemy. She focused on one step at a time. One stall at a time. Only the horses kept her going. She opened her mind to let them in. Their terror filled her like the smoke. Kept her staggering forward. The mares were mindless with panic; as dangerous as live grenades. A frantic hoof caught Maggie's ankle. A tossing head clipped her chin. She hobbled toward the twelfth stall tasting equal parts blood and fear.

A distant beam collapsed, showering sparks and splintered wood. Some burning debris burrowed deep into unprotected straw. One, two stalls flared quickly. The plank-board siding would be next. The front line of the beam fire was gaining on her. Once the embers struck virgin fuel...

Don't think about it. Get the mares out.

She worked frantically, coughing continuously now. The mares grew quieter. The smoke, no doubt. It was killing her, too. Three more stalls to go. The beam fire passed the center mark.

Glowing debris hit dry straw. Here. There. Instant combustion. Too fast. Too hot. Too close. Oh, God, not now. She hadn't played favorites. She'd released the mares in order. But Aladdin's Girl and her foal were in the last stall. And Maggie couldn't breathe.

Something wet fell over her head. A blanket. Deliverance from hell.

"Get out!" Steve shouted in her ear, removing her hand from the stall door. He shoved her aside and took over.

Maggie moved to the next stall. They could make it working together. Her hands were clumsy, her strength almost gone. She opened the door and sagged against it as a bay mare exploded into the aisle.

The inferno neared. It sucked the moisture from her blanket and the air from her lungs.

"We've gotta go!" Steve yelled, pulling her arm.

The newborn filly squealed.

From somewhere deep inside, Maggie dredged up one more surge of strength and pushed Steve away. She staggered to the last stall and slid the door open.

Aladdin's Girl careered past in a blur, the filly close on her heels.

Crack! Shusssh.

It was raining fire. She stumbled back and hit concrete. A massive beam blocked the aisle ahead, creating a wall of flame. Her protective blanket was almost dry. Useless. Would the smoke kill her before the fire? She desperately hoped so.

Oh Scott, Scott. I should've forced you to marry me, you . . . you cowboy.

She would've laughed, but her lungs hurt too much. She would've cried, but her tears dried up as fast as they welled. The next beam would fall any second.

Oh Scott, I wish we'd had a chance.

A figure burst from the fire, shapeless and huge. Hissing and steaming. It swooped forward and stood facing her, silhouetted against certain death. "Maggie!"

The ragged shout was muffled by wet wool. With a soundless cry, she fell forward.

Scott opened his shroud of wet blankets and crushed her against his chest, then stepped back and began wrapping her in the extra blankets he clutched.

Crack! Shusssh!

Shoving her against the wall, Scott covered her body with his. She felt him jerk from the impact of falling chunks of wood.

"No-o-o," she wailed. Unbearable, to die now when life had grown infinitely precious. Not fair! Not fair! She buried her face in Scott's chest and raged against the twists of fate bringing her to this point. The blankets barely steamed now. He must be roasting alive. She hated herself for causing his death. For being glad he was here. For succumbing to the terror she'd held at bay since the fire began.

He pulled away suddenly, dragging the blankets with him. She was alone.

The shock of it left her gasping. Whimpering. Unable to move or care about the devouring flames between her and safety.

The blanket settled over her head again, clinging heavily. Scott ducked under and wrapped more wet wool around them. How had he...? The stall water bucket. Of course.

She huddled close, his solid presence infusing her with relief. And strength. And hope. They might die, but they wouldn't wait passively to be killed.

"Get ready to move," he yelled above the din, adjusting their cocoon to allow a slit of vision. "Okay...now!"

They ran together toward the wall of fire. Maggie closed the gap in their blankets. Better. Now the monster couldn't get them. She stumbled. Scott's powerful arm grasped her waist and lifted her off the ground.

Blinding light. Blistering heat. Swallowed screams.

Her feet hit the ground, and Scott whipped off their burning blankets. They clutched each other's waists and staggered toward the entrance. Almost there. A siren wailed in the distance. They crossed the threshold and lurched into the clear night air.

José, Billy, and Steve stood watching the blazing barn, their shock illuminated by red-gold light.

"*Dios Mío!*" José pointed at the pair with a shaky finger.

They must have looked a fright.

Steve's eyes widened. "Miss Winston!" He ran forward as if to embrace her, but she and Scott tightened their arms around each other at the same time.

"Oh, thank God, Miss Winston. I thought...when the beam fell... Oh, God, Miss Winston, I'm sorry I left you."

She could tell he'd been crying, and she wanted to comfort him. But the air was too sweet, the moment too poignant for her to share with anyone but Scott. They clung together and dragged in wheezing gulps of air.

"Give 'em some room, Steve," Billy said gently. "The ambulance is here. The fire truck, too. Go get the medics and point them this way."

"The horses," Maggie managed. "Find them. We'll be okay."

The men fidgeted, their expressions worried.

"Go," Scott ordered.

They scattered and loped off.

Maggie tilted her head back and took in Scott's soot-blackened face, his singed eyebrows, the holes peppering his shirt where debris had burned through. He'd been willing to die for her. How many women got proof like that?

She reached up and stroked his rugged cheek. "Don't expect to order *me* around when we're married, cowboy. If I'm doing my share of the work, I want my share of making decisions, my share of solving the problems. Understand?"

"Was there a proposal slipped in that speech somewhere, Maggie?"

She tensed. "There was. So...what's your answer?"

His slow grin shone white in his grimy face. "Darlin', I'd be plain *stupid* to say no."

EPILOGUE

Eleven months later

MAGGIE PROPPED her elbows on the H & H paddock fence and pressed as close as her extended belly allowed. A tiny foot kicked in protest, and she eased back, giving her stomach a loving pat.

"Sorry, kiddo, I know you're cramped. Just hang in there two more weeks, and we'll both have room to breathe."

Not that Maggie was complaining. What were swollen ankles and indigestion compared with being Scott's wife and carrying his child? She'd come too close to dying to take the miracle of her present life for granted.

She and Scott had married in a civil ceremony the day after the fire, neither of them wanting to waste time on pomp and fanfare. She'd moved back into Scott's house and continued working as Riverbend Arabian Farm's general manager.

The new brood-mare barn was a constant reminder of Liz's betrayal, but Maggie's heart was too full of love these days to harbor bitterness. She assumed her former teacher was getting help—and all the attention she craved—from mental-health professionals in the Texas penal system.

Maggie repropped her elbows and gazed over the paddock fence. After a long day at Riverbend, this was just what she needed.

The newly weaned five-month-old colt circling Orca was beautifully made and amazingly graceful, despite his long legs. Twist and Shout's smoky gray coat would lighten over time to a stunning pearl gray. Although it was too soon to know if the foal would equal his sire in speed and heart, he showed every promise of doing so.

Thank God for Dr. Lawson's impulsive offer to extract semen from Twister all those months ago. She and Scott had bartered the precious frozen straws to Daniel Brady in exchange for a foal from the Oasis mare of Maggie's choice. She couldn't be more pleased with the result.

Absently caressing her belly, Maggie marveled at the difference in Scott since the fire. He'd finally realized no one could take his pride from him unless he willingly gave it away. Asking Donald Winston for a loan—at current market interest rates—had been Scott's idea. The five-year business plan he'd shown her father included aggressive improvements he felt would pay for themselves in a short amount of time. Her father had agreed, and Scott had paid off the bank in full and on time.

Now her Riverbend paycheck was automatically deposited into an account in her father's name—with Scott's blessing. Nothing else proved the depth of his love for her so unequivocally.

When the loan was paid off, Twist and Shout would be the foundation stud for a breeding operation she would establish at the H & H. While Maggie might never be close to her parents, she'd always be grateful to them for providing the means to keep her and Scott's dreams alive.

Suddenly Twister—as they'd inevitably wound up calling the foal—gave Orca a playful nudge and backed up, snorting in invitation. The huge boar continued rooting for piggy morsels in the grass. Twister advanced cautiously, nipped the Hampshire's white collar and jumped back with a spirited little buck for good measure. Again the hog ignored him. When Twister lowered his tail dejectedly, Orca raised his head and grunted.

The two touched muzzle to snout a long moment, reminding Maggie of a similar scene between a magnificent stallion and a homely runt pig.

A white tissue miraculously appeared under her nose. She snatched it up and dabbed at her eyes. "Don't pretend that doesn't get to you, Scott Hayes, because I know differently."

Scott's chuckle rumbled in her ear down to her toes. Strong arms slipped around her from behind, and she leaned back into her husband's embrace with a sigh of contentment. Had any woman ever been this happy?

He rested his chin on her head. "You ever have any... connections, with this foal, Maggie?"

She'd determined her gift emerged only when an animal was extremely distressed. "No, other than a sense of destiny, a feeling he was meant to be born. You know what I mean?"

"Yeah, I know." He rubbed his cheek against her hair. "You're supposed to be inside resting."

"It's too nice an evening to stay inside." She watched Twister break away from Orca and streak across the paddock, his fluid action a replica of his sire's. "Oh, Scott, isn't he beautiful?"

"Squat and hefty, maybe, but beautiful?"

Maggie lifted her elbow and jabbed him in the stomach.

"Ohh, you mean the foal," Scott said, a smile in his voice. He laughed and teased regularly these days. The somber cowboy with the weight of the world in his eyes had vanished. Another profound effect of the fire.

His hands joined hers over their baby. "I think *you're* beautiful, Mrs. Hayes." He nuzzled her neck. "Have I told you today that I love you?"

He'd mentioned it that morning after an oh-so-careful-but-wonderful attempt to bump up her dilation a centimeter. "No, Mr. Hayes, I don't believe you have," she lied.

"Well, I do, darlin'. So much it scares the hell outta me sometimes. If I ever lost you . . ."

Maggie's vision blurred. "I know, Scott. Me, too. But if we spend our lives worrying about what might happen, we'll miss the here and now. And this moment, this very one right now with you holding me, is so perfect I couldn't bear to miss it." His arms tightened, and she turned awkwardly in his embrace.

The kiss they shared was hot and sweet.

Thump! Their lips curved up at the same time. They broke apart and looked down.

"I swear he's going to be born wearing cowboy boots," she said.

"Nah, that's just her mama comin' out in her. She kicks like The Mule is all. I can't wait to see you two butt heads." Turning Maggie toward the house, he draped an arm over her shoulders and forced her gently into a waddle. They bumped hips in companionable silence.

Her gaze wandered over the changes an infusion of capital had wrought on the H & H. St. Augustine grass now carpeted the compound area. The house and barn were repaired and freshly painted a light, silvery gray. She'd chosen a hue three shades darker for the new front porch and window trim, and the contrast made a pleasing picture. The unseen changes were even more dramatic.

A new irrigation system gave Scott license to plant hardy native grasses and increase the size of the herd. Bandolero's breeding fees had paid for a John Deere tractor that resided in a new storage shed behind the barn. They'd repainted or wallpapered every room in the interior of the house, and Scott had laid down a patterned no-wax vinyl in the kitchen to match the butter yellow walls.

At the back steps, Maggie paused, turned toward Pete's trailer and cupped her mouth. "Seven o'clock. Bring the wine," she yelled.

From his chair on the porch extension Scott had insisted on building for him, Pete nodded and waved. The old wrangler still put in full days, despite the two hired hands the H & H now employed. Scott had made it clear this was Pete's home for as long as he lived, regardless of his ability to work.

She waved back and climbed the steps heavily. "I hope he remembers that Laura and Alec are coming with Ada and your dad."

Scott opened the door, led her to his mother's dainty rocker in the corner and helped her sit. "Are you kidding? I sent him to borrow Dad's circular saw this afternoon, and the traitor wound up playing 'horsey' for hours. When I called, Ada had to pull Sarah off Pete's back."

Maggie chuckled at her mental image of the beautiful auburn-haired one-year-old and the wizened cowhand. Sarah was every inch Laura's daughter, which of course made her irresistible. Pushing off with her toes, Maggie set the rocker in motion. She had every intention of rocking her own child to sleep in the room Patricia Hayes had considered the heart of the house.

"Why don't you go grab the first shower," Maggie suggested. "I feel like resting here a bit."

Scott clumped to her side and shook a stern finger. "Don't get up while I'm gone. I'm handling dinner tonight."

She smiled ruefully. "It would take a forklift to get me out of this chair without your help." She plucked his hat off and perched it on her stomach. "Now go."

He bussed her on the cheek, straightened and headed for the hall. At the doorway he turned as if to say something and stared at her, instead. His expression grew achingly tender. "Ah, Maggie, you look so right sittin' in Mama's chair."

She stored the perfect moment away with all the others this man had given her. "Life is strange, isn't it? Who'd have thought when I turned up in your field over a year ago things would end up this way?"

"What way's that?"

"The only way that counts, cowboy." She swept up his hat, jammed it low on her head and grinned. "The Texas way."

BRIDE'S
BAY RESORT

UNLOCK THE DOOR TO GREAT ROMANCE
AT BRIDE'S BAY RESORT

Join Harlequin's new across-the-lines series, set in an exclusive hotel on an island off the coast of South Carolina.

Seven of your favorite authors will bring you exciting stories about fascinating heroes and heroines discovering love at Bride's Bay Resort.

Look for these fabulous stories coming to a store near you beginning in January 1996.

Harlequin American Romance #613 in January
Matchmaking Baby by Cathy Gillen Thacker

Harlequin Presents #1794 in February
Indiscretions by Robyn Donald

Harlequin Intrigue #362 in March
Love and Lies by Dawn Stewardson

Harlequin Romance #3404 in April
Make Believe Engagement by Day Leclaire

Harlequin Temptation #588 in May
Stranger in the Night by Roseanne Williams

Harlequin Superromance #695 in June
Married to a Stranger by Connie Bennett

Harlequin Historicals #324 in July
Dulcie's Gift by Ruth Langan

Visit Bride's Bay Resort each month wherever Harlequin books are sold.

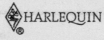

HARLEQUIN ®

BBAYG

Take 4 bestselling love stories FREE

Plus get a FREE surprise gift!

Special Limited-time Offer

Mail to Harlequin Reader Service®

3010 Walden Avenue
P.O. Box 1867
Buffalo, N.Y. 14269-1867

YES! Please send me 4 free Harlequin Superromance® novels and my free surprise gift. Then send me 4 brand-new novels every month, which I will receive before they appear in bookstores. Bill me at the low price of $3.12 each plus 25¢ delivery and applicable sales tax, if any.* That's the complete price and a savings of over 10% off the cover prices—quite a bargain! I understand that accepting the books and gift places me under no obligation ever to buy any books. I can always return a shipment and cancel at any time. Even if I never buy another book from Harlequin, the 4 free books and the surprise gift are mine to keep forever.

134 BPA AW6W

Name	(PLEASE PRINT)	
Address	Apt. No.	
City	State	Zip

This offer is limited to one order per household and not valid to present Harlequin Superromance® subscribers. *Terms and prices are subject to change without notice. Sales tax applicable in N.Y.

USUP-995

©1990 Harlequin Enterprises Limited

Let

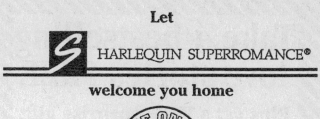

HARLEQUIN SUPERROMANCE®

welcome you home

Welcome to West Texas—and the Parker Ranch!

Long before the War Between the States, Parker sons and daughters ranched Parker land. Eighty-one-year-old Mae Parker aims to keep things that way. And as far as Mae—and almost everyone else on the ranch—is concerned, her word is law. Except to Rafe. And Rafe, thirty-five years old, iron-willed and *unmarried,* is Mae's favorite great-nephew. But he has no plans to buckle under to her by changing his marital status.

That's why Mae invites Shannon Bradley to the ranch. Something about Shannon—the only person other than Rafe who has ever stood up to Mae—gets under Rafe's skin. Still, after years of watching his great-aunt manipulate the rest of his family, he's damned if he'll fall in love to order!

Watch for *A Match Made In Texas* by Ginger Chambers
Available in February 1996
wherever Harlequin books are sold.

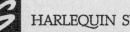

HARLEQUIN SUPERROMANCE®

Emergency!

Dr. Stephanie Sheldon counseled pregnant teens. Now she was pregnant herself after a poignant one-night stand with Dr. Talbot Robichaux. How was she going to explain *that* one to her class?

Well, maybe it would be easier than she thought. Talbot proposed a marriage of convenience, and right now marriage would be very convenient indeed—if it wasn't for his resentful teenage daughter.

There were other complications too: her missing twin's daughter showed up at Stephanie's New Orleans clinic one day. How could she not offer *her* a home? Suddenly this makeshift family was growing faster every day—as were her feelings for Tal!

Look for this heartwarming story from Karen Young in February 1996 wherever Harlequin books are sold.

NML-5

What do women really want to know?

Only the world's largest publisher of romance
fiction could possibly attempt an answer.

HARLEQUIN ULTIMATE GUIDES™

How to Talk to a Naked Man,

Make the Most of Your Love Life, and Live Happily Ever After

The editors of Harlequin and Silhouette are
definitely experts on love, men and relationships.
And now they're ready to share that expertise with
women everywhere.

Jam-packed with vital, indispensable, lighthearted
tips to improve every area of your romantic life—even
how to get one! So don't just sit around and wonder
why, how or where—run to your nearest bookstore
for your copy now!

Available this February, at your favorite retail outlet.

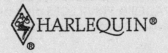

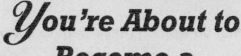

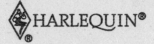